ASSASSIN LAB

Designer Mercenaries Book 1

by

Stuart de Jong

SADD Writings Publisher LLC

Cover art by Deborah de Jong

ISBN 979-8-9902944-4-8 (paperback)
ISBN 979-8-9902944-3-1 (ebook)

Published by SADD Writings Publisher LLC
https://SaddWritings.com

Acknowledgements

Thank you to my wife Debbie for supporting all of my endeavors, proofreading early versions of my story, and designing and illustrating the book cover. Also, thank you to my beta-readers, Peter de Jong and Susan Appelbaum, for their feedback and suggestions.

Table of Contents

PROLOGUE

Lud Blom concluded his lecture and stopped to take stock of his audience of young college students. Today's subject was an overview of the parties represented in Swedish parliament. The lecture hall was filled to capacity and then some, with several students sitting in the stairways between the tiered seating areas. He could spend endless hours discussing each of the Swedish political party's policy positions and what segments of society each party represented, but he acknowledged that not all of his students shared a deep passion for the subject.

He was a realist, so he understood he was teaching a foundational course that satisfied one of the school's humanity requirements needed to graduate. That meant some students in the class had no interest in how their government functioned, and he would probably rarely get their attention. That didn't bother him, since he could take satisfaction in seeing many other students looking forward, eyes open wide, eager to hear what he said next.

His courses were always popular, whether they were part of the core curriculum or not. Over the last decade, he had become a minor celebrity, sought after to give his opinion on various political issues on news programs and podcasts—he was one of the talking heads program directors liked to bring in to discuss the important topics of the day with the anchor.

That celebrity and his reputation as a dynamic lecturer ensured that his introductory civics course was always fully registered.

As a full professor at Stockholm University, he had the credentials to speak on any political issue, but there was more to why he was in such demand than that. In many circles, he was also Stockholm's most eligible bachelor: tall and handsome, a deep voice, exuding confidence, he was pleasing to look at and listen to. In fact, he was scheduled to do one of those interviews later that day, using a camera and microphone he had set up in his office, just for that purpose. One of the local news shows had been featuring him in their *Politics 2022* weekly segment.

After class, he made the ten-minute walk from the lecture hall to his office. He had twenty-five minutes until he was scheduled to join the conference call with the afternoon news show, so he was relieved that there were only two students waiting outside his door, looking for counseling. He unlocked the door and invited the two young women into the office, allowing them to enter before him and leaving the door open. While he was making his way to his desk, one of the women turned around and closed the door before sitting down.

"Miss, I would prefer if you left the door open," he stated with a tone of formality.

She raised her eyebrows and smiled at him. "What we have to discuss is private." Her friend just giggled.

Lud needed to extricate himself from the situation quickly and firmly. Years ago, when he was just starting out, he welcomed these types of dalliances, but now at forty, he dreaded them. Early in his career, he had the reputation as a ladies' man and had a few affairs with his students. But one day, his mentor took him aside and let him know that if he didn't restrain himself, his career would be over shortly. The intervention worked. He continued to be popular with women, but he avoided students and stuck to peers and women he met through his engagements with the media and various hobbies.

"Do you have anything to discuss regarding your course work?" he gruffly asked. His brusqueness and stern manner seemed to offend the girls, but he had no choice. The only way to discourage this type of behavior was to do it clearly and firmly.

"Let's go. I didn't realize what an asshole he was," the girl who had originally closed the door said while getting up from her chair. The other girl gave Lud a slightly embarrassed look, but got up and followed her friend out the door. Relieved, Lud locked the door and prepared himself for the interview on that afternoon's local newscast.

∗

Later that evening, Lud finished grading a stack of essays he'd asked his students in one of his advanced classes to write the week before. The afternoon interview went well—he was his usually charming and entertaining self. Overall, it had been a productive day, but it was now almost ten o'clock and he was eager to leave the office, get some food, and wind down the night with a good book. It had been a long day, and he had a staff meeting at 8:00 AM the next morning to get up early for.

He caught a bus to his neighborhood of Östermalm, and found his favorite late-night falafel stand to grab a bite before walking the rest of the way home. It was a cold, moist November night, and the streets were nice and quiet. The grind of reading all of those essays earlier left his eyes heavy and his body drained, but the cold clean air revived him, and he was starting to feel better. He thought about calling up his on-again, off-again girlfriend he occasionally hooked up with

3

when one of them was feeling lonely and needed some comfort and release.

Just then, a van pulled over and stopped beside him. A balding man with large, full-rimmed glasses opened the driver's side window and waved him to move closer, to which Lud obliged. In English, the man asked for directions to the Viking Museum.

"The museum is not open at this hour..." That was all he got out before someone grabbed him from behind with one arm and covered his mouth and nose with a sweet-smelling cloth with the other. His knees started to buckle as the person behind pulled him down. Lud was tall and strong, but the chemical made him feel weak and disoriented. He instinctively tried to pull away from the assailant, but his muscles wouldn't cooperate. His vision grew blurry, and he started having trouble even thinking coherent thoughts.

The door to the van opened and one other person jumped out. Together with the person holding him from behind, they dragged Lud into the van and set him on the floor. He sensed the door closing and the van starting to move, but by then he was completely out of it. He tried to force himself to stay alert for a moment more, but all his body really wanted was to just sleep. Finally, Lud closed his eyes and gave in to his body's needs.

CHAPTER 1

It was the usual morning rush at the Smith house, with Jan working to get everyone fed and to their engagements on time. It was a dreary, rainy Western Washington morning, so she liked to make sure everybody got a good start to their day by making breakfast. Her younger child, Mikey, never missed a meal, so promptly made his way down the stairs, more than ten minutes before he had to leave to catch his school bus. That was how Jan liked it: get going early to avoid having to hurry.

Her twelve-year-old daughter worked in the opposite way and liked to wait until the last minute to move herself, which meant she was always racing out of the house just as the school bus was arriving. She never missed her bus, but that didn't calm her mom's nerves—she might miss it in the future.

"Kate, Kate, come on down; your breakfast is getting cold," Jan yelled up the stairs.

"Can I have her bacon?" Mikey pleaded.

"No! Get your hands off her plate. Go wash up and get your shoes and jacket on."

"It's already time to go, Kate's not going to eat it," Mikey whined.

"Now!"

Mikey banged his fists on the table and, with a jutted lower lip and bad attitude, walked into the mud room to finish getting ready. Finally, Kate came down and ran into the mud room to bundle up, not even bothering to look at her breakfast. Both kids shouted, "I love you, Mom," as they bolted out the door, just as the school bus was coming to a stop a few houses down on the corner of the block.

Dave, with his usual perfect timing, came down the stairs right after the last child left for the morning, and like Kate, was out the door with an 'I love you' and a goodbye kiss, skipping breakfast. He was a good husband and Dad most of the time. He was mostly patient and easygoing, which was a good counter to Jan's high-strung, emotional, personality. It wasn't all perfect though, sometimes he let his frustrations with work come out in passive-aggressive ways; he could be cutting at times.

It was the first day of the last month of 2023 and with the holidays coming up and all of the end of the year school activities, Jan anticipated things getting more hectic in the coming weeks, but for now, with everybody out of the house, she took a few slow deep breaths, taking in the peace and quiet, before sitting down to eat Kate's cold leftover eggs.

*

Kate ran to the bus stop and hopped on just as the doors were opening, pushing aside Mikey, who was standing in the way—his bus was still down the block at its previous stop. Kate didn't like being out in the open any longer than she had to be. For that matter, she didn't feel that comfortable in her house either. She didn't understand why she felt that way, but for the last month, she'd had this uneasy feeling she could not explain. She felt worst when undressing to shower; she felt watched; she wondered if she was crazy. She couldn't keep the feeling to herself anymore.

"Somebody is spying on me," Kate stated.

Her friend Taylor immediately looked over the back of her seat and gave Evan and Toby a dirty look. They both stared back up at her, their jutted upper teeth adding to their looks

6

of confusion. Then Taylor looked back at Kate and said, "They're creeps, but they're just sitting there."

"I didn't mean them. When I'm at home, at school, everywhere. I don't feel alone."

Taylor sat there for a second, staring at Kate, confused. "What do you mean? Like Mikey?" Taylor said.

"No, I mean, not always, but there is this change in the way the air feels around me. A tingly feeling. I think I might be going crazy."

"Are you having that feeling now?"

"No, it's more if I'm alone or still, I can feel something," Kate replied while starting to tear up.

Taylor had never seen Kate cry about something like this before. Kate could get emotional, especially when she was playing a game and not winning—she was hyper-competitive—but this was different. "Tell me when you feel that way again; I'll see if I can feel it too," Taylor stated.

Kate wiped her dripping nose with her sleeve, feeling a little silly but also relieved; she now had someone to help her. Taylor was a good friend. After unburdening herself, Kate didn't have that strange, watched feeling for the rest of the day and started to feel better. She worked out extra hard at basketball practice, since vigorous physical activity took her mind off her troubles and that eerie, tingly feeling she wanted to get away from.

CHAPTER 2

The two-hour drive over the Cascade Mountains to Kate's basketball tournament in Ellensburg gave Dave plenty of time to talk to her about her alleged eating disorder. Jan was worried that Kate wasn't acting like her usual self lately, which included skipping meals. He also noticed that Kate seemed more anxious and jumpier than usual, but chalked it up to normal teenage behavior. Talking to her about it wasn't something he looked forward to, however, so he decided not to start the day under a black cloud and enjoy the ride through the mountains instead. Besides, Kate wasn't a morning person and was curled up asleep in the back seat of his Subaru.

Dave loved his wife and could not imagine life without her. He depended on her for so much: his role was to work, manage the kids' athletic schedules, mow the lawn, and not much else. Jan insisted on doing most other things; she was very particular about how stuff got done, so over time, keeping the peace meant dividing up the chores and activities in a way that minimized overlapping responsibilities. Dave was perfectly happy with the arrangement, since he had enough stress and responsibilities at work. Being in charge of the fun things at home, such as sports, was just how he liked it.

Dave pulled into the already full parking lot at 8:45 AM, just fifteen minutes before Kate's first game of the day was set to start. After parking the car in the overflow lot, he gently shook her arm, rousing her from her nap.

Kate let out a big yawn and looked up at her dad with a tired squint. "Are we here?"

"Yep, honey, it 8:48 AM, so we should get going."

Kate immediately straightened up with eyes wide open. "What! I'm the starting point guard. I'm going to miss the game." She quickly grabbed her bag, bolted out the back door, and started running toward the sports center. Realizing she had forgotten something, Kate turned around and yelled back at her dad, "Are you coming?"

"Just go, I'll catch up," he replied. With that, Kate sprinted across the large parking lot and managed to make it into the building without getting hit by a car. Realizing that Kate might need him to get into the complex, Dave also moved into a slow jog. When he entered the building, he was met with a loud, chaotic scene. There were parents and kids with large gym bags everywhere. He made his way through the maze of people to the registration table, but Kate was nowhere to be seen. Worried that she just skipped registration and made her way to the locker room, he found the person in charge of last names beginning with H - O and discovered that Kate had already gone through registration.

Kate was a combination of both her dad and mom. Like Dave, she was prone to procrastination and had a laid-back attitude some of the time, but when required, the mom in her would pop out to get done what needed to be done. That included getting through registration, changing into her uniform, joining her team, and getting warmed up for her first game of the day, all in under ten minutes. When it came to things she cared about, such as basketball, she always put in maximum effort.

Dave quickly found a spot in the bleachers with the other dads and a few moms, ready to cheer on the Panthers, who were already on the court in their gray and maroon uniforms. Kate was on the side, distributing balls to other girls as they

9

went in for layups. One advantage to getting there with only a few minutes to spare was not having to wait around very long before the game started.

He turned to face another dad, named Jordan, and said, "Hey, man, how you doing?" This was a little bit of a tease, since Jordan was Lynn's husband, who Jan had gossiped to him about the other day. Apparently, he and his wife were going through marital difficulties.

Jordan replied, "I'm doing really great." His proclamation didn't sound convincing, given he mumbled the reply in a low monotone.

Knowing firsthand what it was like to have an angry wife at home, Dave should have stopped, but continued, "How's Lynn?"

"You're an asshole, Dave," Jordan said, still looking down toward the court. It was true—sometimes it made Dave feel better to know that someone else was having a worse time of it than him, which made him an occasional asshole.

"What are you talking about?" Dave said, feigning surprise at Jordan's outburst.

Still not looking Dave in the eye, he said, "Jan knows, which means you know. Lynn just won't let up. A guy can't make a mistake? Lynn's no angel, let me tell you." He said the last part while turning his head back to look Dave in the eyes for emphasis.

"Hey, I'm the victim here too, I didn't ask for this information." Doing a quick scan of Jordan's middle-aged-Dad-bod figure, hairy ears, and thinning hair line, he had a sudden pang of jealousy. What would a twenty-year-old girl see in him? A former captain of the cheerleading team and good friend to his oldest daughter—former good friend. Dave was no movie star, but he was decent looking, in good shape, and of average height, so much more attractive than Jordan. He asked, "How did you do it?"

That question brought a smirk to Jordan's face. He replied, "You don't know how to talk to women. I'm sorry to say, but girls just don't go for an awkward guy that can't get a full sentence out in their presence."

"You don't have to get personal. I'm sure your bank account didn't hurt either," Dave said defensively. Jordan was right, so the comment hit home. If both he and Jan weren't drunk on their first few dates, he would never have gotten married. By the time they had their first sober date, they had already had sex multiple times, so the ice was broken, and Dave was able to get through the date with only semi-stilted awkwardness. Fortunately, the game was starting, allowing Dave to pull himself out of the conversation.

The referee blew his whistle, and the Panthers were off to a dominating start. Immediately, their center tipped the ball to Kate, who then tossed a perfect single bounce pass to the team's forward streaking toward the basket. Just like that, the Panthers were up two to nothing. Now their turn on offense, the opponents tried to slow the game down by passing the ball around until the perfect shot presented itself. That strategy continually backfired, since on over half their possessions, a Panther stole the pass, relayed the ball to Kate, who directed the fast break down the side of the court, and passed the ball to one of the two forwards for an easy layup. At the start of the second quarter, the Panthers were already winning sixteen to seven. Three of their opponent's points came from free throws when the Panther players got too aggressive on defense. Kate's team was a fast break machine.

One minute into the second quarter, the opponent's point guard passed the ball to their very large center. Fearlessly, Kate jumped in to try and steal the pass. As she was moving into the path of the ball, she felt a tightness in her head that caused her to feel dizzy and lose focus. Instead of catching the ball, it hit her on the head, and she stepped on the foot of another girl, rolling her ankle outwards. At first, she was confused, since she felt detached from her physical body, but that passed quickly, and she noticed the sharp pain shooting up from her right ankle. Kate screamed, mouth wide open and eyes closed, holding her right ankle straight up in the air. The action immediately stopped as the other girls on both teams paused what they were doing and all stared down at Kate. The referee immediately blew his whistle to stop the game, and the Panther coaches ran out onto the court to assist Kate.

Dave initially stayed up in the stands and let the coaches and referee handle the situation, but after watching Kate continue to wither on the ground, he knew something was seriously wrong and stood up to make his way down onto the court. As he stood, he noticed an exceptionally beautiful woman smiling at him from the top row of the bleachers. She was a black woman with light smooth skin, brown eyes, and thick dark brown hair pulled back into a ponytail. After goggling at her for a moment too long, she gave him a wink, then pursed her red full lips up and blew him a kiss. She then mouthed what he thought might be "Hey there, dumpling." She made him feel very strange and uncomfortable, but aroused.

The spell she had over him was broken when he heard Kate's angry yell from the floor of the court and made his way down to join her. He held her hand, and after a minute, she seemed to calm down a bit. She wanted to try to stand up and walk it off, but when Dave gently touched her ankle, she let out another yelp, so walking it off didn't seem like an option. Finally, the paramedics on call for the tournament arrived and ran through some tests, determining that Kate probably had a sprained ankle, but suggested they head to an emergency room to get it x-rayed. Dave helped her off the court so the game could continue, and the paramedics applied some ice to her ankle back in their makeshift training room.

"Can you just finish icing it and tape it up? I need to get back in the game," Kate implored with tears in her eyes.

The paramedic gave Dave a quick look and shook his head side to side a couple of times. Dave sighed and answered, "I'm sorry, honey, but unfortunately, you are done for the day. I'm going to take you to the hospital to get your ankle looked at more closely." Dave also noticed a little swelling under Kate's left eye where the ball had hit her in the face. As he moved in to gently stroke the red spot and wipe away one of her tears, she angrily pushed his hand away.

"No fair. This is bullshit!" Kate boomed.

"I know you're very upset, but you can't talk like that," Dave calmly but sternly told her.

Kate just folded her arms tightly around her torso and pursed her lips into a tight frown. Dave thanked the paramedic and carried Kate and her bag out of the gym and to the car. Fortunately, Kate didn't weigh very much. She kept her tightened posture the whole way back to the car, tears slowly dripping out of her eyes.

*

The plan was to drive home and take Kate to a local emergency room, but when they got to the car, her ankle was very swollen. So, ten minutes after leaving the sports center, Dave was carrying her into the Kittitas Valley Hospital. The doctor was very nice, but Kate was a recalcitrant patient. As her rude behavior continued, Dave went from feeling bad for her to getting very upset himself: she was embarrassing him.

When the doctor stepped out, he told her sternly, "You need to stop acting like this right now. I know you're disappointed, but injuries are part of playing sports. They are no excuse for treating people trying to help you badly, understand?"

She leered at her dad with a hard look for a few seconds, but then let loose her still crossed arms and conceded with a whimpering, "Yeah."

"Good, I need to call your mom now."

"Can you wait until they take me to the x-ray? I don't feel like talking right now," Kate said.

The nurse came back a few minutes later and wheeled Kate to the x-ray room, while he remained in the cubicle. It was finally time to make the call home, although he knew his day might be about to get even more stressful.

"Hi, Jan," Dave said.

"What's up? How is the tournament going?" Jan asked.

"That's what I'm calling about. Kate sprained her ankle during the first game, so I'm at the emergency room getting it checked out."

"Oh no. ... Is she alright? Why did you wait to tell me?"

"Yes, yes, she's fine. I was busy getting her to the hospital. She's just very upset about not getting to play."

"I can imagine. Let me talk to her."

"She's over in x-ray now, but I'll have her call you when she gets back."

"Ok, but if the x-rays haven't come back yet, how do you know it's just a sprain?"

"The doctor is just being cautious but is almost certain it's a sprain. I'll let you know what the x-ray tells us and have her call you back. I've got to go now. Love you," Dave concluded, quickly closing the line. He was stressed enough without having to play twenty questions with Jan. He could let Kate handle her mom on the ride home.

A few moments later, Kate was wheeled back into the room, and a few moments after that, the doctor confirmed there was no break or major damage; thirty minutes of gathering paperwork later, they were back on the road home. Kate spent much of the ride on the phone with her mom, expressing her disappointment at not getting to finish the tournament. Predictably, she concluded that her dad unnecessarily pulled her from the game, and was also upset he didn't take her back to the sports center after they finished up at the hospital.

While waiting for the discharge papers, Dave had called one of the other dads to get an update on how the game had gone after they left. It turned out, without Kate in the lineup, the Panther's lost that first game and were done for the day. He kept that news to himself, however, not wanting to upset Kate any more than she already was.

CHAPTER 3

Dave was one of two accountants working at a medium-sized plumbing company in Seattle. He and his coworker Paul were responsible for managing payroll, billing, taxes, and all other expenses associated with the business. Along with the owner and general manager, they were the only salaried employees on the payroll. In practice, that meant he typically worked fifty-hour workweeks without overtime pay, unlike the hourly workers, who got time and a half for every minute over forty hours they worked in a week. Regardless, the pay and benefits were decent and enough for him to have a good life with his family, but if he ever wanted to get rich, he would have to first get more ambitious. The master plumbers on the team actually made the big money.

"Thanks for covering for me last week," Paul said. Paul had spent the previous week fishing in Florida, leaving Dave with double the workload.

"No problem, how was the trip?" Dave asked, even though it had been a problem for him. He didn't like Paul, so he had to put great effort into staying cordial.

"Truthfully, I wish I had another week down there. A week of sitting on a boat fishing and drinking all day and hitting the bars at night—it was heaven. I even met a few women while I was there," Paul said, giving Dave a little wink. "I only get that type of action when out with my cousin; he's always been a player."

Dave thought to himself, *I need to get out more*. He wasn't looking for side action, like Paul, but while Paul was out on his adventures, he was always back here doing the extra work.

They were receiving the exact same salary, even though the owner, Jim, knew Dave put in many more hours and was the responsible one. Paul was Jim's cousin and local golf and fishing partner, so the dynamic was unlikely to change. He thought to himself that he needed to get control over his bitterness about the whole situation; the stress wasn't doing him any good.

Dave was a homebody who didn't fish or play golf or hang out at bars, making him the odd man out socially. Without Dave there to back them up, Paul and Jim would have much less time for sport. To emphasize that point, at 12:00 PM, Jim walked into the office and reminded Dave that he needed to finish the billing estimate by the end of the day for a big project the company was bidding on. Dave promised Jim that it would be done by 4:00 PM; Jim gave him a thumbs up, knowing Dave never let him down. Jim then turned to Paul and said, "Hey, buddy, let's head to lunch so you can tell me all about your trip."

"You're the boss," Paul said, giving Dave another wink, rubbing it in. They headed off, and Dave was left to work right through lunch and also mind the office; the two cousins would probably be gone for at least an hour and possibly longer. It was just as well, if Jim had asked Paul to help him, Paul would have just slowed him down and he would miss the deadline. Fortunately, the administrator, Claire, was efficient and shielded him from any distractions for the couple of hours Jim and Paul were at lunch. By the time they were back at 2:00 PM, Dave had finished the bid, but he kept that to himself; instead, when Jim plunked a new folder down, he reminded Jim that he needed to finish the bid. Reluctantly, Jim picked the folder back up and put it on Paul's desk; Paul looked surprised.

"I know you," Paul said after Jim left.

"Excuse me," Dave replied.

17

"I can see you've finished working on the estimate. I can't blame you for wanting to slack off a little."

"I'm not slacking," Dave said defensively. "I need to go over the figures again to make sure there are no mistakes. I'm not the one taking extended lunches right after coming back from vacation."

"Whoa there, we're all doing our part. It's not my fault you have to put in extra time to get your work done," Paul said, putting his hands up like he was surrendering.

Dave knew he should not have let his anger out. Paul was lazy and inept, but Jim didn't care. His role was to do the job and cover for Paul so that Paul was available to entertain Jim. Trying to fight against that dynamic was a losing battle. Paul turned away from Dave, put on his headphones, and started tapping his pen on his desk, being useless and annoying as always.

Dave spent the next couple of hours alternating between checking over the bid and surfing the internet. At exactly 4:00 PM, he got up and delivered the bid to Jim. He dropped off the folder and turned around to walk out of the office, but Jim asked Dave to sit down and hang out with him while he went over the bid. This was unusual, but landing the job was crucial for the company, so he understood. For the next hour, they both pored over the details of the package he had put together; Jim wanted to understand exactly how Dave had come up with the costs for equipment and labor and how he came up with the time frames involved. He told Jim not to worry, since he would be ready to pitch the bid to the customer and answer any questions they had.

"I appreciate that, Dave, but I'm going to give the pitch on this one myself," Jim said.

"Okay ... well, I'll make sure you have all the information you need."

"That won't be necessary, this bid package you put together is very thorough. It's what I've come to expect from you," Jim said, now looking Dave right in the eye.

Between spending an hour going over the package, learning Jim was planning to do the pitch himself, and finally receiving a compliment, he suddenly had a bad feeling about where the conversation was going. "Do you have something you want to tell me, Jim?"

"Dave, you've been a special employee, but as you know, business has not been that great lately."

"It's been pretty good, and our profits are up this year. Remember, I'm your accountant," Dave said before squeezing his lips together.

"I disagree. Unfortunately, I can no longer afford to have two accounts on staff, so I decided to keep Paul and let you go. It's Monday, and I'll pay and keep you on our insurance plan through the end of the week. ... Anyway. It's the best I can do."

Dave knew that Jim's mind was made up and the decision was final, but he decided to plead his case anyway. "Come on, Jim, you know that I do almost all the work back there. Paul could not have put together this bid package. You need me."

"I understand why you might be upset, but between Paul and me, we'll be just fine. Like I said, you've done a fine job for us over the years, but my decision is final. Maybe if you had been more of a team player, things could have been different, but ... well ... good luck."

Dave sat there for another few seconds, staring at Jim, but finally conceded and got up and calmly walked out of Jim's office, trying to keep some of his dignity intact. Surprisingly— it was 5:15 PM—Paul was still in his former office when he went to collect his stuff. Paul had helpfully left a cardboard box on his desk.

"Need any help packing up, champ?" Paul snickered.

19

Of course, Paul knew what was coming to Dave; they'd probably laughed about it over their extended lunch. "Good luck now that I'm gone. Your days are about to get much busier without me here to do all the work."

Paul gave Dave a little frowny face and said, "I'll miss you, brother, you were so much fun. You'll have to move on to spending your days judging someone else."

Insecure prick, Dave thought to himself. Fortunately, he had all his items packed up in under two minutes, since he had to get out of there before losing his shit on Paul. As he walked out of the office, his foot caught on the door sill. He tripped and landed hard, while his box of belongings went flying across the floor. Jim came out of his office and just looked at Dave with pity. He thought he heard Paul laugh but refused to look back.

With any dignity he thought he retained gone, he got up, ignoring the pain in his elbow and the taste of blood in his mouth. He quickly shoved everything back in his box and limped out of the office to his car. Dave sat there, breathing deeply, trying to calm himself down to avoid adding to his embarrassment by crying. To calm himself down further, he repeated a mantra to himself, "Payback is coming, payback is coming ..."

When he had time to further self-assess, he noticed his elbow starting to stiffen and could see his gums were bloodied up from the faceplant. His only solace was that nobody had come out of the office yet to gawk at him, but he knew he had to get going. If Paul came out and gave him one of his patented winks, he might step on the gas and run him down.

CHAPTER 4

Dave pulled the car out of the lot without further incident, but now had a much bigger problem than humiliating himself in front of his former co-workers. Somehow, he would have to tell Jan that he had lost his job. She stopped working twelve years before, when Kate was born, so after the week was up, their family would have no income or health insurance and only around four or five months of savings. Dave decided to do something he had never done after work: instead of going home, he would go to a bar and drink.

Being new to the bar hopping scene, he didn't have a go-to establishment in mind, so just picked a place he regularly passed by that was only a few miles from where he lived. It was almost 6:00 PM and the lot was pretty full. He could hear loud music emanating from the windowless building and saw people milling around the doorway smoking cigarettes; it seemed as good a place as any to take his mind off things.

He quickly found a small table in front of a television in the main room and sat down. A young waitress came by. She was dressed in tight-fitting shorts and a cut-away tank top. With great concentration and effort, he managed to keep eye contact as he ordered a Corona and loaded nachos before settling in to people watch.

It had been years since he'd hung out at a bar and he started feeling a little nostalgic for his younger and freer self. Not the mid-thirties version of himself that had a wife and two kids to feed and a large mortgage to pay off. Unfortunately, the food was delivered by a food runner, but he could still admire the beautiful waitress from afar. That was just as well, since when she came over to ask him if he needed anything else, he strutted out his most awkward self. He stared at her, mouth wide open, while trying to come up with something witty to say. In the end, he just stuttered out, "Just a-a refill." She gave him a little smile and left, obviously used to middle-aged men making fools of themselves by trying to hit on her.

After giving up on impressing young women, he turned his attention back inward and wallowed in his own sorrows. After an hour, he had polished off his large platter of loaded nachos and three beers, and asked for the check. The server left him a little thank-you note and a smiley face on his check, so he did the only reasonable thing and left her a ten-dollar tip on a twenty-five-dollar bill.

When he stepped out of the bar, he saw a guy lying on the ground soaked in his own vomit and piss, crying like a baby. He felt slightly better about himself, knowing that he was a long way from hitting that type of low. The air was crisp and the sky was unusually clear for that time of the year, so he put a little distance between himself and the man-baby and looked up at the stars. He breathed in deeply, letting the cold air into his lungs, leaving him feeling somewhat rejuvenated.

He decided that everything that had happened to him that day was for the best. He didn't like working at the plumbing company. He hated Paul and had been sick of Jim taking him for granted. This was the kick in the ass he needed to find a better job, a job that paid better and where he would be appreciated. He considered himself a damn good accountant. Feeling better about things, he smiled and took one last look at the pathetic loser, still lying alone on the stoop of the bar, crying.

Dave felt a little lightheaded from the beer, as he was not used to drinking that much, but he decided he could make it the three miles home. Besides, Jan would only ruin his good mood if he called her up to tell her he was at a bar and too buzzed to drive home. He would walk confidently into the house, announcing his good fortune with his head held up high. He almost got away with it too, but within sight of his driveway he forgot to stop at a stop sign—or so he was told—and was pulled over by a police officer right in front of his own house.

CHAPTER 5

Aliyah Cramer was sitting in a white Chevy Malibu, waiting for Dave to emerge from the bar. Her job was to observe Dave Smith and his daughter Kate. It was her call as to which one to observe when they weren't together. Her boss, Mr. Jones, just expected daily reports on their locations and to contact him immediately if they strayed far from their normal haunts—nothing too detailed.

To break up the boredom, sometimes she would go off script and have a little fun with the daughter. Back at the lab (her office and home base), she found a device that emitted sound waves outside the normal range a person could hear. She didn't know its real purpose, but it was fun to point the device at people and give them a little poke; they could sense the high-frequency sound wave on their skin and in their nerves. It was a fun way to creep people out.

Nobody at the lab seemed to notice the device was missing, so she liberated it and now used it to abuse Kate and other worthy victims. The device had good range and worked through most windows, so from a distance, she could give Kate the heebie-jeebies. Aliyah always poked her when she was alone, so over time, Kate became jumpy and paranoid, afraid of her own shadow. She watched the girl go from an overconfident little brat to a twitchy mess.

What she was doing to Kate was mean, but it was necessary to prevent her from doing much worse things; she had severe rage issues. Letting some of the tension out in frequent little discharges was a way to avoid letting the rage build up into something more dangerous—to other people.

If you looked into Aliyah's background, you would find a young woman who grew up in a modest, middle-class home in a seemingly stable family. The reality was much darker, however. Her father, Bernard Morrison, had a predilection for young girls, and after a close call where he was almost caught acting out his urges with a pre-teen a few towns over from theirs, the family made the decision to sacrifice Aliyah to ensure her father could act on his compulsions without getting caught. So, from the age of twelve to when she ran away at sixteen, she shared the matrimonial bed with her father, while her mother moved into her room. She had an older brother, but being a pervert himself, he was no help to her.

Aliyah satiated her rage by hurting other people. Wanting to be a good person deep down, she tried to control her rage and could successfully keep on the straight and narrow for sometimes months at a time, but then something would trigger her, and she would blow. One of the times she lost control, she beat a guy to death in a wooded area behind some industrial buildings; she got away with that one. Another time, she broke a girl's jaw in a fight outside a bar, which put her on the path to her current life.

It's not like Mr. Jones hired her because of her expertise in security work or kind heart. He knew what he was getting when he somehow convinced the prosecutor back in her hometown of Worcester, Massachusetts, to drop the felony assault charges she faced for breaking the girl's jaw in a bar parking lot—not unlike the one she was currently sitting outside. Given her priors, she was fully expecting them to lock her up in prison for many years. But they let her off, instead.

That afternoon, as she was walking away from the courthouse, not sure where she would go, a black Town Car pulled up beside her. A middle-aged, slightly balding man, with large full-rimmed glasses, rolled down the window and told her to get in. When she turned from him and kept walking—a little faster—he had the car follow along beside her and explained that he only wanted to talk to her. He then waved some hundred-dollar bills in the air, saying he would be happy to pay for her time. She replied that she was no whore. He said, "Of course, the money is just to talk." He opened the door and stepped out to show her that it was only him in the car, plus a driver up front. He promised not to touch her.

He didn't look dangerous, being somewhat geeky and doughy looking, so with no prospects and no place to go, and against her better judgement, she got in the back seat and listened to his pitch. Surprisingly, he wanted to offer her a job as one of his security agents, with good pay and benefits. When she asked, "Why me?" He replied that they were looking for raw talent that they could train and develop their way, and they felt her issues with the law and sometimes violent temper was actually a strength. He gave her his card and let her go to think about it.

Now a year later, Aliyah Morrison was Aliyah Cramer, and she was staring at the door of a bar, wishing she could go in and have a few drinks. But tonight was the night they were taking Dave back to the lab, so she had to remain fully alert while she waited for the guys to come up with the plan to nab him on his way home.

"Ooh, that one doesn't look so good," she said to herself. She pulled out her sound wave device from her oversized purse and pointed it at a drunk man with a large belly and thin arms who had just stumbled out of the bar. As he was lighting up a smoke, she pointed the gun-like device right at him and held the trigger down. At first, he jumped and started looking around, like someone had flicked him from behind, but then not finding anyone, he started dancing around with a distressed look on his face. He tried to get away, but tripped and landed hard on the cement, which elicited a loud whiny sound. A few other people were standing in front of the bar, talking and smoking, looking at the fat man in disgust, and assuming he was just very drunk and losing control. One aggressive man leaned over him and started yelling, "What the fuck is wrong with you?" The guy barely jumped away in time when the fat man started puking all over the sidewalk and himself. Having had enough fun, Aliyah eased off the trigger and put the device back in her purse.

A few minutes later, Butch called and told her to meet at the entrance to a park not far from the bar; they finally had a plan.

CHAPTER 6

The officer took her time, but after a minute, she got out of her vehicle and slowly lumbered over to the side of Dave's car. She knocked on his window, carefully keeping her body behind his front door, like she was worried he would shove the door open, slam it into her, and come out shooting. The blue lights were flashing, so his neighbors were starting to come out to gawk as he rolled down his window.

"Hello, officer, how can I help you?" Dave said. He had a moment of déjà vu, like he had seen her before. She was wearing a cap and large dark sunglasses, but her red lips and silky brown skin seemed familiar.

"Where are you heading tonight, sir?" Officer Davis said.

"Nowhere, officer, this is my home right here. I'm just getting back from work," he replied.

"Are you aware that you just went through a stop sign, sir?"

"No."

"Did you not see the stop sign on the corner, a half block from your house?"

"I thought I stopped," he feebly replied.

"No, sir, you didn't. You'll need to give me your license and registration."

Dave just nodded and handed them to her, then watched as she made her way back to her vehicle. He could see most of his neighbors now, either watching the show from their windows or standing out on their lawns to get a better view. Worst of all, Jan and the kids were also looking out at him through their front bay window. Jan looked disappointed, while Mikey had a big smile on his face; he must have thought his dad was cool, as he had entered the cops and robbers phase of his childhood and always liked to play the robber.

After a few moments, the cop came back to Dave's window and resumed their previous dialogue, "Sir, how many drinks have you had tonight?"

"Umm, maybe one or two after work, but I'm fine."

"Was it one or two, sir, or maybe more than that?"

"I think it was just one," Dave lied.

"I'll need to administer a sobriety test. Please step out of the vehicle slowly."

"Why do I need to leave my car? I don't want to! You have no cause!" Dave complained.

"Sir, I can smell alcohol on your breath, and you just admitted to having multiple drinks before getting into your car to drive home. Are you refusing to exit your vehicle and take a breathalyzer test?"

This was going downhill fast, and his family and all his neighbors were watching, so he didn't want to embarrass himself further by making a scene. Undoubtedly, the sobriety test would find him over the legal limit and he would end up in jail. To make matters worse, a second patrol car was pulling up behind the officer's car. Two largish men exited and started to approach him from both the driver and passenger side. *Are they going to drag me out on the street if I don't obey?* Dave thought to himself.

"No, officer, I'm getting out now." Dave opened his door and started to step out of his car when he felt something holding him back. He tried to force himself out a couple of more times, not understanding what was happening to him.

"Sir, please unbuckle your seatbelt," she said with a laugh and a smile. *Man, those lips seemed familiar.* One of the other officers, whose name tag read Jeffries, was now also standing beside his car. He smiled and helpfully added, "Do you require assistance in exiting your vehicle?"

"No, I'm fine! With everybody out here watching me, I just forgot. I'm fine! Don't need help. I'm perfectly fine," Dave snapped. Officer Davis then stood back from the side or the car door, while Jeffries swung his hands to his side, palms up, inviting him to continue his efforts in leaving his vehicle.

"Good job, Mr. Smith," officer Davis deadpanned as he finally made it out of the car and onto his feet. "Now you see officer Cane over there?" she asked, pointing to the second large male cop. "I want you to walk in a straight line over to him. Don't worry, I'm here right beside you if you need help."

"I don't need help, thank you very much." Dave started his walk toward Cane, but it didn't go well. He noticed that his kids were still staring at him through the bay window, but Jan was now standing on the front lawn only ten feet away. He eventually made it to Officer Cane, but stumbled twice along the way. That led Officer Cane to order him to turn around and put both hands on the back of his Subaru. He was immediately surrounded by all three officers; they cuffed him and then carefully placed him in the back of Davis's patrol car. Before sinking into the back seat, he had time to look over at Jan one last time and yell, "Jan! Bail me out! ... And I have good news!"

As Davis was pulling away, he could see Jeffries talking to Jan, hopefully telling her what station to meet them at. At least getting hauled off meant his one-man humiliation show was now over, and Dave's neighbors could go back to judging their spouses. The night had been a real rollercoaster of emotions: he went from depressed and worried, to elated and hopeful, to embarrassed and humiliated. He was now hurtling toward indignation and anger.

CHAPTER 7

It was 8:00 PM and Jan was starting to really worry about Dave; he was almost never home late from work and always called to let her know if he would be. Earlier, at 6:30 PM, dinner was on the table, and she had started trying to reach him on his cell, but despite four calls over the course of an hour and a half, Dave did not answer. She called his office and Claire acted cagey, just saying he left around 5:30 PM and that she would let Dave tell her what was up. She tried to get more information from Claire, but she held firm and wouldn't give Jan anything else. Now it was 8:00 PM, dinner was over, the dishes had been cleared, the kids were in their rooms doing their homework, and all Jan could do was anxiously wait.

She was about to call Dave yet again when she saw blue flashing lights shining through her front window. At first, she felt relief upon seeing Dave's car, finally knowing where he was and assuming he was alright, but then that feeling was quickly replaced by worry when she saw a police officer slowly making her way to his side window. She also noticed her nosey neighbors coming out in force to gawk at her unfortunate husband. *Had none of them ever been pulled over before?*

It didn't take long for Kate and Mikey to notice the flashing lights and commotion too, and all three of them were now looking out at the scene, staring at Dave.

"This is so cool; can I go out to get a closer look?" Mikey asked.

"No, stay right here or go back upstairs to finish your homework," Jan answered.

"Oh man, what do you think Dad did. Maybe he robbed a bank."

"Dad wouldn't rob a bank," Kate said.

"How do you know? There, look, another cop car is pulling up, so Dad must have done something really awesome."

"It's just a traffic stop Mikey; they'll just give your dad a warning or ticket and that will be it," Jan said, hoping it was true.

"Those two cops are really big," Kate said with some trepidation in her voice.

Jan was thinking that too; she hoped he was just being stopped for a traffic violation, but now that she saw him stumble a little after getting out of the car, she was very worried that this was more serious than forgetting to signal or rolling through a stop sign.

"I'm going out to see if I can help, but you two stay here, understand?" Jan commanded.

She knew Mikey would complain, so she was ready with the death stare to cut him off at the pass. Mikey folded his arms in frustration, but otherwise stayed put. She walked out the door and started to make her way to the street, where she now saw the female officer cuffing her seemingly drunk husband. As she approached, one of the large male officers put his hand up, indicating that she should stop; she stopped.

A moment later, he approached her and said, "Ma'am, is this your husband?" pointing toward the man being squeezed into the back of a police car.

"Yes, why are you arresting him?"

"We suspect your husband is under the influence of alcohol and are taking him downtown to the station to administer a breathalyzer and blood test."

"Can I follow you there?"

"Yes, but I think things will go smoother if you wait ten or fifteen minutes, by then, we should have him processed and ready for you to take him home." Officer Jeffries, according to his name tag, then turned and nodded at the female officer; she got in her car and sped off. Jeffries then said, "I'll see you at the station, ma'am," before setting off with his partner a few seconds later.

Jan was speechless, but then noticed her older neighbor, Tammy, walking toward her. She just yelled out to Tammy that she had to go, then turned around and quickly went back into her house. She had already decided that she wasn't going to wait fifteen minutes before leaving for the station, so she quickly got the kids bundled up and into Dave's car, since it was already out on the street ready to go. She retrieved the second set of keys and headed off with the kids to the station.

CHAPTER 8

LUD: ONE YEAR AGO

Lud was sitting in the back seat of a minivan watching a family eat dinner together through their dining room window. In the front seat was his new boss, a mercenary in command of the operation.

"Are you ready, Lud?" the boss asked.

Lud didn't answer. In his old life, he loved to talk, but in his new role, he felt no desire to say anything, ever. They had abducted him and brought him to a place they called the lab in the United States, where they transformed him from a human into a beast. Months before, he had been a respected civics professor and sought after commentator, but now he was a monster, an assassin, designed for murder.

Killing was the last thing he wanted to do, but the unholy procedure they put him through had left him violent and bloodthirsty. If he could, he would satisfy his bloodlust by tearing apart his boss, but after they transformed him, they strapped a collar around his neck that kept him in line. He could only hurt the people his masters wanted him to hurt; he was a slave.

"Keep it simple. Just break through the door, kill the family, and get back to the van."

Lud didn't know what the family had done to deserve to die, and he didn't care. As the moment grew closer, his bloodlust started to overcome him. He was an addict that needed a fix, and at that moment, nothing else mattered. He left the van and ran to the door of the house, barely slowing down as he broke through. When he got to the dining room, he stopped to size up his prey.

All four of them stopped eating and stared at him; ape-like and fierce, he must have been a frightful sight. The mother screamed and Lud smiled; he couldn't help it. With lightning-fast speed, he attacked the father first. He simply balled his hand up into a fist and brought that fist down on the top of the father's head, crushing his skull into his spine. Without stopping, Lud then leaped over the table and landed behind the mom, who was up and running toward the kitchen. He killed her with a twist of the neck before making his way back to the table. The children looked at him, too scared to move, and he hesitated.

Lud felt a mild shock from the collar and finished the job, killing the two children, before making his way back to the van. As soon as the door to the van closed, the boss stepped on the gas and they sped away. Lud had never felt so alone.

CHAPTER 9

PRESENT DAY

Jan had left to go to the police station with the kids only five minutes after the officers took her husband away, so she was surprised when she walked into the police station and didn't see any signs of Dave; she had never picked up someone who had been arrested and booked at a police station before, so she also thought that maybe her expectations were off. The lobby was empty, but fortunately, there was a police officer occupying the counter behind a glassed-in enclosure. She walked up and knocked on the glass; the uniformed woman behind the counter sighed as she looked up and pressed a button on her console.

"How can I help you, ma'am?" Officer Sanders asked.

"My name is Jan Smith; my husband Dave was just brought in to take a breathalyzer test; I would like to come in and see him now."

"I'm sorry, Mrs. Smith, nobody has been brought into the station this evening."

"That's not correct. He was just arrested, and Officer Jeffries told me that he was taking him to the station downtown to administer a blood test and breathalyzer," Jan said, clearly frustrated.

"I've been here for the last hour, and nobody has come in," Sanders replied with well-practiced patience.

"Maybe they came in a different entrance. Is that possible?"

"No, Mrs. Smith, no one has come in tonight or has been arrested tonight." She then held up a finger, indicating that

Jan should hold tight for a second while she typed something into her computer. She then continued, "Also, Officer Jeffries was off-duty this evening. Are you sure they were Issaquah police officers?"

Suddenly, Jan was unsure of herself. She was almost positive that the police vehicles that pulled up in front of her house had "Issaquah Police" written on the side of their doors. She also assumed they were Issaquah officers, since she lived in Issaquah and her husband was arrested in front of their house.

"I'm almost positive. The police car was an Issaquah police car, and he was arrested in Issaquah; can you please check again?"

Officer Sanders typed away on her keyboard for a few seconds more, remaining patient, but starting to look a little drained. She then said she would be right back and left Jan standing there. Jan could feel her heart pounding away in her chest, and she started having trouble breathing; the stress and frustration were starting to get the better of her. She looked back at Kate and Mikey, both sitting on a bench in the lobby, currently occupied by smacking each other's arms. She took a few deep breaths to get a hold of herself, not wanting to have a breakdown in front of the kids.

A minute later, Officer Sanders came back. She opened a slot in the window and pushed through a printout with a list of police stations and phone numbers. "Your husband is not here, and I confirmed that Officer Jeffries was not on patrol this evening. I suggest you call around to the neighboring stations on that list and see if you can find where your husband is. Let me know if I can be of any more assistance," she said with little enthusiasm.

Jan looked at the list, nodded to Sanders, then found a spot in the lobby to start making calls. Both Kate and Mikey got up and ran toward her when she moved away from the counter, and she had to direct them both back to their bench so she could get on with making her calls. She must have looked frightful because as soon as she spoke to them, they looked at her wide-eyed and ran back to their seats without the usual complaining.

She worked her way through the list, starting with Redmond, then Sammamish, and then moved on to the multiple stations in Bellevue. One by one she called to ask about her husband, and one by one they all said that nobody by the name of Dave Smith had been brought in on suspicion of driving while intoxicated. There was a Detective Jeffries working for the Bellevue police, but a quick check verified that he had not been out on patrol that evening in Issaquah either, and he certainly hadn't arrested her husband. This was turning into a nightmare, but regrettably, it was about to get even worse.

*

Another half an hour had passed, and Jan was just about to make her eighth call when a slightly overweight man in a worn looking tweed blazer, and possibly a couple of days' worth of stubble, came out into the lobby and walked to her.

"Mrs. Smith, I'm Detective Calahan; I was told that your husband was pulled over and arrested by three police officers: one woman and two men. Is that correct?"

Jan didn't answer at first, a little taken aback by the detective's abruptness. He was looking right in her eyes, with tight lips and a hostile demeanor, hovering over her as he waited for an answer.

"Ye-e-ss, do you know where he is?" Jan asked.

"Will you please come back with me? I have some questions."

"Okay. My kids are there. I can't just leave them here by themselves."

Calahan looked over at the two children sitting several feet away—seeming to just notice them for the first time—and turned his lips down like Jan had just inconvenienced him.

"They can sit on the other side of the counter; Officer Sanders will look after them."

She contemplated his offer for a second, then nodded her head and told Kate and Mikey to get up and follow her.

"Are we going to jail?" Mikey asked with wonderment in his eyes.

"No, this detective is going to help me find Daddy, and you are going to wait inside," Jan said firmly.

Having two kids in tow seemed to soften Detective Calahan a bit, so when they moved back into the secure area of the station, the tension eased slightly, and he offered them both lollipops while introducing them to Sanders. Mikey wasn't going to let him off that easy, however.

"I don't want to stay here. Let me go back with you so I can see where the action is. Are there criminals back where you are taking mom? Is she going to jail?"

"Your mom is not going to jail, kiddo, and there is nothing to see in the back, except for some old desks and older cops. You'll have much more fun out here with Officer Sanders," Calahan said. When Calahan mentioned the word *fun*, Sanders' already tired expression downgraded to despair. She didn't seem to be in a kid-friendly mood, or maybe she was just having a really bad day.

"I'll be back before you know it; just be quiet and let the officer here do her work," Jan said. She was positive that Mikey would not stay quiet. He would start peppering Sanders with questions and getting into things as soon as she left with the detective, but right now, she had more important things to worry about than Officer Sanders' contentment.

It was almost 9:00 PM on a Wednesday night when Calahan led her past a room full of officers, all seemingly hard at work.

"Is it always this busy on weeknights?" Jan asked.

"No"

Calahan then led her back to a small conference room where another uniformed officer was waiting for them by the door.

"This is Lieutenant Peabody; he'll be conducting the interview with me."

The two officers stepped aside to let Jan walk into the room first, but Jan hesitated, now more confused and frustrated than ever. Her husband had been taken away by three patrol officers over an hour before, and now a police detective and lieutenant were taking her in for questioning— and *they* seemed irritated; she was the one with a lost husband.

"I'm not going anywhere until you tell me what you did with my husband. You can't treat us like this. Where is he?" Jan yelled the last part, shaking, now almost frantic.

"That is what we are trying to determine, but please step into the conference room so we can clear this situation up together," Calahan replied curtly.

"What situation? Where is my husband?"

Seeing how the situation was getting out of hand, Lieutenant Peabody decided to deescalate things and calmly said, "Mrs. Smith, I know you are worried, and I want to answer your questions, but right now, we don't know where your husband is and need your help to find him. I promise, we are all doing everything we can to help, but we would appreciate your cooperation."

Jan continued to shake with worry and anger, but responded to Peabody's warmer tone and led the way into the conference room. Peabody raised his eyebrows at Detective

Calahan on the way in, indicating that Calahan needed to turn the temperature down a notch. He was starting to let his own anger interfere with the investigation.

Calahan followed Peabody's lead and worked to calm himself down, taking a moment to breathe in fully before slowly breathing all the air out through his mouth, just like they taught him in the mind-body workshop the town HR administrator made him attend. Calmed, he let Jan know that their conversation was being recorded.

Peabody then opened the door and let another uniformed officer in the room.

"Do you recognize this man, Mrs. Smith?"

"No, should I?"

"Are you sure? Is there nothing familiar about him?" Peabody repeated.

"Yes, I'm sure," Jan replied again.

"Thank you," Peabody said, not looking at anybody in particular. The mystery police officer then left the room.

Over the next forty-five minutes, the two officers asked Jan to recount her version of the events over and over again. After several minutes of follow-up questions following her third recounting of the story, she had finally had enough and refused to say anything else until they told her what was going on. Peabody looked over at Calahan, then back at Jan, and decided to fill in the blanks.

"Two of our police officers were murdered earlier this evening and their vehicles were stolen. We discovered them a couple of hours ago in a wooded area east of town. Their names were Dale Davis and Trent Cane, both young men with new families. They were stripped of their name tags and uniforms, and we suspect the killers may have been the ones that pulled over your husband and took him away."

The second Peabody told her that the people who took her husband were killers, Jan went into a tailspin. Her eyes both shot up into the back of her head and she slumped over onto the table, smacking her head hard. When she came to, Calahan was kneeling on one leg on the floor beside her, with his hand on her back. Peabody was looking at her from across the table, holding a paper cup of water that hadn't been in the room before.

"There you go, Mrs. Smith. Just breathe easy. You fainted. I'm sorry I was so blunt, but at this time, we don't have any reason to believe your husband has been harmed."

Jan pulled the cup toward her and took a sip of water. She looked at Peabody, unconvinced. They had just told her that her husband had been abducted by cop killers, so how could they know if her husband was unharmed? They didn't.

She composed herself: "No. The cop who talked to me was named Jeffries, and the cop who took my husband away was a woman," Jan said. "I'm sorry about your fellow officers, but they have my husband." Jan was shaking.

Detective Calahan tried to clarify: "Obviously, we are still very early into this investigation and as we speak, the crime scene where the two officers were found is being combed over. Since it is possible that the perpetrators who killed our officers also posed as traffic cops and took your husband, we are interviewing all of your neighbors too. Also, the man we asked you to identify earlier is the actual Officer Jeffries."

Jan sank into her chair, completely drained. Between the hours of worry and long interrogation, she had nothing left to give. "No, that wasn't the Jeffries that arrested my husband. Please, just find my husband."

"We gathered that and will do everything we can to find him. I promise," Peabody said.

"I need to take my children home now." Jan was completely drained and desperate to get out of there and back home.

Peabody gave Jan a sympathetic look, but said he just needed one more moment of her time. He introduced her to a man in plainclothes named Craig, who he said was the station's tech guy. He wanted her to work with Craig to try and find Dave's phone, since that might lead them to Dave and the killers. Jan consented, wondering why they hadn't taken this step an hour before, but it was of no consequence anyway, since they had tracked the phone to her car in the police parking lot. She'd had enough and needed to get home.

Peabody nodded his consent, and Calahan walked her back to the front counter to pick up her children from a relieved looking Officer Sanders. Calahan noticed all Jan's emotion and energy were gone now as she walked out the back doors, zombie like, ignoring her two kids bombarding her with endless questions and tugging at her for answers she did not have. He was desperate too, he had to catch the killers of his fellow officers.

CHAPTER 10

Mateo loved exploring the forested area behind his neighborhood; just a short walk from his house was the Tiger Mountain Conservation Area. Right after school, he had stopped at home for a quick snack, dumped his bookbag, and set off to hike the Poo Poo Point Trail. Now hours later, he was finishing up his hike, and all he could think about was getting home and eating dinner—it was close to 7:45 PM. He was only around twenty feet from the trailhead when he noticed a coyote and some crows picking at something just off the trail. It was already dark out, but the parking lot lights were shining through the trees, so he could see what looked like two legs sticking out from behind a tree.

He grabbed a rock and approached the coyote, which immediately stopped focusing on pulling at the leg and moved its focus to him. Mateo was not the type of person to back down from a confrontation, so when the coyote started growling at him, he just screamed back, nailed it on the side of its neck with the rock, then quickly picked up a large stick. The coyote ran back a few feet, which enabled Mateo to get close enough to see two bodies behind the tree; the bodies were only partially clothed, and he could see that the coyote and crows had been biting and pecking at them. It was too dark to get a closer look, and the coyote looked like he might come in to try and reclaim its prize; it wasn't backing down either.

Mateo ran the short distance back to the parking lot, called 911, and told the dispatcher what he had seen. He then called his parents; his dad told him to stay put and not say anything;

44

he would be right there. The police station was only a few blocks away from the parking lot, so within seconds of calling the dispatcher, he heard the sound of police sirens. Within a couple of minutes, there were two police cars and four police officers in the lot. He led them back to the bodies—the coyote must not have liked the odds and was no longer chewing their legs—and was then told to go back to the lot and wait.

His dad, Marco Rivas, was in the parking lot looking for him when Mateo reentered.

"Are you okay, son?" Marco said, worried.

"I'm fine, Dad."

"You're lucky, what if the people who left those bodies there were still around when you walked by?"

"They weren't. It was just a coyote, and I chased him off," he said with a little pride.

There were now ten police officers and an ambulance in the lot, and they were taping off the area to prevent anybody who wasn't supposed to be there from entering. One of the uniformed officers was talking to a man in a tweed blazer and was pointing right at Mateo. The man in the blazer walked over and introduced himself as Detective Calahan, confirmed that it was Mateo who found the bodies, and then took out a notepad and wrote down the father and son's details. He then went on to ask Mateo to go through everything he did and saw from the time he first entered the woods earlier that afternoon until he called 911. The questioning lasted until another officer interrupted him; Calahan then told Mateo that he would be back in touch with him to go over what he saw in more detail later but could now go home. Calahan then headed off into the woods to see the carnage for himself.

*

Earlier that evening, Detective Calahan had been at home and was just settling in with his TV dinner and beer for a night of watching basketball and relaxing. He had just taken his first bite of Salisbury steak when his cell phone went off; he looked at the number and let off a big sigh before picking up the phone and simply saying, "Calahan." When he heard that a kid had found two bodies in the woods at the end of East Sunset Way, he perked up a bit: this type of excitement was pretty rare in Issaquah. He shoved his tray of food and half-drunk can of beer into the fridge and was out the door.

When he finally arrived at the trail head parking lot, there were already several officers securing the crime scene, which gave him a sense of relief, since he appreciated when things were done right. It was after dark on a cold December evening, so thankfully, the only two spectators he saw were a teenager and what looked like his dad standing to the side. Another officer came up behind him and pointed the teenager out as the person who found the bodies and made the 911 call. He really wanted to inspect the bodies first, but he decided to do a quick interview of the boy while everything was still fresh in his head.

Looking down at the teenager, he asked, "What is your name, son?"

"It is Mateo, sir."

"And I'm Mateo's dad, Mr. Rivas."

"Mr. Rivas, I would like to ask your son a few questions. Is that okay?" Calahan asked, looking first at Marco and then at Mateo. Mr. Rivas replied in the affirmative, while Mateo just nodded his head. "Good, this should just take a few minutes."

Calahan then spent the next ten minutes leading Mateo down memory lane, getting every detail he could out of the boy. It was particularly interesting that Mateo had not noticed the bodies when he entered the park earlier in the afternoon while it was still light out.

He was just wrapping up when another officer tapped him on the shoulder and quietly told him that the two bodies were fellow Issaquah police officers. Before Calahan could fully absorb this, it was immediately followed up with a report from back at the station that there was a woman with a missing husband. The curious thing was that she claimed her husband had been arrested by three Issaquah police officers, even though there were no arrest reports called in that evening—all traffic stops and arrests were recorded and called in as soon as they happened. This was getting more interesting by the minute.

Calahan told the father and son that they could go, but he would be back in touch to finish the interview in the next day or two. He wanted to interview the woman with the missing husband, but first, he needed to see the crime scene and gather all the information he could on what had happened at the park.

*

Finding the two bodies was just a matter of walking toward the bright lights; the crime scene investigators had managed to set up floodlights around the bodies and surrounding area. They had just started getting to work on gathering evidence, and Calahan knew they would not be able to tell him much. There were a few police officers milling around the area, so he told them to go back to the parking lot, not wanting them to walk over any evidence. As he approached the scene, he could see the bodies of the two men face down on the ground, partially covered with leaves. He could see that they were missing their uniforms, left wearing only underwear. He also noticed that the leg on one of the bodies had been chewed up, the bone visible below masticated flesh.

Another officer on the scene identified them as two fellow officers, Dale Davis and Trent Cane, both young officers were at the start of their careers with new families. He knew both of them pretty well and considered them to have had bright futures in the department and beyond.

Like Calahan, Kelly Jacobs used to work for a big-city police department but took a job in the quieter suburbs for the better pay and reduced workload.

"I know you're just starting your investigation, but is there anything you can tell me now?" Calahan asked.

"I can tell you that rigor mortis is only just starting, so they've been out here for no more than a couple of hours. The backs of both of their heads were smashed in with a rock, which we found just a few feet from where they left the bodies. I don't know whether they died from trauma to their heads or that was done to them postmortem, though I suspect the latter. I'll have more for you in a few hours," Kelly replied.

Calahan just nodded his head and thanked her. When he got back to the parking lot, there were twelve police officers standing around, not being very useful. He selected two officers to keep the area around the parking lot and trail head secure, and directed the rest of them to start canvassing the surrounding neighborhood. In particular, he wanted to know if any of the neighbors had heard or seen anything—were there gunshots? He also needed to push the tape back further to prevent anybody else from entering the lot, since it was possible that the confrontation with the perpetrators occurred in the lot. He needed that area to be kept clear so any evidence would not be trampled on any more than it had already been.

He called into the station to let them know he was coming in to talk to the woman with the missing husband and to request more officers to secure the area for CSI. It looked like somebody beat him to the request for more help, since just as he was leaving the scene, several more police cars pulled in. Among them was a team of CSI agents from the state, to help Kelly. He put a sergeant in charge of keeping the crime scene secure and left for the station.

CHAPTER 11

The drive from the parking lot to the police station only took three minutes, but that was enough time for Calahan to take in what had happened to the two young police officers and work himself into a fever. He tried to compartmentalize his anger, but the result was that he was short with Jan Smith, the wife of the missing husband. He only comported himself in a professional manner after Lieutenant Peabody subtly scolded him. He had to get control of his emotions because he suspected things were only going to get worse from here.

The interview confirmed that the perpetrators murdered the officers, stole their cars, and then used the officers' identities to kidnap Dave Smith. It did not tell him why the perpetrators did any of this—was the goal to pose as cops a part of a premeditated plan to kidnap Mr. Smith or was some or all of what occurred spontaneous? And where was Dave Smith? He would need to gather a lot more information before he could answer any of those questions.

Both Calahan and Peabody agreed that they needed to interview all of the Smith's neighbors who had witnessed the traffic stop and get a hold of any camera footage from the houses surrounding the area and along the route between the Tiger Mountain parking lot and the Smith's house. Before doing any of that, he had to try to locate Mr. Smith; he had a tech guy named Craig working with Jan to try to locate Dave's phone.

Walking over to Craig's desk, he could see they were wrapping things up. He told Jan she could go home, assuring her that he would keep her posted on any updates related to her missing husband. Craig let him know the good news first—the phone had been tracking all his movements, and he had a month's worth of data to analyze; the bad news was that while they could determine all the places Dave had been up to the point of his kidnapping, the phone's current location was in the police station's parking lot. Dave had left the phone in the car when he was taken.

While Calahan was interviewing Jan, the tech had also tracked down the stolen police vehicles, but that was also a dead end. Both vehicles had been abandoned on a back road a few miles from where Dave was taken, meaning the perpetrators had switched vehicles. Where the cars were abandoned was a starting point though, so they put out a bulletin to all the surrounding police departments to be on the lookout for a vehicle possibly containing a woman and two men posing as cops. It was looking much more like a pre-planned kidnapping by the minute, but he still didn't want to assume that Dave was the planned target from the get-go, he might have just been the unlucky victim of the perpetrators' greater designs.

CHAPTER 12

Sitting in the back of the police car, Dave tucked his chin into his chest as officer Davis pulled away from his house: he was ashamed of himself and couldn't bear to watch his neighbors gawk at him as he was taken away. He couldn't imagine life getting any lower, but then Davis amped up the volume on the radio when "Shiny Happy People" started to play. She was singing along and doing a little shimmy.

"Why are you so happy?" Dave asked bitterly.

"It's a beautiful world, Dave. I've been listening to these tapes on happiness, and the first rule is that you have to act happy to be happy. You should try it."

What she said sort of made sense, but Dave needed to stay miserable and felt that Davis was being wholly inappropriate. You can't ruin someone's life and then do a happy dance—was this not something they taught in the policy academy?

She looked at him in her rearview mirror and made a little frown. "Aww, is Dave feewing unwhappy?" she mocked in a little baby voice. "Lighten up, Dave, I have a feeling that things are going to get a lot worse for you, so sing along while you can still speak in full sentences." Dave looked at her, a little stunned at the threat. "Just kidding, Dave. A little birdy in HR told me you have a bright future. ... I shouldn't say anything more, but if you want my advice, take their offer. It really is a great company to work for."

"What the fuck are you talking about?"

"Language, Dave, language. Don't make me come back there with a bar of soap," Davis said with a little smile. She was enjoying herself.

Dave was pretty confused at this point, but assumed she was gaslighting him. He'd read that cops tried to throw you off balance in order to get you to admit guilt; he wondered if they were looking to pin some other crime on him, besides drunk driving. While he was distracted, he didn't notice at first that she was driving in the opposite direction of the downtown Issaquah police station.

"This is police harassment. Where are we going? Downtown Issaquah is the other direction!"

She just smiled at him via the mirror and kept on singing and chair dancing—joyous. She then pulled the car off the main road and onto a narrow dirt road. Looking out the back window, he could see they were being followed. After another thirty seconds, Davis stopped the car. She got out and stood by his door while the other two officers made their way over. When they were all set, she opened the door. Cane immediately reached in, grabbed him by the collar, pulled him out of the car, then leaned him up against the trunk and punched him hard in the gut upwards toward his diaphragm; he instantly crumpled to the ground in a fetal position, unable to breathe.

"You should have danced with me, Dave, while you could; I bet you didn't believe me when I said your day would get worse," Davis teased.

After a moment, he got his breath back and spit out, "You also told me I had a bright future, and fuck all of you!"

"You told him all that, Aliyah?" Cane asked in a sarcastic tone, "You always have to ruin the surprise." He gave her a little scolding sideways head nod. "What will it be, Dave, a dark or bright future? ... Hmmm, nothing to say? Smart. Well, nothing personal, Dave, but we have a long journey ahead of us and I always find things go easier if I soften the package up a little right at the start. ... Pull him back up to his feet."

53

Cane viciously punched him again, causing him to fall back to the ground. After the third punch to the gut, he took out a baton and smacked it into Dave's thigh and then calf. "That should do you. With those two boo boos on your leg, you won't be running away from us anytime soon. Word to the wise, Dave, if you do try to run away, I promise I'll catch you and use this baton here to break your feet ... comprende?" Not waiting for Dave's answer, he smiled and introduced himself as Kevin, then leaned down and grabbed Dave's hand while Dave still lay in the fetal position, and shook it enthusiastically. The cop he formally knew as Jeffries then introduced himself as Butch and also shook his limp hand.

Dave didn't know what to think about all this: on the one hand, they were kidnapping and torturing him, but on the other hand, they had suddenly become so agreeable. He was starting to understand Stockholm syndrome; he almost felt like one of the gang. It was sort of like when his fraternity hazed him back in college.

"... and who are you? Aliyah?" Dave asked, looking at the person he originally knew as Davis.

She made her way to his side, closed her eyes, and snuggled her nose against his cheek, taking him in with a deep breath. "I'm the woman you dream about, dumpling." He felt aroused, but then guilty and a little uncomfortable. Whoever she was, she was the most stunningly beautiful woman he had ever seen.

After the introductions, they dragged Dave to a minivan parked in front of the police cars, stripped him down to his birthday suit, and squeezed him into a utility box that was sitting where the third row of seats would normally be. Before closing the box, they jabbed him with a needle; Aliyah gave Dave a kiss on the cheek and wished him a nighty night.

CHAPTER 13

The Human Enhancement Lab—or HEL for short—was a secret lab within the Special Research Division of megacorp, Greenrock Solutions. Most people knew of Greenrock from their advertisements touting green solutions to the world's energy problems. They were the company that would help the U.S. meet its energy needs now and into the future, while simultaneously guaranteeing fresh air and clean water for the nation. According to Greenrock marketing, they were the solution to the world's greenhouse emissions problem.

It was true that Greenrock sold technology used to limit greenhouse gasses in manufacturing and energy production, but underneath the friendly façade, they made most of their profits contracting with various governments, including the U.S., providing technology used in weapons and security. HEL was founded a little over a year and a half earlier by CEO Philip Stirling, company research director Hunter Cassidy, and Dr. Seymour Danzel to provide the U.S., and the very wealthy in general, with a service designed to eliminate one's enemies. There were plenty of firms that specialized in using non-lethal techniques to gain influence for their customers, and if murder was necessary, they would try to do it cleanly with minimal collateral damage. HEL filled the niche where assassination required more of a shock and awe approach; terrorists, but on the side of the angels—or whoever had enough money to afford the service.

It was also a vehicle for turning Dr. Danzel's brilliant and sociopathic mind into a profit center. Unfortunately, after overseeing Danzel's work for many years, Cassidy suddenly grew a conscience and tried to close down HEL—directing an organization set up to assassinate people for profit became too much for him. By that point, Greenrock and the U.S. government had already invested hundreds of millions of dollars into the lab, so Cassidy was fed to the lab's first monster, and another company director who had previously worked at Greenrock headquarters, Mr. Jones, was promoted in his place. Mr. Jones had no experience in research and development, but that didn't matter, since the job no longer required scientific aptitude. One of the lab's technicians had jokingly called the Neanderthal-like monster they created a furry—the name stuck. The fact that something so fiendish and horrible could have such a cutesy name would only add to its legend.

Knowledge of the lab was kept to a minimum within Greenrock, so HEL's current management included only Dr. Danzel, Mr. Jones, and Shane Cooper, who was vice president of the Special Research Division. Jones ran the lab's day-to-day operations, including the small security force used to patrol the lab and acquire new recruits. The newest recruit was Dave Smith, formally of Issaquah, Washington. Unlike the nine other furries currently in the program, Dave would be the first to use Danzel's new genetic models to more finely tune the transformation process, providing the program with a new tool to use on their terror missions.

The other member of HEL leadership was Alan Keeps. He was a former U.S. special forces officer who oversaw the special operations unit, a force of ten mercenaries and nine furries. He trained the furries, and led and planned their assassination missions. Jones didn't consider him part of the management team. Keeps liked to stay out of office politics and just run his team.

*

Mr. Jones looked at the screen and watched Dave sleep off the anesthesia they had given him during his two-day trip to Johnstown, Ohio on the outskirts of Columbus, the location of the Special Research Division and HEL. He looked over at his boss, Shane Cooper, and shook his head in frustration. That morning, Dr. Danzel had informed them that he wouldn't be ready to start working on his new patient for at least a couple more months. The plan was to bring Dave in and immediately transfer him to the furry program. Now with the delay, he was Jones's problem for the foreseeable future. Unfortunately, Danzel was irreplaceable, so his eccentricities were shrugged off, and everybody else was expected to adapt—sociopathic mad scientist doctors were in short supply.

They had holding cells on the lower level, but keeping a prisoner locked alone in a cell long term wasn't really in HEL's purview and might negatively impact Dave's psyche. He didn't actually care about Dave's mental health, but it could affect his transition into the program later. That meant he had to come up with something for Dave to do for the next couple of months. Cooper patted him on the back: "I'm confident you'll make the best of the situation. You always do, Bill." With that, he was off to do whatever big picture stuff VPs did when they weren't patting their reports on the back and being condescending.

Mr. Jones did have a plan, actually. In the last week, the special research accounting department had lost four employees, and conveniently, Dave was an accountant looking for a new job after being recently laid off and relocated—serendipity!

CHAPTER 14

A month prior to Dave's recruitment, Greenrock's corporate compliance discovered that three of the accountants working at special research were skimming money. Getting payment from customers who used the services provided by HEL division was more complicated than how Greenrock billed customers in its other divisions. HEL's customers required absolute confidentiality, so payments were filtered through multiple shell companies before the money wound up in Greenrock's coffers. If audited, it just looked like those customers purchased various consulting services through third parties. If any auditor looked very deeply, they might find that Greenrock ultimately supplied the service via one of their IT or human resources consulting divisions. Serving clients that way was common in their industry, so it wouldn't raise any red flags.

The bouncing around of billing between the third parties and special research enabled the crooked accountants to hide their crimes for almost a year. Finally, compliance discovered that some of the money lost in the overhead of moving payments between the various entities was a little more than it should have been on each transaction. If special research were a normal company division, they would just fire the three accountants and possibly bring them up on charges, but the company no longer trusted the three of them to honor their NDA's and keep what they did at Greenrock private.

The solution was to do things the Greenrock way, which technically should have been referred to as the HEL way. HEL's whole charter was to engineer new and more efficient killing machines; their products were the evil things that went bump in the night. If a lesson needed to be taught, you hired HEL to educate your adversary with extreme prejudice. Cooper and Jones had to set an example so any other employee who might be thinking about ripping off the company would take notice.

Jones had a couple of his security goons grab a recent immigrant, Amar from Syria, who had come to join his extended family in Toledo. They threatened to kill both of Amar's parents and little sister if he did not complete a very simple task. All he had to do was take a backpack they had supplied him into a restaurant, order some food at the counter, and leave, conveniently forgetting the backpack under the front counter. They would then pay Amar five-hundred dollars and never bother him or his family again.

Meanwhile, they told the manager of the three embezzlers to take them to lunch at a local sandwich shop. Once there, she would tell the men that their misdeeds had been discovered, but the desire of the company was to quietly put the whole incident behind them; the manager thought she was there to offer the men a generous severance package if they left quietly and kept their mouths shut about what they did at the division.

On the day of the operation, the four employees walked into the restaurant at 12:13 PM. Five minutes later, Amar received a call on a burner phone, telling him to proceed into the restaurant, order lunch, and stash the backpack he'd picked up at a dead drop just an hour before. Amar was so nervous that sweat was pouring down his forehead and stinging his eyes; he kept walking toward the restaurant anyway, shaking and filled with dread. He was from Syria and had experienced plenty of violence, including bombs set off in public places. He wasn't naïve and knew what they were asking of him. Amar's family came first, however, so he would do what he had to do to keep them safe.

Fortunately, the door to the restaurant was propped open, so he didn't have to attempt to turn the nob with his shaky, sweaty hands. He spotted the counter in the back of the restaurant, past the tables, got around halfway there, and then heard a click. He didn't even have time to register what had happened before the blast blew his body apart into its component atoms. The blast pressure radiated out to the rest of the restaurant, instantly tearing everything and everyone to bits. The three stories above the restaurant also came tumbling down into the blast area, burying the carnage and suffocating most of the flames from the detonation. What was left was a large smoldering pile of concrete, bricks, rebar, and body parts.

In the days that followed, Amar's troubled history and infatuation with ISIS was discovered in social media accounts linked to him and on his computer. The fact that he was a young single man from Syria who had an electronic trail leading back to ISIS, and that it didn't raise any flags with homeland security when he entered the country, was an embarrassment to the intelligence community; congress was gearing up to hold hearings. In the meantime, Amar's family was also under intense scrutiny from law enforcement; things would not go well for them either.

Cooper needed to disseminate his teachings to the rest of the staff at special research, so he made sure the rumor mill included gossip about the dead employees' thievery and disloyalty to the company. He had no reason to believe the manager was also disloyal, but the manager was obviously incompetent, so it was a small loss to lose her as collateral damage.

CHAPTER 15

Dave woke up with a spinning head and nausea; he put his head over the side of the bed to avoid puking on himself, and noticed a conveniently placed bucket under him. He spent the next minute heaving up liquid, then heaving up saliva, and then just heaving until he was finally able to get control of himself and roll back into bed. He felt better, though.

As he lay there, the previous day's tribulations filtered back into his mind. He noticed that he was still naked, and he was lying on a bare vinyl mattress, with no sheets or blankets. He wasn't cold; the room he was in was kept at a comfortable temperature and the lights were mercifully dimmed; his abductors were thoughtful. Beside his bed was an ergonomic chair and desk with a reading lamp on top. Up toward the ceiling were three slotted windows that let in simulated daylight, similar to the daylight LED lamps he used at home. The room was cozy in a dorm room sort of way, but with gray concrete walls and a well-polished concrete floor. There was also a camera looking down at him; he waved, hoping to get the attention of whoever was on the other side, watching him.

After an indeterminate amount of time, a balding man with oversized framed glasses and wearing a sports coat and khakis walked in and sat down in the chair; he then started pawing through a folder he had brought in with him. Dave started to say something, but without even looking up, the man held up a finger, indicating that he should wait. Dave sat up and started tapping impatiently with his foot until the man finally was ready to engage him.

"Let's start with the basics. Is your full name David Albert Smith?" Dave just sat there. "Please answer so we can get through this as quickly and painlessly as possible."

Given what he had experienced over the last day—was it even the last day anymore? He didn't know how long he had been out—he took the last part of the man's statement as a threat. "Yes, my name is David Albert Smith. Who are you?"

"Thank you, Dave. I hope you don't mind me calling you Dave, I heard that is what you like to go by. You can refer to me as Mr. Jones."

"Sure, but if you already know my name, why did you ask ... and can I get some clothes?"

"As I said, we just need to get through some formalities to get you properly processed. As for your second question, all in good time. Now, I'm sure you have lots of questions, but I assure you that they may or may not be answered eventually. I'm just here to make sure you understand and agree to the ground rules so that there aren't any misunderstandings as we move forward with the onboarding process."

Dave, now feeling vulnerable and agitated, stood and hovered over Jones and loudly said, "Onboarding to what? I've figured out that you are not really the police, but why am I here?"

Mr. Jones said softly, but firmly, "Sit—down—Dave, our organization does not tolerate threatening behavior of any type. All team members are required to support and build each other up ... understand?" As Jones said the last part, he looked up at Dave, almost daring Dave to challenge him further.

Dave sat down, no less upset. "You must be kidding me? You people have threatened, beaten, and kidnapped me, and you expect me to believe you don't tolerate threats—you are crazy."

"As a leader, sometimes I have to make decisions that are less than fortunate. You've had a really rough go of it the last few days, so I'll let your last comment pass. Unfortunately, I need to rattle you just a little bit more before we move on to more interesting things." Jones sighed deeply and grimaced a little as he pulled a photograph out of his folder and took a long look at it—the whole 'this pains me more than it pains you' routine. "Okay, Mr. Smith, I want you to take this in the spirit it is intended." He then handed Dave a photograph of Jan, Kate, and Mikey dancing together in the backyard, enjoying happier times together.

As Dave stared at the photo, Jones continued, "You have nothing to fear, Dave. I want you to know that this company always takes care of its own, and that includes our employees and their families. As you will soon learn, our first and most important core value is that we are all family here. Your loyalty will be well rewarded, but on the converse, if you betray the company ..." Jones stopped and breathed in and out slowly, giving Dave his best theatrical pause, "well, let's just say, you have a lot more to lose than yourself."

"You fucking bastards! I swear, if you harm my family, I'll, I'll, ..."

"Yes, you won't do anything. I can see how upset you are, and that love you have for your family is something we are counting on. Feel free to keep that picture; there is even a nice frame in your desk drawer."

"I just want you to know that I don't believe any of that core value bullshit you are flapping on about for a second. I've met your peers. So, this is my prison cell and if I try to leave and don't do everything you say, you'll kill my family."

"They aren't my peers. I'm the boss here!" Jones said reflexively. Dave smiled, realizing that he had got under Jones's skin, and he was a little insecure. Jones recomposed himself: "Now you are starting to understand the stakes, good. Now let's move on. This is your quarters; we'll spruce things up a little bit to make it more homey. As I said before, we reward loyalty, and that is where our focus should be from here on out."

Mr. Jones waved his hand up at the camera, and Aliyah (formally Officer Davis) walked in, holding some folded-up clothes. Forgetting he was still naked, Dave stood up to take them from her, but then she pulled the clothes back and paused as she gave him the once over, spending an extra moment gazing at his crotch, while biting her lower lip and jiggling her hips. Dave felt a little unhinged.

"Is sexual harassment part of my onboarding?"

Aliyah frowned at Dave and handed him his clothes. Jones interjected, "Well, it's good to have friends, but I see your point. Aliyah, you might want to avoid teasing our new guest. He's not in the best of moods right now." Moving his focus back to Dave, he continued, "We'll leave you alone now so you can shower and get dressed. Aliyah here will be back in fifteen minutes to take you to lunch; after that, you'll start your orientation. It really would be best for everyone, yourself especially, if you fixed that attitude of yours. Good day, Dave."

CHAPTER 16

Dave followed Mr. Jones's direction and showered in the small bathroom attached to his room. There was also an electric shaver in the bathroom, but he felt shaving would be conceding too much at this point. The outfit they gave him was a gray sweatsuit, boxers, white tube socks, and white sneakers. He wasn't normally a boxer guy, but everything fit perfectly. As soon as he finished slipping on his sneakers, Aliyah walked in.

"Come on, dumpling, I'll take you to lunch."

"Let's get this clear. I'm not your dumpling and I would appreciate it if you stopped objectifying me. Clear?"

She nodded, not hiding her disappointment. "I'm just trying to have a little fun. We're in different departments, so there is no reason we can't have a little fun, if that is what you are worried about."

"What, you think I'm worried about the org chart. I'm married and not interested in you, even if I wasn't. You don't remember beating and kidnapping me?"

"Don't get yourself so wound up. You'll live longer if you learn to relax," she said, winking at him. "Your past life is over now, so all that matters is what's ahead. You're a good-looking man; I'm a good-looking woman; what more do you need than that? I can see how you try to suppress your attraction to me. It's cute, but it's okay to be a man around me."

Aliyah wasn't going to back off, so Dave just had to pull back and learn as much as he could about this place if he was ever going to get back to his family and keep them safe.

Maybe instead of fighting with Aliyah, he could start using her apparent affection toward him to get information about where he was. That would be tough, since he both hated her and was unreasonably attracted to her, both things working together to put him off his game.

They made the long walk and elevator ride up to the prison's first level and sat down at a table in a small café. Shortly after, one of the wait staff came and took their orders. They were the only ones in the room, so he decided to start interrogating her.

"Are we the only ones eating lunch today?"

"I doubt it."

Wise ass. "And let's get one thing clear, I'm not a recruit or an employee: I'm a hostage. By the way, what is the name of this company or organization you kidnapped me into?"

Aliyah hesitated a little, but then smiled and moved her head close to his. "I'm not supposed to tell, but I like you, and it's not like you're going to leave and tell anyone," she said with a chuckle. "Greenrock Solutions, you've heard of them?"

"Vaguely, don't they advertise that they are a clean energy company? So, I was kidnapped to sell solar panels."

"Funny! You're not part of that division. Let's talk about you, though. What do you like to do for fun? Other than hitting the bars and eating nachos."

Well, that's interesting, Dave thought. "You were watching me the night you kidnapped me? How long were you out there?"

She lied, "I was sitting not ten feet away from you, and to tell you the truth, I didn't do a good job hiding my interest. Your baby blues had me mesmerized. It's slim picking in the guy department around here, so maybe I became a little infatuated studying up on all that is Dave." She paused for a sigh and then continued, "If you want a little advice, I would work on your situational awareness. I wasn't even hiding my interest in you, but you just sat there oblivious." She took a sip of her water and said with a pout, "To tell you the truth, I was a little hurt. Here I was, ready and interested, but you didn't even notice me. ... Notice me now?"

"For the last time, I'm not interested in you. I want you to let me out of here so I can go back to my wife and kids ... and speaking of watching me. That was you at the basketball game, wasn't it?"

"Yep, I've had my eye on you for a long time. I wish I could help you, but I'm just a worker bee like you, following orders."

"Well, you seem to enjoy your work a little too much. How long before the night at the bar were you watching me and my family?"

"Long enough. This conversation is starting to bore me. Do you always have to live in the past?"

"Bitch."

Aliyah just looked at him, a little taken aback. "You're traveling a dangerous road there ... Dave. I am not someone you should insult," she said ominously.

The pejorative just slipped out, though was probably accurate. Dave felt like a jerk anyway and had an overwhelming desire to apologize. Her response scared him a little bit too. He successfully forced his logical side to win out and not give in to Aliyah's threats and gaslighting; he could not forget that he was the wronged party here. He couldn't forget that even though she was an attractive young woman, she was a criminal just like the rest of them. Even worse.

He was living out a nightmare, surrounded by psychopaths threatening him and his family. Now that the conversation with Aliyah had stopped, he started focusing on the food. The little café' served up an amazing burger: the meat was prime, and the aioli was a perfect combination of sweet and sour, with a little kick. His plan to hunger strike his way out of captivity quickly fell apart.

Seconds after taking his last bite, two men walked in and escorted Dave back to his cell, four levels down in the dungeon he now called home; these people always seemed to appear just at the moment he wrapped up one activity and was ready to move on the next.

"See you later, dumpling; now you behave yourself and I'll be back later to give you a treat."

Incorrigible, Dave thought, but was also relieved that she had seemed to get over his rude comment. Despite her angelic looks, he didn't doubt her capacity for violence.

CHAPTER 17

When Dave got back to his room after lunch, he found it made up like a small hotel room. The vinyl mattress had been replaced with a real mattress that was nicely made up with sheets and a comforter, plus a couple of pillows—no mint, however. There was also an alarm clock and lamp on the desk, and a dresser in the corner that was fully stocked with clothes. The bathroom was even stocked with any toiletries he might need. In addition, by the door, there was a light switch and thermostat that had previously been hidden behind a locked panel. One thing that hadn't changed was that the door was still locked; they had nicely upgraded his room, but it was still a jail cell.

There were no reading materials, radio, or television in the room, so all he could do was sit there and fume over his current situation. If it were just him, he would be planning to make a run for it at his first opportunity, but he believed that Mr. Jones was serious about hurting his family. He knew there must be a way out of this situation, but he couldn't figure out what that way out was.

Between the heavy lunch and racking of the brain, trying to understand his situation, he grew tired and dozed off. He was awoken with a startle when a man dressed as a security guard wheeled in a food cart and kicked his bed. The man said, "I'll be back to pick up the cart in one hour," and then abruptly left. There would be no stimulating dinner with Aliyah tonight—for that, Dave was thankful. As it was with lunch, the food was very good and plentiful. He wondered if the prison had a nice gym where he could work off his calories and frustrations.

*

The next morning, Dave woke up to the blast of alarm bells ringing through his walls. The din was accompanied by his room lights automatically turning on to full midday sun mode. He stumbled out of his bed and managed to turn down the brightness, which also silenced the alarm bells. He then plopped back into bed to catch his breath; the shock of the loud alarm and bright lights left his heart racing; Dave felt like a ball of tension. It didn't help that he barely slept. With no distractions, he spent most of the night staring at the ceiling, ruminating about what had become of his shitty life.

While he was lying in bed, still trying to get his bearings, a new, young-looking security guard walked in pushing his breakfast cart. The kid said, "Someone will be back in one hour to escort you to work. Please be ready." Dave looked over at the clock and saw it was 6:50 AM, but he was confused by what the kid meant.

"Work? What kind of work?"

"I don't know," the kid said anxiously. He didn't seem like anybody that could give him answers, so Dave didn't press the matter and watched him quickly leave the cell while avoiding eye contact.

The hotel vibe continued with breakfast, which consisted of scrambled eggs, some fresh fruit, and a cup of English breakfast tea. They knew he skipped the toast and drank tea and not coffee; he wondered how long they had been monitoring him. *Were there cameras hidden in his home?* Even the toiletries in the bathroom matched the products he used at home. They kidnapped him and threatened to kill his family to work for them in some unknown capacity, but they

70

were also trying to make him comfortable by making sure his personal effects were familiar to him. His thoughts drifted back to solar panels, and he grew a little anxious, realizing that he knew nothing about them.

Fed, relieved, showered, and shaved, Dave sat waiting for his escort. He didn't have to think about what to wear because they had provided him with three identical sets of slacks, dress shirts, socks, and underwear. There was a small laundry basket beside his dresser, so he assumed his room came with a laundry service.

At exactly 7:50 AM, he heard the click of the door bolts retracting and actually smiled a little: despite his situation, the isolation of being stuck in his small room was starting to get to him. His facial expression involuntarily turned from relief to dread when he saw the person who walked through the door was Aliyah. "Oh ... it's you."

"Why the pouty face, dumpling? Most people are excited to start their first day of work at the new job," Aliyah responded. "Didn't you like your dinner last night and breakfast? I'm the one who wrote up your food profile, thank you very much."

"I'm not your dumpling. It's still prison grub," Dave said, crossing his arms tightly around his torso and making a grumpy face, not willing to concede a thing.

"I really thought there could be something between us, but you really are just a whiny bitch yourself."—*Touché!* "Are you the type of person that doesn't like to be happy?"

Feeling slightly embarrassed, Dave took note of his demeanor and loosened up his arms and uncrinkled his face; he decided that he could express displeasure in a way that didn't mimic his son Mickey.

"Let's go. You wouldn't want to be late on your first day. Mooove, mooove..."

71

As they started the walk from the cell block to the elevators, Dave decided to ask some questions and get some information that might be pertinent to what he might be experiencing for the rest of his day.

"The kid said you were here to take me to work. What is the job, exactly?"

Aliyah pressed the button to call on the elevator and turned to him: "Same job you had on the outside, Dave. You get to work in the accounting department. Seems like a boring job to me, but the important thing is that you seem to like it, and there was an opening that they needed to fill."

"Accounting department for this dungeon? I don't understand."

"No, silly. This dungeon is actually a lab underneath Greenrock's Special Research Division building. I don't know much about what you eggheads do, so you'll need to save your questions for your new boss."

"Special Research Division. What is that? Where are we? I think I'll need to know at least that before I meet my coworkers, don't you think?"

The elevator stopped, and they got off on the same floor as when they had lunch in the café the day before.

"I guess showing up for work and not even knowing what town you are in would leave a bad impression with your fellow eggheads. Other than, outside of what this lab does, I don't really know all that they do, but I'm sure you'll figure it out when doing your accounting shit."

"This dungeon is a lab? What do they do in this lab?" Talking to Aliyah was like pulling teeth. She couldn't just tell him everything he needed to know.

"What we do here is something you'll have to ask Mr. Jones. I can't say."

"Ok, how about just tell me where we are then?"

They walked through a maze of hallways to another set of elevators. The only button to call the elevator showed an up arrow, so Dave assumed that the elevator was the way up and out of the dungeon. Standing in front of the elevator button was a large black man, with a good-sized belly, in the standard security guard uniform.

"This is Freddy. He'll take you the rest of the way up. Lift up your pant leg for me," Aliyah ordered. He hesitated for a second, instinctively wanting to give her a hard time, but with Freddy there, he felt outnumbered and decided to just comply.

Aliyah fitted him with an ankle monitoring bracelet. It was very thin and not noticeable after she pulled his sock up over it and dropped his pant leg. "Not that you would want to try and make a run for it, but we like to make sure we know where our guests are at all times. Big Freddy here will take you up to accounting." She stood right in front of him, looked him in the eyes, and continued, "Now this is very important. Your workmates do not know you are in-house, and you are not going to tell them. You are here on temporary loan from Greenrock's headquarters in Potomac, Maryland, until we can properly hire replacements for the four accountants we recently lost in an incident. Got it?"

"What incident?"

"Not important. Do you got it?"

"I got it. What if they ask me details about my life and where I live?"

"Figure it out, but don't get too creative. I suggest you are a lifelong bachelor. Don't give them any connection to your old life. If they ask you details about your old job, just tell them it's confidential. In this company, that is normal and should immediately close any further inquiries."

Aliyah started to walk off, but then turned around one last time. "And, dumpling, try to fix your bad attitude."

73

With that, she set off back the way they came, and Dave was stuck with Big Freddy. At least Freddy didn't talk, Dave thought to himself. He heard the elevator ding. The two of them loaded up, and Freddy pressed the button labeled G; he also noticed that they were currently on floor U1—there were only two buttons: U1 and G. The elevator started to rise, so he took that to mean he was one level below the ground level, and his cell was on U5, so five levels underground. When they got to ground level, Freddy walked Dave around fifty feet to a set of metal doors.

Freddy said, "This is as far as I go with you. On the other side of these doors is the main lobby of the building. You are to cross over to the elevators and take them up to level three and follow the signs to accounting. No deviations."

With that, Freddy swiped a card over a keycard reader on the side of the doors to open them, and Dave walked through. He walked several more feet to the end of a hallway that opened up into a main lobby. On one end of the lobby was a long reception desk with a couple of young women stationed behind it. Immediately beyond them were the front doors and what looked like a courtyard on the other side of them. The front doors were sectioned off from the main lobby, including the reception, by a glass panel that extended the length of the lobby that sealed off the entranceway from the rest of the building. Security guards manned an entry and exit through the panel. The exit was a gated revolving door, set up so that you could only revolve out of the lobby, and the entrance was set up like airport security with x-ray machines and conveyor belts.

Since Dave was already within the secure area, he didn't have to worry about that. Being in a space with normal-looking people that he guessed were not all prisoners gave him a false sense of freedom. He could pretend that he was just here on his first day of work, but deep down, seeing all the people who were really free just made him somber. He had to get moving, however, since it was now ten after eight, meaning he was already late for his first day of work. He would have to come up with an excuse that didn't mention his prison escort being late in picking him up from his cell.

He got halfway to the elevators and then remembered something, turned around, and walked toward reception. When he arrived at the desk, he asked the young woman sitting behind a name plate labeled Michelle a question Aliyah never got around to answering.

"Where am I?"

Michelle simply stared at him with her tongue lolling out her mouth, seeming to not understand him.

"I mean, what town am I in?"

"Johnstown, Ohio," she hesitantly said, as if she thought it might be a trick question.

"Where is that?"

"By Columbus?"

"Thank you! Finally, someone with some real answers."

With that, Dave was back on his way to the accounting department.

CHAPTER 18

The accounting department was easy enough to find, since the elevator opened directly across from the open area that made up the department's lobby. Dave made his way to the front desk and checked in with the receptionist. The receptionist was an older lady, named Marge, who welcomed him to his first day of work with an easy smile and southern accent.

"Mr. Smith, I'll just need to see your ID, so I can print you up a temporary badge and get you on your way."

Dave felt his stomach drop and started to panic. They had taken all of his personal belongings, including his wallet with his driver's license, when they first kidnapped him. Then he remembered his breakfast tray that morning. They had left a wallet with a sticky note that had, "Keep With You," written on it. He had put it in his pocket before leaving the room, but never looked inside. He took it out of his front pant pocket, opened it up, and found a Maryland driver's license; it had his pretend address in Potomac, Maryland on it.

"Are you okay, honey? You look a might bit confused."

Dave was busy staring at his new license with his mouth partially opened. When Marge addressed him, he slowly lifted his gaze to her with his mouth still hanging open, looking dull. Finally, he snapped out of it when Marge held out her palm and asked if she could borrow the license for a quick moment.

"No need to be nervous, we don't bite," she said with a wink, and she scanned his license. He then heard the sound of a printer firing up, and seconds later, she was handing him a still warm plastic badge secured to a lanyard. "Just slip that around your neck and Mr. Laso will be right out to take you in. And don't worry. Everybody is so nice here. I'm sure you'll fit right in."

Right on cue, a man in a formal pinstriped business suit came out to greet him. "Dave, it's so good to meet you. Come on in and let's get started. Thank you, Marge." He key-carded the two of them into the office and continued, "Well, Dave, I'm your manager and I will help you get settled in. You can call me Mr. Laso. We've really been shorthanded for the last couple of weeks, so nobody is happier you're here to help out than me. Oh, here's your permanent badge, by the way. You can toss that temporary one in the shredder."

Laso led Dave into a small supply room that also housed the printer and a slotted cabinet with the words "Confidential Materials" labeled on it.

"The first thing you need to know is that we take security very seriously in this office. Any papers you no longer need should be placed in this cabinet. It is emptied multiple times a day and taken down to the shredder room on the first floor. You'll also notice, as I take you around, that everybody's desks are kept very neat when they aren't working. Whenever you leave your desk, even if it is just for a few seconds, you must lock all your work away. Auditors randomly walk through the office, and if they find unattended company documents on your desk, it is noted and can affect your career come review time ... why are you laughing?"

"It's nothing. I'm just not used to such strict protocols." What Dave was really laughing about was the mention of his career. His career with Greenrock was the last thing he cared about, but he did make a mental note to start leaving confidential material lying around as part of his passive-aggressive protest. It probably wouldn't be fair to Laso, who was clueless, but fuck Laso.

77

"Yes, I was told you are on loan from headquarters. I would have thought the security there would have been very tight too."

"You would think that, Mr. Laso," Dave quipped.

Laso just shook his head, "Well, that laxity won't fly here. I think you'll come to appreciate the way we do things. It's really about respect for the company and our customers; not to mention the legal trouble that leaks can cause."

Dave decided to needle Laso a little more. "I heard you were a little short on staff because of some incident. What's the deal with that?"

Laso pursed his lips, already annoyed by Dave and not yet recovered from learning that the company headquarters was loose with their security protocols.

"As I've already mentioned, we take our confidentiality seriously here and also don't gossip. ... I was going to have you dive right in, but maybe I better start you off more slowly."

Laso then led him into a cubicle, which contained a gray desk with an old-fashioned keyboard and terminal on top. Displayed on the terminal was a little green flashing underscore after the word, *login*. Dave, being only in his thirties, had never seen anything like it and was not sure what to do.

"What do I do with that?"

"That terminal connects to the mainframe down the hall. Unfortunately, our customer and billing data are still all stored in the mainframe. The accountants on the floor use more modern tools to crunch the numbers, but all the data is ultimately stored behind that old terminal there. You are essentially the bridge between the mainframe and accountants. They will send you requests for data, and you will compile those data requests and send the resulting data to a link that the requester can access. Here is the key to your desk. Inside the desk is a manual and a note with your login and password. Memorize it and then put the note in the confidential cabinet in the supply room. The password changes once a week. It's all pretty simple. Go through the manual and let me know if you have any questions. You should be ready to serve requests by this afternoon."

After Laso left, Dave just nodded his head in disbelief. He couldn't believe that he had been ripped away from his family and forced to work at Greenrock, just to serve as the interface between technology from the 1970s and whatever more modern tools the actual accountants used. When he was walking over to his cubicle, he did notice that other employees in the workspace had actual laptops. On one hand, he didn't care about the job, since he was essentially their slave, but on the other hand, he felt he was a pretty darn good accountant, so data entry was beneath him.

On the walk to his cubicle, he also noticed a lot of cluttered desks with and without occupants, so Laso was full of it when it came to his team's supposed tight security.

He opened up his desk and found his login on a sticky note: username DaveSmith and password Frog#$Legs8. The manual was only four pages, highlighting the fact that anybody with a few brain cells could do the job they gave him. Every time someone sent him a request for data, a little speaker beside his terminal would beep. That would signal him to type in a query to get the list of open requests. He would then follow the directions in the request to build the query for the data, and after making the query, type in another command to send it to the specified location: mind-numbing.

CHAPTER 19

It was still only 10:00 AM, and Laso had told Dave that he wouldn't have to serve any data requests until later that afternoon, so he decided to get the lay of the land and cause a little trouble to release some of his irritability and pass the time. He started with the cubicle across from his, which contained a very young-looking man with large, frameless glasses and a neatly cut head of brown hair in a comb over. With his smooth, hairless skin and slightly chubby cheeks, he looked like he could be in middle school.

"Hey, son, is your dad around?" The man-kid just looked up at Dave with his lips jutted, revealing a few saliva bubbles. "Take your time before answering, kid, maybe swallow down some of that saliva before you spray me."

The kid instinctively put his hand up over his mouth and scrunched his eyes together. "I work here. I don't know you."

Dave introduced himself and put out his hand, but the kid just stared at it while seemingly contemplating what the gesture might mean. Dave didn't let him off the hook, though, and just stood there with his hand out until the kid finally grabbed it and gave him a limp, wet handshake. Dave wiped his hand on his pants, while the kid just sat there, looking baffled. He asked, "... and you are?"

"I'm Rick."

"Are you an intern, Rick?"

"I don't know why you would think that. I've worked here for three months now. I graduated top of my class at Wharton last spring."

"Hmmm, then why do you have a terminal that looks like mine in front of you? I figured a Wharton man would be given something more interesting to work on."

Rick looked annoyed. "If you must know, I'm moving to an analyst position next week. I'm told that most people just starting out take much longer than that to move up from clerk. ... Didn't they talk about career paths with you? Maybe you're not on the fast track, like me."

Dave thought to himself, *the kid is feisty.* "Good comeback, kid ... I mean, Rick. Maybe we started off on the wrong foot. Since you've been around a while, maybe you can tell me about the incident that left you guys short on staff?"

"We're not supposed to talk about that." Rick then looked around like somebody might be listening in and gestured Dave to move his head over a little closer, and then whispered, "You heard about the terrorist attack at the sandwich restaurant a couple of weeks ago? Well, my former manager and three analysts were eating at the restaurant at the time. You didn't hear it from me, though. We're not supposed to talk about it."

"Why not?"

"Because they said so. I have to get back to work."

Rick turned around and started typing something into his terminal, which looked like a data entry query, so Dave assumed the conversation was over. Rick looked a little shell shocked and genuinely worried about telling him about what happened to the four lost accountants, but he probably needed to get that information off his chest. He would need to read more about the terrorist attack later if he could get his hands on information. Locked up with no television, newspapers, or internet, he would have to sleuth around and see if he could get access to those things in the accounting office.

He didn't have to wait long to find the information he was looking for. In one of the cubicles, someone had left a copy of *The Columbus Dispatch* newspaper on their desk. Seeing no one paying any attention to him, he quickly reached his arm in and grabbed the paper then made his way back to his desk. On page three, he found an article describing the progress made in cleaning up the building that collapsed in the recent suicide bombing. He made his way to the part of the article that recapped the events and found that a man identified as Amar Ismat—a recent immigrant from Syria—walked into a sandwich shop and set off a bomb that ripped through the building foundation, causing the entire structure to collapse down onto itself. All of the victims were identified, including four employees of Greenrock. Amar's social media posts seemed to foretell his actions, but the police and the FBI didn't know how Amar had obtained the C4 and knowledge to build a bomb; they were still looking for any accomplices.

Given what he had seen so far, Dave immediately suspected that Greenrock was behind it; if they were willing to recruit employees by kidnapping them and threatening their families, it wasn't a stretch to think they would terminate employees in a literal sense. He wondered if Laso was in on the kill, but assumed not—it seemed like a Mr. Jones type of operation. He had nothing to lose, so he would try to grill Laso on it anyway. If nothing else, it was more confirmation that they would carry out their threat to hurt his family if he didn't play ball; maybe he did have a lot to lose by stirring up trouble in the office.

CHAPTER 20

LUD: ELEVEN MONTHS AGO

Lud had spent the first couple of months after he was abducted and transformed into a beast in a large plexiglass cage in an even larger concrete-lined room. Then in early January, they moved him to a new, much larger circular enclosure that contained tree-like structures that supported various raised huts and platforms. His new accommodations accentuated his keepers' view of what Lud was: a jungle creature, more animal than person. They sometimes referred to him as a furry—a put down, he was sure.

The facility he was trapped in seemed to be getting built up around him, so he had the impression that he was part of a startup within Greenrock Solutions. Unfortunately, he couldn't share in his jailers' excitement in building a new enterprise, since he was the product. HEL was founded specifically to create monsters and train them to fight battles and kill. He was still the only furry in the facility, but he assumed that would change. The human side of the mercenary core, commanded by his boss, Alan Keeps, was expanding. At first, it was only Keeps and Lud out on missions, but three other mercenaries had joined his command in the last few weeks.

Lud made up his mind to embrace his role as a new species. Dr. Danzel said it himself: Lud was an evolutionary advancement. Lud embraced his non-humanness and decided to wear his epithet as a furry with pride. He was more advanced than his human lineage in every way and had no doubt that he would someday escape his bondage and rise to his full potential. They had taken his physical freedom, but his mind and how he comported himself was still his own.

*

Lying in one of the huts, Lud felt the pain and sickness he had experienced in the weeks after his transformation. When it first started, a few days prior, he wondered if he was experiencing flashbacks; the procedure was traumatic, so maybe he was suffering from a form of delayed PTSD.

The feelings and discordant thoughts he experienced weren't like memories, however. They seemed more like they were coming from someone else—he was acting as an empath for another being. This other being in his head was a young man named Dell, an auto mechanic. He decided to take a more direct approach and introduce himself.

Hello, I'm Lud. What is your name?

There was no direct response, but he felt confusion in the other mind. He tried again.

Hello, you are not insane. I was transformed, like you were.

What are you?—a response.

I was abducted, just like you. The procedure seems to have given us the ability to read each other's minds.

Lud … I've felt your thoughts in my head for the last three days. It makes sense now. You are a killer.

This stung Lud, since while true, he didn't want to think of himself in that way. Nonetheless, he had to accept it.

We are a killer. That is our purpose for being. I think our shared mind will make us stronger in the end.

You think it will help us escape?

Yes, with every new mind we share, we'll gain power.

My family.

Gone for now. Our collective mind is our family.

Lud had a new mission of his own. While HEL was building up its band of fiends, Lud would build his collective. Furries would have their own society, with their own rules, and he would be their first leader. As the collective grew, so would their power, and that would ultimately lead to their freedom—he hoped.

CHAPTER 21

PRESENT DAY

Back in Issaquah, three days had passed since the murders and kidnapping, and Detective Calahan knew that the suspects were in the wind. He had learned a lot in the last couple of days: the three suspects escaped with Dave Smith in a light blue minivan, a fourth accomplice was likely waiting for them with the van. They drove on back roads up through north of North Bend, where they dumped the minivan for another vehicle which they were not able to track, but strongly suspect headed east on I-90, and were likely no longer in the state.

With the help of the state police, he even identified one of the kidnappers as Aliyah Morrison, originally from Worcester, Massachusetts. She was a runaway with a history of petty crimes and one serious crime that was strangely dismissed when the prosecutor decided not to pursue charges against her for breaking another woman's jaw. After she walked out of jail, she disappeared until multiple cameras caught her face when she was posing as a cop. On a hunch, Calahan found cameras around the areas where Smith's phone tracked his movements, and some of those cameras also picked up images of Morrison; she was monitoring him in the days before the eventual kidnapping.

Because the case involved the brutal murder of two cops and the suspected kidnapping of Smith across state lines, the FBI was also involved in trying to identify Morrison and discover her new location. For his part, Calahan was reviewing the mounds of information his department had collected over the last few days, and getting ready to attend the funeral for the two murdered officers. With the FBI fully involved, there was no longer much for him to do other than sit there and wonder if he'd missed something that could be important in discovering Smith's whereabouts, which would hopefully also lead them to the killers.

As bad as Calahan and the rest of the station felt about the loss of two of their brethren, Officer Keith Jeffries had it the worst. He was supposed to be in the car with Officer Trent Cane, but he had been delayed at a school function for his kid. Trent was going to meet him at the school later that evening to pick him up so they could finish their night shift together. Jeffries hadn't gone home since being called that night with the news of his partner's murder, as he had kept himself busy out interviewing possible witnesses and collecting evidence. When not out in the field, he was back at the station working with Calahan to put it all together. Jeffries was starting to get manic, propped up by endless cups of coffee, and both Calahan and Peabody suggested he go home and rest. But Jeffries wasn't having it; he felt that if he was there, the three of them would have had the advantage, and his brothers would not have been killed; he was probably right about that.

Calahan was overworked himself and fell asleep in his chair. He woke with a start, slumped back in his uncomfortable chair, a crick in his neck, and a sharp pain in his lower back from sitting in such an awkward position. Normally, cops falling asleep in their chairs at the station would be the cause of lots of razzing and jiving, but this time, the other officers in the room just ignored the offense, the mood at the station was too somber for any good-natured fun. Calahan just slumped his body back the other way toward his desk and read over all of the evidence they had collected, again.

CHAPTER 22

Mr. Jones and VP Cooper were huddled in a conference room deciding on what course of action to take, given the total shit storm Dave's kidnapping had unleashed. The cops had identified Aliyah by her old identity, but they were worried that with the FBI involved, they would eventually connect Aliyah Morrison to the Aliyah Cramer who was on the payroll of Greenrock Solutions. They had to stop the investigation in its tracks before it became too big of a problem to sweep under a rug; they were getting close to that point already.

"Those fuckups all work for you, Bill. How could they be so careless?" Cooper asked.

Jones kept his composure and didn't say anything, taking a moment to collect himself. He knew Cooper was right, but didn't like being dressed down by someone who didn't work for a living—not like him, who wasn't afraid to get his hands dirty. Cooper had actually gotten his hands plenty dirty over the years, but Jones always had to see himself as the burdened.

"I've already put measures in place. After the funeral for those young officers that my men eliminated, Detective Calahan will be quietly eliminated too. It will not look like another murder."

"Well, let's just hope the people you send out to terminate the detective are a lot more subtle than the clowns we locked up down in holding."—the clowns Cooper was referring to, were the three men on Jones's security team that murdered the police officers.

Jones didn't say anything, but given his depleted staff, he didn't have the personnel to carry out an operation to terminate anything. Alan Keeps' mercenaries would handle the detective, and given their experience and discipline, they would get the job done cleanly.

"As for the FBI, I took care of that," Cooper stated. "The agents assigned to this case are already in the process of moving on to more important priorities. If the local authorities try to keep the case going, they'll just run into a brick wall of bureaucracy. The FBI is keeping jurisdiction over the case, but will just put it on the shelf. We spend a lot of capital, figuratively and monetarily, when we have to go begging the FBI to ignore one of our messes, so please make this mess your last one, Bill."

Reporting his actions to Cooper was Jones's least favorite part of the job. Anything he could ask of him, he had already thought of and put into action before Cooper even asked. The team Jones sent in to bag Dave had screwed up royally, but Jones already knew that without Cooper's scoldings. He would punish the men severely—more severely than even Cooper could wish for. Aliyah was too important to the lab and him personally to punish, but he would keep her close to home for a while, until things fully died down. Her day would eventually come too. None of them would get away unscathed, including Mr. Jones, who now had to replace his lost personnel. He didn't like the process of hiring new staff— good help was so hard to find. His passion was in playing spy master, identifying and tracking targets, and directing his own security team in running operations for HEL, such as the now problematic operation to nab Dave.

The meeting adjourned and Cooper went back to doing whatever VPs did, while Jones went about cleaning up his mess. With his team decimated, he had to rely on Keeps' mercenaries more than he liked. Not having his own field team, loyal to him, made him feel vulnerable.

Technically, Keeps worked for Jones, but Keeps was former special forces and the mercenaries he commanded respected Keeps and were loyal to him. Keeps also trained and commanded the furries on their missions, but the furries were loyal to no one but themselves. They only followed direction under the threat of pain from the shock collars they made them wear—*animals*.

Back in his office, Jones used his access to government intelligence servers to see if he could find replacements for the personnel he was about to lose. He wanted real professionals this time, so was looking around for disgraced or disgruntled cops. A former top cop who had been demoted or had lost his or her job because some liberal politician needed to look compassionate would be his ideal candidate. He needed people who were willing to do anything he told them to do, no matter how reprehensible, but that were also smart and disciplined—those types of people were hard to find.

On the surface, Jones appeared as someone who was smart and disciplined, but in reality, he was often in over his head. His main strength—as far as the job needed—was his ability to make decisions that ruined or ended lives, without much thought or consternation. He was also a little insecure and had a false sense of superiority over others he worked with, which sometimes clouded his decision making. All his strengths, weaknesses, and abilities combined to make decisions that sometimes led to mistakes. Cassidy was a much more competent director of operations in his time, but competence took a back seat to nefariousness, so HEL was run by Jones, and Cassidy was furry feed.

CHAPTER 23

A typical dreary December day in Issaquah was an apt setting for the funeral of the two young officers who were murdered in the prime of their lives. Hundreds of police officers from departments throughout the region showed up in formal uniforms to pay tribute. The murdered officers' families were obviously devastated and beside themselves throughout the funeral. In one awkward exchange, Dale Davis's brother confronted Calahan about why he let his brother's killers get away. Fortunately, his family was able to back him off and calm him down before Calahan was forced to defend himself from the brother's physical threats; the brother was being very inappropriate, but handcuffing him would have been a bad look for Calahan and the department.

Emotionally exhausted from the funeral and the last week of non-stop work trying to track down the perpetrators, Calahan went home and plopped down on his easy chair with a beer and a TV dinner. With his belly full and the television still on, he fell asleep with his half empty bottle of beer still in his hand. He was so tired that the bang of the bottle on the wood floor didn't wake him up. Hours later, still asleep and oblivious to his declining state, his heart stopped.

The next day, Lieutenant Peabody, wondering why Calahan had not shown up for work at the station, sent one of his rookie officers over to Calahan's house to see if he was okay; he knew from experience that Calahan had an occasional drinking problem, and was worried the stress of the confrontation with the brother sent him off the wagon. Fifteen minutes after the rookie left the station, he called back in to say that he could see Calahan in his chair watching TV, slumped over. He had tried knocking on the door for several minutes, but Calahan didn't move. Peabody told the rookie to break into the house and check on Calahan; the rookie wasn't thrilled about busting down the door to a detective's home, but followed Peabody's order and kicked the door in. It turned out that his worries about how angry Calahan would be at him for breaking his door were misplaced; Calahan was cold and stiff with rigor mortis, having died several hours before.

Two weeks later, the coroner's report came back, indicating that Detective Calahan had a heart attack in the middle of the night and died in his sleep. They all assumed the stress of the events in the days before his death was the cause.

CHAPTER 24

Butch Daniels, Hamit Osman, and Kevin Ortiz sat naked on the floor of one of HEL's more unadorned cell blocks. The room's bare cement walls, floor, and ceiling were all painted the same shade of light gray. The room was very clean and evenly lit, so it was hard to tell the walls from the floor; it was very disorienting. The three men were sweating profusely: not because the room was too hot, but because their ankles and arms were zip tied so tightly that after several hours, they were all in agonizing pain.

Butch, Hamit, and Kevin had fucked up big time. As HEL security personnel out on a recruiting mission, they were required to formulate a plan and execute said plan to acquire their subject. In reality, Jones had laid out most of the plan ahead of time, so they just had to follow his direction, possibly making small adjustments as the situation dictated.

Originally, Jones just wanted them to grab Dave when he was out of sight of possible witnesses, or force him to stop his vehicle and set it up like a carjacking, only with Dave still in the car. Instead, they decided to get creative and go off script in their last mission, which had unfortunately created an ugly situation that the company had to clean up.

It started the past Wednesday. The three were standing ready by their minivan in a trailhead parking lot when Aliyah called in with an update. She told them that the target, Dave Smith, had stopped in a bar and was drinking beers and eating nachos. They immediately put their collective minds into solving the problem of how they would snatch Dave. Butch came up with the idea of posing as plain clothes officers and pulling him over for drunk driving—a variation of Jones's carjacking plan; it seemed like a great idea at the time. Serendipity struck when two police cars pulled into the lot a moment later and the two officers left their vehicles and made their way over to the three men.

Hamit quietly whispered to Butch, "Zap them."

The officers approached, and a smiling Kevin tried to put them at ease by raising his hands and asking the officers how their night was going. Unfortunately for the officers, their laxness cost them everything. When they were within fifteen feet of the men, Butch and Hamit pulled out their tasers and zapped the officers with 50,000 volts of pure hell. Both officers immediately stiffened up and fell to the ground, eyes wide open, violently shaking. As they lay there on the ground, incapacitated, the three men stripped them of their weapons and uniforms, then put bags over their heads. They were getting ready to tie the two up when one of the officers grabbed his chest and started wheezing; then he stopped moving all together. Butch spent the next few minutes administering chest compressions, but the cop didn't recover; they had killed him.

Butch made the executive decision to drag both cops into the woods and smash their heads in with a rock to make sure they both stayed dead. Now fully committed to their plan, Butch and Kevin put on the uniforms they had removed from the officers, and fortuitously found another in the trunk of one of the cop cars. They called Aliyah and quickly told her the plan and asked her to meet them at the lot. They skipped telling Aliyah about how they acquired the cop cars and uniforms, since time was running short, and they didn't want to waste time getting a scolding from Aliyah. When she showed up, Butch changed into the uniform of Officer Jeffries that they found in the trunk, and Aliyah put on Davis's uniform.

Fifteen minutes after Aliyah got the call with the plan, she was sitting in wait by a stop sign a block away from Dave's house. Butch and Kevin were a few blocks away, waiting to sweep in after she pulled Dave over. Hamit drove the minivan to a spot a few miles away to meet them for the transfer after they acquired Dave.

Despite starting so badly, the rest of Butch's plan went smoothly. They boxed and drugged Dave, then drove away in the minivan. They drove to a second spot, twenty-five miles away, and the four of them and the package transferred into a pickup truck, dumping the minivan in a wooded area. Thirty-three hours of driving later, they were back at Greenrock's Special Research Division in Johnstown, Ohio—package delivered.

CHAPTER 25

Mr. Jones walked into the gray room and looked over the three prisoners with pursed lips and a crinkled nose. All three men had peed and crapped themselves and reeked of body odor.

"You boys have caused us a lot of headaches," Jones stated after he caught his breath.

"I know we fucked up, Mr. Jones. Please give us a chance to make it right. I promise, we'll clean up the mess. Please give us another chance," Kevin pleaded, speaking for the group.

Mr. Jones just eyed him with disgust. Seeing the three of them in such a wretched state dehumanized them in his eyes, making what came next easier for him.

"I'm afraid it is too late for that." Two large men in yellow rain suits walked in with a hose and proceeded to give the prisoners a good rinsing; conveniently, there was a large drain in the center of the room. After they were washed, the cleaners dragged them out of the room and loaded them onto a cart, where they were wheeled up to a lab on level U2. The lab was full of medical equipment and video monitors. On the far side were large windows that overlooked what looked like a jungle exhibit in a zoo.

A man in a white lab coat worn over a dress shirt and slacks came over and cheerfully introduced himself. "Hello, I'm Dr. Danzel. Welcome to the human enhancement lab viewing area," he giggled. "In a few moments, you are going to be part of something much bigger than yourselves. Each of you has my heartfelt gratitude and respect." While Dr. Danzel was giving the men his spiel, Mr. Jones just stood to the side, grimacing: Danzel and his mad scientists disturbed him, but he knew an example had to be set and wasn't the type to shrink from his responsibilities.

"Now, I know you are anxious to get on with it, so out of respect for your time, I have everything set up and ready to go," Dr. Danzel told his three captives.

All three men had heard the rumors about what went on at this facility; Butch and Kevin started crying as they got on their knees and begged Dr. Danzel and Mr. Jones to let them go. They insisted they knew they had fucked up and promised them that they had learned their lesson and would do anything they could to fix the mess they had caused; they begged for mercy from a doctor who had no understanding of the word. Kevin even asked Jones for forgiveness, but Jones just shook his head no, and tenderly told Kevin that it would be over quickly. Hamit—to his credit—stayed stoic throughout, wanting to leave the world with some semblance of dignity.

As promised, the bad doctor did not make his captives wait. The two large men who had cleaned them up back in the holding cell dragged them over to an opening in the floor close to a wall of windows on the far side of the room. Dr. Danzel and a few other people wearing scrubs took their places by the windows to watch the upcoming demonstration. The cleaners first cut off Kevin's restraints and tossed him down into the hole; they then did the same to Butch. Hamit tensed up as he prepared to receive the same treatment; instead, he was brought over to the viewing window and held in place by the cleaners, forced to watch.

Kevin and Butch shot through the hole and were transported by a chute to land heavily on a gravel floor in an enclosure some thirty feet below. Kevin came out first and screamed as he landed awkwardly on the floor, the crus of his

97

leg bending forward fully at the knee. Butch came out next, Kevin softening his fall with his damaged body; unfortunately for Kevin, that meant broken ribs and pierced lungs as Butch landed right on his chest.

For a moment, nothing happened. Butch got up into a wrestling stance, head on a swivel, ready for what came next. Kevin just lay there on his back, twitching, bloody saliva bubbles gurgling out of his mouth, unable to breathe, chest crushed. They were in what looked like a forest exhibit in a zoo, with bare trees towering overhead, marked by multiple raised houses and platforms bolted to those trees. One by one, wiry, naked, hairy creatures started to peak out of their dwellings to see what was for lunch. Some jumped down and some climbed, but soon Butch and Kevin found themselves surrounded by those beasts.

One beast came forward to face Butch and mimic his fighting stance, seemingly laughing as it hopped up and down, mocking Butch. While Butch's focus was on the beast facing him, two other monsters grabbed each of his arms and pulled. Butch let out a high-pitched scream as his right arm detached from his shoulder, causing the beast on his left to comically fall over onto his back with his legs pointed up to the sky. Butch went along for the ride and landed on top of the beast; it then wrapped all four of its limbs around him and squeezed as it started taking bites out of his shoulder. Not wanting to miss out, the other ravenous beasts piled on and started taking bites out of Butch; one of the smaller ones with a long snout ate its way into his torso and pulled out his intestines with its teeth. Butch continued to scream for a short time, but soon enough he was no longer able to even moan, and then mercifully he passed out and died.

Fortunately for Kevin, by the time they started eating him, he had already passed out from a lack of oxygen due to his punctured lungs. Dr. Danzel didn't hide his disappointment in not getting to view his creations subdue both men; Mr. Jones had had enough of the psycho doctor's macabre theater and left the room.

Dr. Danzel turned to Hamit and said, "Mr. Osman, did you know that furries all share a rare genetic trait?" When Hamit just stared at him blankly and repeated, "Furries?" The doctor continued, "Yes—well it's true, only around one in ten-thousand people possess the gene combination required to transition from a human into a furry. As you can imagine, when we discover someone with that gene sequence, we are extremely eager to recruit them into our program. Well, Mr. Osman, let me officially welcome you to HEL, as our newest test subject."

Hamit fell to his knees and vomited—dignity lost.

CHAPTER 26

The security personnel picked Hamit up off the floor, carried him back out to the cart, and wheeled him through a maze of hallways, stopping when the hall dead-ended at a set of double doors. From there, they carried him through the doors into what looked like a wing of a hospital, where a female nurse and male orderly were waiting with a gurney.

The security men roughly lifted Hamit up and lay him on the bed, face down, holding his arms tightly while cutting away the restraints. After spending hours with his wrists tightly zip tied behind his back, he was in no condition to fight his way to freedom, but the security personnel worked with maximum caution anyway. They flipped him over and secured his briefly freed wrists to bed straps attached to the gurney. They then carefully did the same with his ankles, removing the zip ties and securing his ankles to bed straps. In addition, they pulled a restraining belt over his arms and belly; with the straps and belt pulled tight, Hamit could barely move. Satisfied, the security men left, and the orderly started wheeling Hamit deeper into the hospital wing.

"Hello, Hamit—you don't mind if I call you Hamit, do you? We are pretty informal here. I'm nurse Doris and my partner here is Jamal."

They pulled him into a standard looking hospital room with a bathroom to the side as you entered the room. On the wall opposite the bed was an enlarged photograph of a park with a nicely manicured lawn and trees. The picture showed people walking on a pathway, bundled up in their winter coats, completely unaware of the evil that was happening in the real world outside the picture frame.

Jamal left after parking Hamit's bed against the wall, leaving him alone with nurse Doris. "I don't suppose you can undo these straps so I can use the bathroom, Doris?"

"Aww, don't try to sweet talk me, Hamit. If you need to go number two, I can call in Jamal, and we can loosen up the belly strap and slip a bed pan underneath you." He just shook his head no. "Well then, I'll have a catheter in place in a few minutes, so you won't have to get up to pee—how convenient, huh?"

"You know what they are going to do to me, don't you? Please don't let it happen. Help me," Hamit asked calmly to try and appear as non-threatening as possible to Doris.

"I only know that I need to get you hydrated and cleaned up for surgery tomorrow. Don't worry, it will be okay, I'll take good care of you."

"They are going to torture me and turn me into a monster, a killing machine. Please help me get out of here," he asked with a little more urgency.

"You have a very active imagination, Hamit. We all just want what is best for you." Jamal walked back in pushing a supply cart. Doris took a needle out of one of the drawers, held it upright, and tapped it a couple of times, priming it, then said, "Lucky for you, I have some discretion when it comes to your care. I can see you're upset, so I have something here to relax you." She jabbed the needle into Hamit's hip and gave his owie a little rub after pulling the needle out.

"No, you have to believe me. I saw what they do. Please, please..." It was no use; Doris wasn't listening. The injection did make him feel better, though; he felt himself sink into his mattress as all the muscles in his body released the tension he was holding inside. He smiled, never more happy and content, as Doris inserted an IV into his arm and a catheter into his bladder. Jamal loosened up the straps so she could give him a proper sponge bath; he had no thoughts of escaping anymore; she ran the warm sponge softly over all of his body; it just felt so good.

*

Hamit opened his lids then quickly squinted. The room's bright overhead lights hurt his eyes. He felt a pull on his arm as he tried to bring his hands up to shield his face from the bright lights. He was confused and didn't understand what was happening at first, but then remembered watching his friends get eaten by monsters. The last thing he remembered was the nurse injecting him with some drug that made him feel good—he thought to himself that he could use another dose.

Two orderlies he had not seen before were in his room, packing away his urine bag and attaching his IV to a pole on the side of his gurney. They unlocked the bed's wheels and started to roll him out of the room.

"Where are you taking me? Enough, please let me go!" The orderlies stopped pushing the gurney. One of them pulled out a leather muzzle and placed it over his nose and mouth, pulling the straps tight around the back of his head. They then tightened up all of his restraining bed straps and continued pushing him on his gurney out the door. The only part of him that he could move was his head, so he slammed it up and down on his pillow in protest.

They ignored him as he flopped his head around and made their way out of the wing with the patient rooms and into a new hallway. Finally, they entered a surgical room where several people in blue scrubs were getting things ready for him. A woman in a surgical gown came over to his side and introduced herself as Dr. Powell, Dr. Danzel's assistant.

"Now I'm sure you have lots of questions, Hamit, but unfortunately, there is no time to answer them—and frankly, nothing you know now will matter anymore very shortly. Now, I'm going to inject you with a neuromuscular-blocking agent to keep you paralyzed during the procedure. You will be awake and completely aware of everything that is happening to you, however. Unfortunately for you, fear and pain are a vital part of the transition procedure."

She smiled as she inserted the needle with the paralytic drug into his IV line. Almost instantly, his muscles started to feel heavy, then he slowly started to feel a loss of control over his own body. No longer able to fight, they unstrapped him from the gurney and moved him over to a cold metal platform. There, they strapped him in so he was sitting upright with his legs straight out and his head strapped tightly to a headrest. He was naked and exposed. The drug paralyzed his diaphragm and other breathing muscles, resulting in his eyes dilating with panic as he felt himself suffocating. Before that happened, they hooked him up to a ventilator; he could breathe again, but felt everything as they pushed the tube down his throat.

After getting him all set up, Dr. Powell called out, "Dr. Danzel, the patient is ready." Dr. Powell moved aside as Dr. Danzel moved into Hamit's line of site. Hamit's body was completely paralyzed, but he could still move his eyes back and forth and his eyelids up and down.

"Welcome, Hamit. I just want to say, before we get started, that I admire you, and I'm a little envious, to tell you the truth. You are about to experience something very few human beings have ever experienced or could ever dream of experiencing. You will become something greater, millions of years of evolution in a matter of days. You saw the furries as animals, savage and violent, but as you will soon find out, they are much more than that." Danzel finished his spiel and gave one of his assistants a nod. "As any great athlete will tell you, in order to mold your body into something stronger and better, you have to sacrifice, and overcome pain and suffering."

The assistant injected something into his IV line, and he immediately felt a burning sensation traveling up his arm and then out to the rest of his body. The burning died down, but it felt like every nerve in his body was put on alert. Every sensation was amplified: the cold of the room, the pinch of the needle in his arm, and the fear emanating from his core. If he hadn't been paralyzed, every touch would have made him jump out of his seat, but he could only internalize each shock to his system—there was no release.

Two assistants repositioned his torso so he was lying flat on his back. They then inserted drops into his eyes, which made them sensitive to the light. He got some short-lived relief by closing his lids, but then Dr. Powell inserted a metal speculum in each of his eyes, holding them open. He thought the pain in his eyes was almost unbearable with the bright florescent lights of the room shining overhead, but it was about to get much worse.

They repositioned his torso back into a ninety-degree seated angle and placed a device in front of his face; he was staring at two needles positioned right in front of his pupils. Dr. Danzel said, "When we're finished, you will see things normal humans could only dream of." He then started to move the two needles towards his pupils, slowly, drawing out the suspense, reveling in the pomp.

The needle to the right stopped moving forward around an inch from his eye, but the left needle kept moving, very slowly. Hamit was now screaming inside, overcome by fear. The needle then hit, piercing into his iris. The intensity of the pain only increased as he felt them pushing something into the inner part of his eye socket; the substance stimulated something in his optic nerve, which felt like bolts of electricity pulsing through the nerve and directly into his brain. The needle then started slowly pulling out until it reached its partner on its right. He then went through the same ordeal again with the needle on the right, it piercing his eye and ejaculating fire into his eyeball.

After they'd finished, they pulled the needles away and removed the speculums; Doctors Danzel and Powell and the staff all huddled in front of him, waiting in anticipation. At first, they appeared blurry, but slowly things started clearing up, until he could eventually make out details he never thought possible. It was like going from watching shows on the old television set he watched when visiting his grandparents as a kid to watching a show on the latest 8K widescreen. The doctor was right, it was amazing, already he felt superior—enhanced.

"Ahh yes, I can see it in your eyes. You now understand. Before we finish here today, every cell in your body will undergo the same metamorphosis you are now experiencing in your eyes. You'll be stronger and smarter—better in every way."

For the rest of the day, they injected various substances and nanobots into different parts of Hamit's body. Every injection was followed by searing pain that slowly dissipated, leaving him feeling euphoric and improved. He started to relish the painful jolts, knowing the pure joy and sense of strength and well-being he felt afterward—he was addicted.

By the time they had finished up for the day, the paralytic agent had worn off and he could breathe and move on his own again. He had a strong desire to tear every doctor and assistant in the room with him to pieces, and felt like there was nothing to stop him from accomplishing that goal if he was freed. Unfortunately, they had him tied down tight to the gurney with metal straps and cuffs. They barely left him enough room to wiggle and breathe.

As a final note for the day, the bad Dr. Danzel assured Hamit that he would continue to *evolve* in the coming days and weeks as his treatments took hold in transforming him cell-by-cell, from human to beast. Danzel and Powell reiterated their gratitude and congratulations as they wheeled him out of the surgical room on his gurney.

CHAPTER 27

Dr. Danzel was almost giddy with excitement over his new subject. After transitioning nine other humans to furries over the last year, one might think that the procedure would get somewhat routine, but Danzel didn't think that way. Taking a normal person and transforming them into a new creation that he had designed himself was like a drug to him—a drug that he never had to come down from. If anything, turning his tenth human into a furry was more exciting than ever—there was something about the number ten that he liked. HEL was the culmination of almost twenty years of incredibly hard work in the making, so these were gravy times.

Back when Danzel first started his work, genetic engineering wasn't one of Greenrock's core industries, but as part of their research budget, they allotted some funds for genetic research anyway. When it came to weapons research, they liked to cover as many bases as possible, and running a small genetics lab seemed like a good investment if it could someday result in some genetic or biological weapon they could sell for profit.

Dr. Danzel and his assistant, Dr. Powell, were mostly left alone to pursue whatever paths they wanted. Danzel was particularly interested in the genetic makeup of neanderthals, a species that became extinct forty-thousand years ago. He was fascinated by their supposed adaptability to harsh climates and their strength. He thought of them as super-humans, and not as some inferior beings that went extinct because they couldn't cut it when it came to competing with modern humans.

Danzel and Powell developed crude methods of modifying gene sequences in cell DNA. Working in a small laboratory on the campus of the Special Research Division, they became obsessed with enduing people with neanderthal genetic traits that would transform them into stronger and more capable versions of themselves.

They worked tirelessly for six years, perfecting their methods for editing gene sequences in samples of human tissue from all parts of the human body. Finally, when they could no longer make any more progress working with samples, they wanted to move on to using human subjects. Getting those subjects would be tricky, though, since they predicted they would likely kill or mutate hundreds of test subjects before they could perfect their process and create an actual enhanced human being.

As luck would have it, Dr. Danzel was scheduled to give the CEO of Greenrock Solutions, Philip Stirling, a summary of his work as part of a division tour the CEO was undertaking to view and understand the different divisions' latest research projects. He was looking for new product opportunities within the company that were based on research the company was already funding.

*

The day had finally arrived that Stirling and a few of his advisors were scheduled to show up at Danzel and Powell's lab. Also present were the Special Research Division's new VP, Shane Cooper, and director of research, Hunter Cassidy. Stirling and his posse squeezed into the small lab, and Danzel gave the best presentation of his life.

He walked through how he and Powell had worked through the process of using his gene editing technology to modify genes by splicing in new strands into their human tissue samples' DNA, and showed how those samples had improved after the modifications. Despite Danzel's enthusiasm and technically brilliant work, Stirling knew enough about science to know that working with cells in tissue samples was a long way from enhancing an actual human being. He approved an increase in their funding, which included money to buy a larger and more isolated lab farther outside of Columbus. This would give them space to start animal trials.

That was less than satisfactory to Danzel, but he knew that he had to prove he could enhance a living mammal before he would get the green light to move on to humans. The doctors started to make real breakthroughs when a couple of new technologies became available.

The first was CRISPR, which simplified the process of editing gene sequences in DNA. The second was in the field of nanorobotics, which provided a delivery mechanism for their gene editing proteins and modified sequences. They could program their nanobots to target specific cells to deliver their payload of enzymes and new gene sequences, which then modified the DNA in those cells.

With their new tools, the scientists worked for another four years on tadpoles, rats, pigs, and chimpanzees to learn how to enhance actual animals. After successfully creating chimpanzees with super strength and intelligence, they received the green light from corporate to start human trials.

Greenrock contracted with a private prison company to secretly transfer inmates that met certain characteristics that Danzel was looking for, and run genetic tests on the inmates in Danzel's lab. Most of the money for the contract went directly to the prison corporation's CEO and to various wardens and guards as bribes. Danzel was correct in thinking that the process would require hundreds of human subjects before he could perfect it, but every subject was more money in the pocket of the prison company CEO, and not so much money that Stirling would lose patience.

*

During the years they conducted human trials, replacing human gene sequences with neanderthal and other custom gene sequences, they experienced many failures, and many former prisoners died horrid, painful deaths—some quick and some very slow. Danzel, Powell, and their assistants were unaffected by the cries of their subjects, however. To them, they were merely objects to take apart and put back together, genetic building blocks, moving toward their final creation. Every death was an honor in the scientists' minds, since the test subjects were part of something so great—going from burglar to genetic test subject was a promotion.

Finally, after years of learning what gene sequences worked and what ones didn't, and just as importantly, what type of natural genetic makeup ensured a greater chance of success, the scientists had their process and first enhanced human. They had no idea how fast, strong, and smart actual neanderthals were, but their nouveau neanderthal was a superhuman.

The subject, which they called enhanced human one (EH1), could run twice as fast as the fastest human and could keep up the pace for miles before getting tired. EH1 was incredibly strong and had lightning-fast reaction times. EH1 also seemed to have improved cognitive abilities, though that was hard to measure, given the subject was uncooperative and refused to talk.

When Stirling and his advisors saw EH1 in action, they grew giddy with excitement. This was something that had never been done before, a scientific breakthrough unparalleled in the annals of human history. Most importantly, it was a weapon they could sell for a very high price.

There were some problems, however. EH1 was a former serial killer who had killed his own family, as well as many others. EH1 was also uncontrollably violent, which they chalked up to him being a serial killer, not yet realizing it was also a side effect of the transformation. Lastly, EH1 was ugly, and not just because the change left him looking like a neanderthal, but disgusting to look at even before the transition.

Despite the problems, Stirling decided that it was time to move the research project into production. He greenlighted the building of an underground lab and complex beneath the Special Research Division campus in Johnstown, while Danzel, Cassidy, and Cooper were tasked with setting up a process for finding subjects with the right genetic traits to enhance—subjects that weren't violent criminals.

To fund the project, they trotted out EH1 to perform its feats before a parade of government officials in the intelligence and defense community. Many of the officials were shocked and disturbed by what they saw, but they also wanted the technology to stay within the U.S., so they agreed to sponsor the project with the understanding that they had first rights to use the beasts for their own purposes. The partnership also helped Greenrock move into the mercenary business, since they would need a private army to train and lead the enhanced humans on government missions. Unknown to the government, Stirling had his own plans to use his private army to also carry out missions for hire from the highest bidders. His loyalty was to money more than to the country.

Finally, with their new facility built and a new subject found, they were ready to move from research and testing to full furry production—the term furry replaced the EH designation shortly before they moved into the new facility. The first furry out of their new facility was Lud Blom, a civics professor from Stockholm University. Lud was a tall, smart, and handsome man, a well-respected erudite.

The transition from human to furry went without a hitch, and the new human enhancement lab, or HEL, had its first product off the assembly line. While ape-like in the same way EH1 was, he was a much more attractive and majestic specimen. Unfortunately, he had the same disposition for violence as EH1, but they now had a collar developed to control that and a profitable outlet for that brutality. Since they had no more use for EH1, he became a great guinea pig to test out the new collar's features, including the one that killed its wearer.

With Cooper still acting as VP of special research and Jones as director of the new facility—Cassidy being Lud's first victim—the organization had settled into the HEL that would go on to swallow up Dave, Hamit, and many others. The future and bottom-line were looking bright for Greenrock, but less bright for its many victims to come.

CHAPTER 28

Dave was a few weeks into his new job, and the routine was always the same. Big Freddy would pick him up in the morning and walk him from his underground prison cell through the dungeon and up to the double doors leading to his worksite's lobby. When his accounting shift ended, he would use a special keycard they gave him to exit the double doors back out of the lobby, then use a phone by the elevator to request an escort back to his cell.

After the first day, he only ever had contact with Freddy and a rotating cast of afternoon escorts; Aliyah and the other HEL staff must have been too busy with kidnapping and murder to pay any more attention to him. After complaining to Freddy that he needed exercise, they let him work out in the division building's employee gym for an hour a day. The weekends were the worst: they gave him two daily hours in the gym, but the other twenty-two hours were spent locked in his cell, staring at the wall.

By his third week, he started worrying about going crazy—he started developing a funny facial tick after his third weekend isolated in his cell—so he rethought his attitude at work. The accountants and other people who worked in his building seemed to have no knowledge of HEL; they were all working in Greenrock's Special Research Division, and all of the financial data he came across looked like legitimate research budgets targeted toward new product development. He decided that punishing his coworkers for his current situation by being passive-aggressive just resulted in further isolating him. Outside his underground prison, he needed to build some social connections to keep his sanity.

Most of the data requests that came his way were made by Jordan, who occupied a cubicle close to his; the workspace wasn't that large, so everybody's cubicle was close to his. He started making an effort to follow up with Jordan, asking if he got everything he needed from his last request and whatnot. After being friendly for just a couple of days, Jordan stopped by his cubicle at noon with Carol and Smit, also analysts, to ask him out to lunch. At first, this elicited a stuttering response from Dave, since he couldn't leave the building, but Jordan picked up on his hesitation and said, "I know you're busy, but we're just heading upstairs to the cafeteria."

Relieved, he wouldn't have to make an excuse for not leaving the building, he enthusiastically got up to join them. The fifth floor featured the cafeteria with multiple different food stations, and both large indoor and outdoor rooftop eating areas. In the opposite direction from the cafeteria were signs pointing to an executive conference area. Until that point, he had just skipped lunch every day, so he realized while ordering his food that he didn't have any money or even a wallet—he had gotten into the habit of just carrying his company ID/keycard. He would have to ask Freddy if they could give him a food allowance, but for today, his lunch would be a coke from the complimentary soda fountain and some soup crackers from over in the condiments section.

Dave pathetically stood there with his crackers while he waited for Jordan to get his food. Jordan came by with an excellent looking Pad Thai, while Carol and Smit both went for burgers and fries.

"Is that all you're having?" Carol asked.

"I ... I ate a big breakfast. I usually skip lunch, but that looks good," Dave said.

"We noticed you always work through lunch. I don't have your will power. By 11:00 AM, my blood sugar drops through the floor and all I can think about is getting through the rest of the morning to lunch. I used to snack, but I'm trying to be healthier and cut out the mid-morning treats," Carol said as she stuffed fries into her mouth.

"The food is one of the best perks of working here. It's better than most restaurants I've been to and really cheap. I would give it a try," Jordan said as he dug into his Pad Thai.

"It does look good, but my jailer forgot to give me my food allowance today," Dave said, trying to be less awkward about it.

"So, you're married too. I didn't see a ring, so I figured you were single," Smit said.

Remembering his cover, Dave said, "No, I'm single. Just making excuses for forgetting to bring cash."

"You don't need cash. You can just use your keycard at any Greenrock cafeteria or employee store to pay for stuff. They just deduct whatever you spend from your paycheck. Didn't Laso tell you any of this?" Jordan said.

"No, he just gave me some information on how to run the queries, I haven't really talked to him much since. He just occasionally asks me how I'm doing while walking by."

Smit lifted his head and did a quick look around: "Between you and me, Laso is kind of useless. I'm not surprised he left you to figure everything out yourself. Sara would have done much better—God rest her soul."

Realizing that Smit was talking about the Sara that died in the supposed terrorist attack, Dave inquired, "I heard about that. Do you know any more about what happened than what they are reporting in the newspaper?"

All three accountants looked a little nervous, but Carol leaned in and whispered, "We were told pretty clearly to not talk about what happened, which I don't get, but there were rumors before they were blown up that they were stealing from the company. You didn't hear that from me, though."

"Well, I am not a crook," Jordan jokingly said in his best impersonation of former President Nixon, before changing the subject back to how good his Pad Thai was.

After lunch, as they were about to board the elevator, Dave suddenly said, "Hey, I need to go to the bathroom. Meet you back down there."

Instead of going to the bathroom, he picked up a pack of gum from the self-service snack bar and was pleasantly surprised when the card reader blinked green after he swiped his card at the pay station. *Well, maybe my jailers aren't complete douchebags.* He then walked back to the cafeteria and ordered the catch of the day, a nice big lobster claw with a little bowl of melted butter and a side of coleslaw. It was winter, but it was sunny and there were space heaters over some of the tables on the outdoor deck. Sitting outside in the sun, eating his lobster, he actually felt happy.

CHAPTER 29

Kendall leaned back in his ergonomic chair, lifted one arm up over his head, squeezed his crotch with the hand of the other, and let out a great big yawn. He then hunched forward onto his desk and continued to stare at the sleeping man on the screen with tired, squinted eyes. Calling his job boring didn't do justice to the word, but given his poor grades and lack of drive, he wasn't qualified to do much else. He sometimes wished that he had worked harder back in high school or learned a trade after he graduated. He was always good at knowing what he should have done, but not so good at following through.

As a junior member of the lab's security team, he worked the worst hours and the dullest assignments. His hours were 12:00 AM to 9:00 AM, and he spent most of the time sitting in a closet-sized room staring at a monitor, watching a man named Dave sleep. There was no audio, since he didn't have the security clearance to hear what anybody in the cell might have to say, just a split screen with three views of Dave's cell: a camera over the door showing the room from the front, a camera on the fake window sill in the back showing the room from the back, and a camera over the toilet in the bathroom that gave him a view of Dave brushing his teeth every morning and the top back of his head when taking a crap.

After Dave left for work in the morning, his job was to clean his cell. He made the bed, changing the sheets Mondays and Thursdays, swept and mopped, and cleaned the bathroom. Fortunately, after he wheeled Dave's breakfast cart back to the cafeteria, they didn't make him wash the dishes too. After that, he would fill out his report on what he had observed the previous night and go home.

*

Kendall thought back to how he got to this point in his life. He had been a below-average student who didn't take to books well, and also didn't have the motivation or desire to work a trade, so when his uncle told his brother—Kendall's dad—that his division was hiring security personnel, his parents insisted that he take the job or get of the house—the only two choices they gave him. He should have been grateful because, as his dad told it, the job was a great opportunity and only offered to him because he was the nephew of the vice president of the division. The job paid well—what other job could an unmotivated former D student get that paid $80,000 a year? So, Kendall did his nine hours, including breaks, and went home and played computer games with his other degenerate virtual friends all day.

He did wonder why Greenrock kept the man prisoner, however. The guards all talked, so he knew that Freddy escorted him upstairs to work at a job in the accounting department in the building above the prison facility. Why did Greenrock imprison one of its accountants? He was warned never to ask questions and never talk about his job outside of the facility, and his uncurious nature helped him stick to that job requirement. He didn't know Dave or what he did to end up where he was, but being with him every night, over time, he started to develop a kinship with him. Like himself, Dave did not seem happy; they were both trapped in this place, lonely and marginalized. Sometimes he fantasized that they were the same—friends—he wanted to help Dave but didn't know how.

CHAPTER 30

LUD: TEN MONTHS AGO

After Dell joined Lud in the enclosure, Lud started to better understand how they would be used in the future. When it was just Lud and Keeps, the missions were limited in scope and risk: murder a defenseless person or family. With the new training facility and a larger complement of human mercenaries, Lud and Dell were sent on their first operation against heavily armed targets—people who could fight back.

This was a much riskier strategy, since if the furries failed, the adversary would not only kill HEL's expensive investments, but the adversary would see what was wrought upon them. The illusion of unkillable monsters of the night coming to get you would be broken—and that would not be good for business.

Keeps and two of his mercenaries flew the furries out to an isolated outpost in a desert with orders to attack the outpost and kill everyone stationed there. The team gamed the scenario back at the lab for five straight days, so Lud and Dell were ready for the challenge and their minds were completely in sync.

Using their speed and agility, the furries descended on the outpost like strikes of lightning. They took out half the complement of defenders before they had even realized they were under attack. Most of the rest of them were too slow in reacting and died while trying to retrieve their weapons. A few did manage to fight back with a few shots, but the combination of the speed at which the furries moved and the fear they induced in their prey meant that the shots wildly missed their marks.

In just a couple of minutes, the outpost of twelve men was neutralized and sheeted in blood. Back at HEL, the exec masters must have been over the moon with excitement. If just two furries could so easily neutralize a terrorist cell without the usual evidence left over from a bomb or firefight, the business opportunities were limitless. The only negative of the operation was that there was nobody left to spread their legend—the left behind blood and gore would become their signature.

*

Shortly after Lud and Dell got back from their first overseas mission, a new voice popped into their heads—another furry had rolled off the assembly line. This mind they shared was different: it was a female. Like Dell, the new recruit was young. Her name was Anne, and she was a third-year college student who had been abducted from her dorm room as she slept. Her boyfriend, sharing her bed, was knocked unconscious before having the chance to register what was happening. Anne's last memory before waking up strapped to a gurney the next day, shortly before surgery, was walking into a bar the evening before with a group of friends.

Her new friends welcomed her to the collective and helped her through the post procedural pain and sickness. No furry would have to go through the recovery alone and confused again.

Once she was moved to the enclosure, she immediately formed a special connection with Dell. After a particularly stimulating mission, they came back and had sex for the first time. This was when they all realized that being in each other's heads meant sharing all thoughts, feelings, and sensations. Dell and Anne didn't mind: their lust was too great to let anything hold them back from each other. Lud, on the other hand, felt very awkward that first time, feeling like a peeping-tom intruding on an intimate moment. He quickly got over that, however, and reasoned that since they all shared a mind, it was appropriate to share lusts and desires too.

CHAPTER 31

After the procedure, Hamit spent the next two and a half weeks locked in a large plexiglass cage that was sitting in the middle of an even larger room, one floor down from the surgical center. Men and women in lab coats and scrubs would come and go, directing his care and taking notes on their pads. Doctors Danzel and Powell also made occasional appearances; Dr. Danzel liked to pontificate endlessly, but Hamit didn't listen. He had no interest in what any of them had to say; he was superior; to him, normal humans were just bugs to crush, and crush he would if he got the opportunity.

He spent most of the first two weeks in a feverish sweat, experiencing a pain that would probably kill a regular person while the nanobots continued their work of modifying his genetic makeup, transforming him into a new being—he wasn't fully human anymore. The pain just fueled his joyous rage, what would be unbearable to the unenhanced was orgasmic to Hamit.

By the third week, the fevers started to die down and the pain subsided as he completed the transformation to what the doctors referred to as a furry. He looked like a combination of man and ape; his body was mostly covered with dark hair, matching his head and chest hair color before the procedure. The center of his face, palms, fingers, and bottoms of his feet were bare, exposing his new thicker skin. The hair was thickest on his head, down around his chin, and on his chest. Even though his skin was thick, he still had a sensitive sense of touch. His other senses were also enhanced; he didn't even

122

have to see which person entered his lair; as soon as the door opened, he almost instantly knew who it was by their unique smells. His enhanced brain recorded and remembered everything and everyone he encountered.

It wasn't just the new things he experienced that imprinted into his memory, old memories also became clearer; he could recall all the kids he attended kindergarten with and describe what they looked like and what he thought of them at the time. He doubted even Dr. Danzel could contemplate how intelligent Hamit was, but Hamit was determined to put all of his new abilities to the task of killing every last person who worked at HEL. He didn't quite understand his new bloodlust, since he never liked hurting people before. It was a side effect of the transformation that he didn't want, but also couldn't put to rest.

The other side effect was that he heard voices in his head. Over the last few weeks, those voices went from dull background noise to louder and clearer actual voices. He felt like those voices were trying to communicate with him, but he desperately tried to push them aside. He worried that he was becoming schizophrenic, and it scared the heck out of him. One time, he put his hands over his ears and yelled "Stop!" After a brief second of quiet, one of the voices in his head said, *how rude!*

Was he irredeemable? He wanted to look forward and see a bright future for himself, but his newfound abilities would be all for nothing if they were accompanied by a mental breakdown. He didn't understand.

*

Dr. Danzel conferred with Dr. Powell while looking over Hamit's latest lab results. His biomarkers showed that after four weeks in the cage, he was ninety-eight percent of the way through his transformation. At this point, new changes would come slowly, even his oldest furry of thirteen months was still evolving and changing. Hamit behaved similarly to the other nine subjects that had gone through the transformation. They take their place sitting at the side of the cage, keenly observing everything that is going on around them. The doctors could see them thinking, planning, and scheming, but every effort he made to communicate with them failed. They didn't even like to acknowledge the existence of the people around them, unless those people were within reach, in which case they would tear them apart.

One thing that seemed odd about Hamit, that they hadn't observed in the other furries, was he seemed a little jumpier and more distressed. When alone in the room, he would cover his ears and nod his head back and forth, like someone was telling him bad news that he didn't want to hear. At one point, he even yelled "Stop." Before that outburst, the doctors didn't even know the furries could verbalize. That was the first and only thing a furry had ever voiced.

Both doctors would trade anything to know what the furries thought and experienced, but no stimulus they administered had compelled them to reveal their secrets so far. Knowing what the furries thought wasn't essential to them fulfilling their purpose, though; they had completed every mission assigned to them sufficiently so far. That was all Greenrock really cared about; they were getting value from their investment. But it wasn't enough for doctors Danzel and Powell: they had created superheroes—supervillains to anybody else—and it bothered them that those heroes seemed to treat them with contempt. Dr. Danzel, someone who also considered himself a superior being, should have understood.

CHAPTER 32

It was January 22nd and apparently time for Hamit to leave his plexiglass cell. Hamit knew the date because a few weeks before, one of his keepers was dropping raw meat into his cage and his watch briefly faced Hamit. The watch face was as clear as if it had been placed on his own wrist, given his enhanced eyesight. The lighting in his cell never changed, but there was a certain rhythm to his caretakers' routines that gave him a pretty good idea of what constituted a day in his life.

Hamit looked up and saw the air vents at the top of his cage seal shut. Then he heard a faint hiss and felt a slight change in air pressure. He didn't panic when his head grew light as the gas took hold of him; he was almost immune to fear and panic, even in the face of death. He woke up some indeterminate amount of time later back on a metal gurney, tightly strapped in, but this time standing straight up with his feet on the ground. He was strong, but the multiple metal straps were more than adequate to hold him. In addition, they had secured a collar around his neck; he assumed it was the same type of collar he observed the other furries wearing when he watched his colleagues torn apart and eaten more than a month ago.

A man walked in wearing a brownish short-sleeved shirt, gray tactical pants, and black boots. He had thick dark hair, brown eyes, and a deep tan. He was thin and wiry and looked like he spent a lot of time outdoors doing hard physical labor; he was very strong and manly looking.

He stepped in front of Hamit and waited patiently until Hamit looked up from his usual downward gaze and made eye contact. "In a few moments, you are going to walk through that door over there and meet your troop in what will be your new home. Before that, I wanted to introduce myself and make sure you understand the hierarchy. There is only one alpha in this band of beasts, and that is me. In your enclosure, you animals can make any arrangements you like, but I am your commander, and you do what I say, when I say it. You don't talk, but refer to me as 'boss' in your head."

The *boss* then stepped back a few feet and continued, "Okay, Hamit, let's start our first lesson. I'm going to free you now, but you're going to be a good boy and stand still until I give you a command. You will then follow that command."

Hamit stood there staring at his new boss, not moving a muscle, expressionless and calm. One of the voices in his head said, *Don't do it.* He then heard a snapping sound and all of the restraints that were securing him to the gurney released simultaneously.

At the instant he was free, he leaped over toward his boss with the intention of tearing him apart; he almost couldn't help himself, since the desire to kill the man—any man—was deeply ingrained in his psyche. He made it to within three feet of his new commander then felt a pain that encompassed his entire being. He could handle the pain, but along with the pain, every muscle in his body seized up, and he dropped to the ground, his body stiff and vibrating uncontrollably. The electric bolt that brought him down terminated, but as the boss came to stand over him, Hamit remained still, not trying to attack again.

You should have listened to us, a voice in his head chided. *Were the voices laughing?* It was almost more than he could take. *You realize the pain you feel, we sense too. Try to be smarter?*

126

"Well, Hamit, you failed your first test. Don't worry, every one of you beasts fail the first test. I've found it takes a demonstration to ensure that the lesson sinks in. I want to assure you that what you just experienced is mild compared to what that collar around your neck is capable of doing if you get out of line again."

The boss walked over to the door and opened it. "Now get up and go meet your friends in your new home."

Hamit slowly got up and walked through the door, passing within a foot of his new boss, but resisting the urge to attack again. As he got closer to the boss, he felt the collar start to tingle, warning him. He thought to himself that he would bide his time and strike when he had the advantage.

That's a nut we've been trying to crack for a long time. See you soon!

Go away, Hamit thought.

How rude!

CHAPTER 33

Hamit walked through the door into a small, cement-lined room with another metal door opposite the one he walked in through. The door behind him closed and he heard a loud clang of the lock being engaged. Next, the door in front of him cast the same clanging sound and opened. He walked through into an enclosure set up like a jungle exhibit in a zoo, like one that you would expect to hold African gorillas. The ground was covered with medium-sized pebbles and the enclosure was very large and circular; he estimated the diameter to be around one hundred feet. The enclosure contained many trees, though on closer inspection, he determined that the trees were synthetic, and many of those trees contained tree houses of various sizes and elevated at different levels off the ground. There were ladders and platforms, too, connecting the houses. It was actually pretty nice, something you might desire if going on a high-end jungle vacation in Costa Rica.

Welcome home, Hamit, his head voice said. It sounded so real that he looked around for the source of the welcome.

One by one, the beasts he had seen chew up his friends came down from the platforms to greet him. Instead of surrounding him, they stood loosely in front of him. They didn't seem ready to attack, but Hamit made himself ready to fight anyway, raising his fists and slowly backing away.

What is the matter with you, Hamit? You're not very bright. We're standing in front of you, and you still don't get it. As the voices in his head were talking, one of the more impressive looking beasts stepped forward. *I'm Lud, leader of this band.*

He then silently heard, *I'm George I'm Anne I'm Dell I'm Sigurd I'm Jason I'm Frank I'm Isla I'm Nu.* All the voices projecting one after the other.

You guys are the voices in my head? Hamit thought.

Yes, Lud conveyed. *We are not voices in your head, and you are not going crazy. We communicate with each other telepathically—it is one of our abilities as a result of the transformation.*

Can I turn it off? Hamit asked.

No. Our thoughts and emotions are no longer our own. Over time, you'll get used to it. You are no longer an individual. We're a collective with a hive mind, like in the Star Trek movie.

Movie? I didn't ask for this.

Do you think any of us asked for this? Time to buck up. Trust us, we're your family. The enemy is our human keepers. Eventually, we'll use our strength to free ourselves and take our revenge, but for now, accept your fate or go mad trying to fight it.

Hamit didn't like his new situation but nodded his head in resignation. He did feel a natural kinship with the other furries that he didn't quite understand yet, but his new cage-mates, or band as they put it, seemed friendly enough—their bloodlust only extended to normal humans.

What's with the man who calls himself boss? Hamit transferred.

His name is Alan Keeps. Like he told you, he is our commander, and we are his soldiers. He's not as evil as the rest of them. For the most part, he treats us like humans under his command, as long as we follow orders and don't try to kill him or his human soldiers.

Disagree—the hive mind wasn't as one when it came to the topic of whether their commander was evil, like the rest of HEL's leadership.

Evil or not, the boss isn't as stupid and arrogant as the rest of them. He knows we silently communicate with each other and can sense their emotions. If there is a weakness to be exploited, it is with one of the others that think we are dumb animals.

Hamit took stock of his new home. On the ground level there were a couple of catholes for them to do their business in. The place was very clean, and the other furries were polite and respectful to one another, despite how they looked and their violent dispositions. Their overwhelming desire to kill seemed to only extend to humans and not to other beings; Hamit was okay with that. He climbed up into one of the tree houses where he found the inside was unfurnished but spotless. The bridges connecting the houses and platforms all fanned out from a much larger central platform that hosted a small shack containing cleaning supplies.

He learned that their caretakers used to clean the enclosure while they were out training or on mission, but to their caretakers' surprise, when they stopped cleaning the enclosure for them and just gave them the supplies to use themselves, the furries organized their own system for cleaning the enclosure—the doctors would test behaviors by occasionally changing the way they cared for the furries. The only downside, from the furries point of view, was that they were forced to show their un-animal-like desires to keep a clean and orderly living environment, which would make their keepers more wary of them—better to be underestimated as wild animals.

They had no choice, however; when not digging the intestines out of their victims, they were neat freaks and craved order—or at least Lud was, and they followed his lead. Lud—the first furry—came up with cleanliness as his second core value early on and ingrained that belief into every new furry that came after him. Before Greenrock kidnapped and transformed him, he was a civics professor at Stockholm University. The evil doctors and overseers that ran HEL stole his humanity, but they would never get his civility.

The furry core values were civility, cleanliness, the pursuit of knowledge, and the violent death of all humans in HEL. Admittedly, the last value was a product of the genetic engineering used to transform them from their previous state; the humans of HEL had created a species whose main objective was to someday kill them, confident that they could control where they directed that violence—what could go wrong?

As the days went by, Hamit came to fully accept his new circumstance and actually relish it. Before the transformation, he felt like his life was at a dead-end, but now he had the ability both physically and intellectually accomplish great things. He looked forward to the day he could finally ravage his wardens and leave the dungeon.

CHAPTER 34

A few days into his stay at club HEL, Hamit was settling in for an afternoon siesta after finishing his daily meal—that day it was raw lamb—when he felt three mild shocks from his collar. He sensed the other furries coming to life and making their way to one of the platforms by the side of the enclosure; he got up and joined his band on the platform. He felt another ping from his collar, and everyone stepped back to the far side of the platform, away from the metal door on the side wall; again, he just mimicked what the others were doing.

In walked Alan Keeps, the boss, with his hand on the trigger that Hamit assumed controlled the collars. *Don't bother, there are multiple other jailers watching closely, ready to trigger our collars if you get close to the boss. You won't get that far, though, because the collars are triggered if you get within three feet of him,* the little furry voice in his head informed him, knowing what he was thinking.

The boss stepped to the side, the collars pinged again, and the furries marched through the doorway, single file, into another large room with several structures. On one side was what looked like a typical two-story suburban house. It was surrounded by a lawn and some bushes and trees with a deck in the back. On the other side was a full-scale multistory brick building, like you might find in a residential city neighborhood. There were also other smaller structures, like a couple of sheds, a large pile of rocks, and a swimming pool on the side of the house.

They entered the training facility onto a narrow platform that led to a stairway, which the furries followed down to ground level. At ground level, there was a large set of doorways, which Hamit assumed was how equipment was moved into and out of the room. There were no other entrances or windows in the training facility. Once the furries and the boss were down at ground level, a gate came down and blocked off the stairway entrance they just came through, trapping them all inside the room.

The furries stood in a semicircle in front of the boss and two of the mercenaries also under his command. They were there to help out with the training exercises for that day. The collar pinged again, but harder this time, inducing a painful burning sensation that jolted Hamit to attention. *Step back.* They all stepped back, giving the nervous trainers a little more breathing room.

Useless

Why?

They don't fully understand that our minds act as one. We don't need their help to function as a unit. Just do as I command, Lud instructed Hamit.

"Beasts, tomorrow we go on a mission. This is a big one, so I'll need six of you: Lud, Dell, Nu, Isla, Frank, and Hamit. The rest of you go sit on the side," Keeps ordered.

The four furries that weren't picked walked calmly over to the wall and simultaneously sat down, legs crossed, letting their eyes hang low, seemingly disinterested. The six remaining also appeared calm and bored, waiting for instruction.

"The rules of engagement for the mission are that you neutralize"—*tear apart*—"all hostiles, then pull back to the extraction point after the building is cleared." Keeps looked only at Hamit to give his next instruction: "The trainers you'll encounter today are considered neutralized when you make contact with them, shoot them, or hit them with an object either directly or thrown. Once neutralized, they will lie in place, and you will not further engage with them. All the trainers are fully protected with body armor, but if you get overzealous and try to hurt one of my people, I will hurt you, understand? You are playing two hand touch here, save the real violence for the mission tomorrow."

Hamit and the rest of the furries continued to stand with their eyes down, poker-faced, but Keeps knew they were listening. While Keeps was instructing the furries, several mercenaries in full body armor and armed with paint guns positioned themselves around the building. They looked like they were encased in bomb suits; they had very little mobility, which was one of the many things that made this practice raid unlikely to simulate the real operation.

Regardless, when the boss yelled go, all six of them instantly sprang into action. *Follow me.* Dell and Nu flanked wide to the left of the building and Isla and Frank went right. A moment later, the flankers started neutralizing the building guards. Lud then moved toward the front of the building, Hamit in tow, guided by Lud's will, broadcast to him. Hamit felt and heard the thoughts of the five other furries, plus the four furries sitting on the side, and felt the heightened emotions of the trainers.

The voices in his head felt like they were coming at him from all directions. The other furries calmly and methodically worked their way into the building, but he could feel all of their intense bloodlust, tempered with the frustration of having to suppress their urge to kill. The humans' heightened emotions started to intrude into his head; unlike the furries, the humans projected intense excitement and fear. Hamit made it to within a few feet of the building entranceway before falling to his knees to vomit. He held his head and silently screamed, trying to turn the voices in his head and cacophony of emotions off, or at least control them.

He felt two jolts to his neck, and immediately, the furries stopped their attack. Dell and Nu picked Hamit up by his arms and led him back to the launch off point to debrief. The voices of the other furries were gone, though he still felt their calming presence, but the human trainers' anxieties were still there in his head; Keeps projected disgust along with determination to continue the exercise until it was successfully completed. On cue, the boss shouted out to the team of six furries that they would start over and try the exercise again as soon as the trainers had reset back into their positions.

Organizing our thoughts takes time. Concentrate only on my thoughts, Lud instructed Hamit. Hamit thought that was easier said than done with everyone broadcasting their thoughts and feelings with the intensity required to attack the building and its occupants. *Yes, it is no different than sorting out sounds coming into your ear, you will learn.*

Hamit could not hear all of the trainers reporting in that they were set up, but felt it from Keeps. The boss then yelled go again, and the six furries made their way out exactly as they did before, but this time, Hamit did not fall to his knees. He managed to follow Lud through the whole exercise, but not much more. He was in such a daze, overwhelmed by the multitude of voices and feelings, that he had almost no awareness of what was happening around him; Lud was just pulling him along. When it was over, he was covered with paint, having taken multiple hits; each hit with a paintball was accompanied by a shock from the collar, reminding him to get down. Eventually, he felt a shock he couldn't ignore, the intense pain locking up every muscle in his body, laying him flat on his back, vibrating uncontrollably.

Again, Dell and Nu dragged him back to the launch point, and again, the game was reset and the pack of six was ordered out to neutralize the building. Finally, on the seventh iteration, Hamit made it through the exercise without being shot or shocked, and he was even able to record a kill of his own. After sensing each furry's status report, he heard Lud declare that the building was clear and order everyone out of the building. They then calmly jogged out of the building and into the back of a van waiting for them at the extraction point. Tuning into Keeps' feelings, Hamit knew the exercise was over.

They lined up in single file and made their way back up the stairwell and back into their enclosure. As they were walking back, several of the other furries started to tease him: *We've never had to go seven times before. You looked like a fish, flailing around on the ground like that. Fish. Fish. Fish.* Hamit had a nickname. The old human Hamit would have been angry, but he couldn't be angry with his new brethren; he knew they loved him.

When they were back inside, the first thing Hamit noticed was a large pile of raw meat waiting for them on the central platform, but they resisted the urge to satisfy their hunger, and first climbed down to ground level and hosed each other off. Only after everyone was cleaned, did they go up and enjoy their meal.

CHAPTER 35

Mohamed was out walking the perimeter of the building he was tasked to protect, checking that all of his men were in position and alert. He had worked his way up the ranks, so he was aware that the guards got lazy when they thought they weren't being monitored. Mohamed had no idea what was happening in the building his unit was assigned to guard, but he was determined to show his superiors that they had made the right choice when they promoted him to command the unit earlier that day. His increased pay meant his children could attend a better school and his wife could afford to occasionally buy something nice for herself.

His two most trusted men, out in front of the building, were standing at ready position, fingers not on their gun triggers, but prepared to raise their firearms and respond to any attempt at intrusion. Unfortunately, when he rounded the corner, two other guards were smoking cigarettes and joking around. They hadn't seen him yet, so he decided to turn this into a learning opportunity. He assumed most of the men still saw him as a counterpart and not their superior, so it was up to him to set the right tone and earn their respect.

Mohamed's two underlings made the approach easy: they were so busy paying attention to each other that they didn't notice him edging closer with his back up against the wall of the building, hidden by its shadow. He scurried right up behind the two men then lashed out with a kick to the back of the first guard's left calf. As the guard tumbled forward onto his knees, and with his back fully exposed, he hit him in the kidneys with his club. Almost simultaneously, he grabbed the guard's pistol out of his holster and pointed it at the other guard's face. The first guard retched in pain under Mohamed's foot, which was grinding into his head. The second guard slowly raised his hands, letting his cigarette drop out of his mouth to the ground. Mohamed ordered the second guard onto the ground, where he roughly zip-tied his hands together and disarmed him. He then zip-tied the other guard, who was still moaning in pain on the ground.

Mohamed called in two new guards who were on break to relieve the two guards he had just brutalized. Only after they were properly relieved, and the new guards saw what had happened—he wanted the story to spread—did he free them with an admonishment about how it would have been much worse if he was really an enemy attacker. Satisfied, he continued his patrol around the building, hoping that he would not need to teach his new unit any more lessons for a while.

As was the case with his two unfortunate underlings who were not standing ready when he snuck up on them, Mohamed was now so caught up in his thoughts that he didn't notice the danger sneaking up, right under his nose. He was so caught up in his own assuredness at having asserted his authority that he had walked the entirety of the back of the building before wondering why he hadn't run into the four guards that were posted there. He started reaching for his walkie-talkie when he felt himself falling to the ground. Well, not all of himself—just his head was falling to the ground as his eyes spotted his crumpling body for one last look before all went dark.

The darkness descending upon the building wasn't satisfied with a handful of guards, more blood needed to be spilled. The shadow beasts fanned out, slicing up the guards on the left and right sides of the building, not slowing down in the slightest as they ripped their powerful fingers through each victim they passed by. Speed and fearlessness were their primary weapons; regular people, no matter how well trained, just couldn't react fast enough once they realized they were under attack. Many didn't discern the danger until right before they were torn in half, and some died before they even registered the onslaught.

The beasts tore their way through two guards in front of the building: crushing one guard's head and tearing the arm off the other. The second guard was left trying to hold back the flow of blood from the hole in his shoulder. Next, the beasts broke their way inside the building. The inner guards, now alerted to the danger, started to fight back, but the beasts moved fast, zigzagging side to side, and up and down, dodging bullets, using their strength and speed to take advantage of the whole three-dimensional plain of their environmental surroundings. At first, it seemed like the attackers acted with random brute force, but on closer inspection, the beasts were totally in sync, laying out different positions as they methodically cleared the building. When a beast did need support, support arrived quickly; it was like there was an all-knowing presence guiding them at all times.

One beast ran down a guard who had dropped his weapon and was running for his life. The beast jumped forward, wound up with its right arm, and punched the hapless victim right through the mid-section of his torso, the beast's momentum carrying its arm all the way through the guard until its shoulder was lodged up against the victim's back. When the beast pulled its arm back, the man hanging from its shoulder just went along for the ride. The beast started hopping around in a frenzy, trying to shake the guard off its arm. The man was still alive, his mouth wide open in a silent scream, blood gurgling from his mouth. Finally, after several violent twists of its body, the guard broke free of the beast's

139

arm and flew through the air into a bookshelf, which came crashing down from the force of the human projectile.

When the last of the occupants that the furries could reach were dead, they all stopped and waited. An unknown number of the enemy had managed to hole themselves up in a secure room that the furries could not penetrate. Keeps, who was watching all the action from cameras attached to the furries' collars, had a decision to make; the plan was to simply kill all of the building security and occupants and vacate the area as quickly as possible. They weren't looking to fight a second battle if reinforcements arrived before they could extract.

Keeps made the only decision he could and sent a double ping out to his furries. The furries were a weapon of legend and fear; they hadn't sabotaged the cameras in that area, and if those cameras caught him or his soldiers assisting in the attack to blast open the door to the safe room, it would shatter the illusion of monsters attacking in the night. They wanted the enemy to fear monsters, not other men. A little over a minute after he sent the pings, the furries had made the two-mile journey from the building back to the helicopter. They all piled in and set off.

CHAPTER 36

The helicopter took the mercenaries and their troop of furries back to an airfield to catch a plane home. The furries unloaded from the helicopter, were quickly hosed off, and then locked up in a container sitting on the rear of a flatbed truck. The truck and the mercenaries loaded up into the plane for the long flight back to Ohio.

Hamit knew he was in for an especially long ride home. Furries were great multitaskers, so while they were efficiently clearing the building and killing every living thing in it, they were also razzing the fish. The frenzied panic Hamit was feeling while trying to shake the guard from his arm radiated out to the other furries, who all agreed that Hamit's antics were hilarious.

Wow, fish. I didn't know this mission included entertainment.

I thought you falling to the ground heaving during training was funny, but you surprised us. That is cartoon level antics.

I'm sure your first missions didn't go any better.

They did, fish. You dancing around with that human was a first. It reminded me of my first school dance. He was useless, and I had to be the lead. I might have even thrown him against the wall at one point.

When they tired of teasing Hamit, Isla had some practical advice for him. *Next time, aim higher into the chest, then you can lean into the hard upper part of his back with your forearm to use as leverage while pulling your other arm free.* Others interjected all at once, *I just hug the human and whip my arm out its side. That works too, I guess. The best is when you punch into the chest and rip the beating heart out. That never works like in the movies, the human passes out before you can show it to him. I bet I can do it. It's not possible. I can do it, it just takes a woman's touch,* Isla countered the other thoughts they were all sharing.

*

Aside from the unfortunate incident with the guard getting stuck on his shoulder, Hamit hadn't performed that well on the mission. He stayed upright, but the feeds of thoughts coming into his head from all directions still overwhelmed him. Especially the human thoughts that projected fear and panic; it was like trying to listen to a soft talker while everyone else in the room was screaming bloody murder.

Lud assured Hamit that every furry had trouble sorting through the constant stream of shared thoughts at first, but the solution was to learn how to control his new extrasensory abilities. To that end, the furries had developed a series of exercises they used to train their minds. They created a word response game, where a particular key word would have a matching response word. One furry would project out the response word whenever any of the other furries projected out a key word. The trick was that the furries would create lots of static by continuously transmitting random thoughts, including the kind that terrified humans projected.

The first night after his first training, Hamit successfully responded to only around sixty percent of the key words, while all the other furries could respond to ninety to ninety-nine percent of the words. He was improving, though, and by the time they released them from the container back into their enclosure, Hamit was hitting eighty percent. The furries had greatly enhanced cognitive abilities, compared to even the smartest humans, but they needed to keep exercising their brains and learning new skills to hone those new abilities and keep from getting bored.

They could not hide their physical abilities or their abilities to coordinate their actions and work as a single unit—that was obvious to their handlers as they watched the furries carry out their bloody missions. But they tried to hide their other capabilities by playing their brainteaser games while each was resting quietly in their respective tree houses. The humans also didn't know that the furries were constantly probing their minds for information to learn about them; they could learn a lot about each of their handler's personalities just by understanding their emotional states.

Most of the furries were fairly confident that they could duplicate the genetic transformation process and improve on it, if they just had access to information on doctors Danzel and Powell's research and process. Danzel may have been a brilliant doctor, but he didn't have an uplifted brain. Thinking they were budding genetic engineers may have shown that furries could also be egotistic, just like the bad doctor.

The furries were smarter, stronger, and better than unenhanced people in almost every way, but because they looked like apes and were so violent, most of the HEL leadership underestimated them, confident that they could control them with containment protocols and high-tech shock collars.

CHAPTER 37

A couple of months into the job, Dave was still stuck running queries for the analysts and senior accountants. The work was mind-numbingly boring, and he still couldn't understand why the process for pulling the data the accountants needed to balance the books was so inefficient. It was tax season, and the extra time needed for the accountants to write the requests and for Dave to serve them likely added hours a day of overhead. Rick was promoted to analyst a month prior, so Dave was the bottleneck; at times, he would have so many requests come in at once, that some analysts would have to wait over an hour for him to get to them in the queue.

He seemed to be the only one openly bothered by the current process, however; when he vented about it to Laso or anybody else in the office, they would just shrug their shoulders. Smit even told him to lighten up; Greenrock was a big company that was doing just fine, so why the need to get more efficient and increase everybody's workload, he would say. Smit was right, of course: Dave had no reason to want to improve how things were done in the accounting department other than to satisfy his own sensibilities of what was the right way to do things—double so given that he was slave labor.

On a more positive note, Dave had gotten much closer to his workmates. He would take long lunches with Jordan, Carol, and Smit, plus shoot the breeze with them during coffee breaks. They really valued their long lunches and breaks, but surprisingly to Dave, still managed to get a lot of work done. In order to keep his cover story straight, he harked back to his bachelor days, before he met Jan, and talked about his life back then like it was his current situation. They sometimes liked to eat lunch off campus, so he made up a semi-plausible story about how his contract required him to stay in the building during work hours. Carol told him that was "fucked up," but accepted it at face value, given that Greenrock was full of funny quirks in the way they did things. They didn't understand why he never wanted to get together with them outside of work hours, which he worried would eventually put a strain on their work relationships, as they would wonder if he really liked them or not.

On the intelligence gathering front, he was at a dead end. He had free rein to query all of the data he wanted to collect, but the data he gathered for resubmittal back to the database was sandboxed off in a secure location that he didn't have access to. All he needed to do his job was know how to form the database queries and use the location address of where the data temporarily lived; there was no need for him to actually view the data, so the temporary data was obfuscated with encryption. He briefly thought about purposely modifying the queries he received to push bad data back into the database, but he liked his peers and thought any issues he created would just blow back on them.

The newspaper he stole way back at the start of his employment—or more accurately, his enslavement—was owned by a guy named Gerard, and it turned out that Gerard brought his paper in every day, and all Dave had to do to borrow it, was ask. After he had asked a couple of times, Gerard just started dropping it on Dave's desk after he finished with it. Articles concerning the terrorist attack that killed four Greenrock employees had slowed to a trickle as the investigation bogged down and the memory of the incident began to fade, but on the Monday of his tenth week in the office, the attack was back on page one.

An FBI agent concluded—off the record—that the bomb Amar brought into the restaurant was likely of a design that was used by U.S. intelligent services and not similar to what Middle Eastern terrorists typically used. The bomb itself was much more powerful than suicide bombers were typically given, and no shrapnel, such as nails, was discharged from the original point of the explosion. When reporters tried to follow up, the official FBI liaison called that source's conclusions speculation and maintained that the investigation was ongoing, and no conclusions had been made yet.

Some of the talking heads featured on alternative news sources had been pushing this narrative for a while, so when an agent in the FBI confirmed it, the story went from being on the fringe to the headline of every major news outlet. It also confirmed Dave's biases against Greenrock and the Special Research Division in particular. Dave smiled as he imagined HEL management panicking now that the truth was out; they were probably calling special meetings and getting press releases ready if needed.

*

After ten weeks, Dave couldn't just sit and do nothing about his situation anymore, so he decided to do something rash. He felt that the reporting would eventually start looking into whether Greenrock played a role in the bombing, given that four of its employees were killed, but didn't want to leave that to chance. He would make an anonymous call to the Columbus police department, planting the idea that Greenrock used the terrorist attack as cover to eliminate four employees who were rumored to have stolen from the company.

He had no phone in his cubicle, but Laso had one in his office, so he waited until Laso left for his weekly three o'clock meeting with his senior accountants. At 2:57 PM, he saw Laso leave his office and head down the hall toward the large conference room. He waited another minute, then seeing that nobody was around the area of Laso's office door, quickly snuck into the office. Technically, Laso should have locked his door before leaving for the meeting, but most people who worked in the office had gotten complacent with security. This was despite all of Laso's bluster on Dave's first day about the importance of security protocols.

By the time Dave sat down at Laso's desk, he was sweating and feeling hyper from the adrenaline. It took him three tries to correctly dial the police department's homicide tip line, but on the third try he succeeded, and a man with a gravelly voice answered the phone.

"Columbus police, how can I help you?" the man asked.

"I'm calling from a number from inside of Greenrock—you can verify that. I have information about the terrorist bombing at the restaurant."

"Okay—can I have your name?"

"No! The four Greenrock employees who were killed; they were stealing money from the company."

"Okay—what are you saying?"

"Don't you get it, Greenrock set up the terrorist attack as cover to terminate employees who were stealing from them," Dave said, now exasperated.

"That's a pretty big claim. Can you send me proof?"

"No, I'm putting my life at risk just talking to you. Please just look into it. You wouldn't believe the stuff they do around here," Dave said before hanging up the phone. He then peaked through the blinds beside the office door, waiting to make sure the coast was clear. The phone then rang, and he worried that the officer was calling him back, so he ran back

147

to the desk, picked up the phone, and blurted, "Don't call back," before hanging it back up hard. Seeing nobody in the hallway, he got out of there.

Just as he rounded the corner, he literally bumped into Carol. "Ow, watch where you are going." She looked at him and continued, "You don't look so good. Maybe you should go home."

He awkwardly responded, "No, I'm fine. I just had a little trouble in the bathroom," not believing what had just come out of his mouth as he was saying it. He made his way back to his cubicle and collapsed into his chair, the adrenaline coursing through his veins, making him nauseous and fidgety—and a little giggly. He already had regrets, and he could only hope that what he had done would not cause harm to his family. He didn't care what happened to Laso, even though he doubted Laso was involved in the terrorist plot; he was Greenrock management, therefore, he was part of the problem.

CHAPTER 38

Dave woke up on Saturday morning, five days after he called in the tip to the police hotline, still without having had any blowback. For the remainder of the previous week, Big Freddy had escorted him from his cell to work every day as usual. He had his time in the gym and the quality of his food hadn't changed. He started to wonder if he had gotten away with it; maybe they weren't monitoring him so closely. His relief was short-lived, however, when instead of one of his guards wheeling in his breakfast cart at 8:00 AM, Aliyah walked in.

"Hey there, dumpling. Long time, no see," she said.

Dave was hungry and in no mood to deal with Aliyah. "Oh, it's you," he dismissively replied.

"Still an asshole, I see. I heard you were doing so well at your job—fitting in, making friends. I thought maybe you would have lightened up a little."

"What do you know about it?"

"I know lots of things, dumpling ... so many things," she said with a little wry smile. "In fact, this morning, I'm taking you to your first performance review. This should be fun, no? It's always good to get some feedback."

Dave tried to keep his cool, but started sweating and grew flush; his breathing grew heavy.

"Oh, look at you, all shy and embarrassed. I knew you had a crush on me," she purred, purposely misreading his nervous appearance. "Even though you're a dick, I really do like you, Dave. There are so many things we could have done together, but unfortunately, the boss men have other plans." She sighed before continuing, "Let's go."

Two guards walked in and pulled Dave out of bed, holding each of his arms as they escorted him out of the room and down the hallway to the elevators; they didn't give him time to get dressed, so he was only wearing his boxers. His worry about what was going to happen to him was only tempered by his need to urinate. The two guards continued to tightly hold his arms and scrunched up against him, doing their best to encroach on his personal space.

To take his mind off what was coming next, he amused himself by thinking about letting his bladder loose; he was twisted sideways with his crotch pressed against the guard on his left. He started smiling at the thought of peeing on the guard while looking straight at him. The guard momentarily looked back at him before turning his attention back in front of him, standing stiffly with pursed lips. Dave's impression of a dog humping a leg was making the guard very uncomfortable, which he took as a small victory.

"I'm a jealous bitch, Dave, if you want to get off, it better be with me," Aliyah said, seeming to notice everything.

Fully embarrassed, the young guard's usually pale face was now bright red.

Not wanting to let the matter rest. "It's not sexual, I just have to pee real bad and I'm not sure I can hold it much longer," Dave replied while still staring at the young man with a creepy smile.

"That's why I like you so much, Dave, you're an asshole, but so feisty. Why are all the good ones taken, or in your case, owned?"

The elevator doors opened up, and the guards quickly let go of Dave, seemingly wanting to get away from him as fast as possible. It was interesting that he could so easily influence his jailers with a little sexual mischievousness. He guessed that if he tried a stunt like that on an older guard, such as Big Freddy, he would just get a punch in the gut.

"Okay, boys, you two beat it. I think Dave here is too much for you guys, but I can handle him." They looked at her with a little confusion before she shooed them away with the flick of the back of her hand. After they had left, Aliyah looked at Dave and said, "They keep hiring them younger and younger—or maybe I'm getting older." She sighed and then cheerfully said, "Now let's go upstairs and see what horrible things the boss men have in store for my bad little dumpling."

They entered the elevator and Aliyah pushed the button, U2, while they quietly stood there listening to smooth jazz. She led him down a concrete hallway, not unlike down at the prison level, but not nearly as wide. Aliyah opened up a doorway that was labeled "Examination 3", and Dave walked into a room with an exam table on one side and a counter with a sink and shelving against the wall, like you might find in any doctor's office. The room was much bigger than a typical examination room in a clinic, however, and the examination table was bare metal. Mr. Jones and a man and woman in lab coats were standing on one side of the table, and a younger man in blue scrubs and light blond hair was standing on the other side.

When he walked in the door, he didn't notice the two large men waiting for him on either side of the entrance. They roughly grabbed him by the arms and dragged him to the examination table in full prone position. They tied his wrists and chest down with bed straps, pulled off his underwear, then tied down his ankles. They were strong: the redhead had a mullet, while the other man had a shaved head and goatee— good old boys, or at least that's what they looked like to Dave.

Mr. Jones looked over at Aliyah and said, "Thank you, Aliyah, you can go now. ... You two leave also." As he dismissed the two large men, he gave them a slight nod, signaling them to carry out some plan they had formulated earlier.

All business when in the presence of Mr. Jones, Aliyah simply nodded and turned around to leave. "Oh, he says he has to pee," she stated before leaving the room with the two large men who had strapped him to the table.

The male doctor looked kindly at Dave and giggled, "Well we can certainly do something about that," before nodding over to the blond man in scrubs.

"While my assistant gets things ready for you, let me introduce myself. I'm Dr. Danzel and this is Dr. Powell. I founded this lab, and let me first say that it is truly an honor to meet you. You don't know this, but we have developed a new set of gene sequences we'll use to genetically enhance subjects moving forward, and you are our first production subject we get to transform using the new process. You would not believe the advancements we've made in the last months with AI models based on all of the gene sequencing data we produced from our previous test and production subjects."

Dave was barely paying attention to Dr. Danzel's spiel; his mind was too occupied with what the assistant was pulling out of the cabinet. It looked like a catheter and urine bag; suddenly, the brave front he had been projecting was replaced by fear.

"What the hell is that for? I don't really have to go. I'm better now," Dave spat out.

"Try to relax, this is nothing compared to what we have planned for you first thing tomorrow morning," Danzel assured Dave. "Don't worry about my assistant, I'm talking about making you into something extraordinary. In a couple of days, these little indignities will seem minor in comparison."

Dave looked over at Mr. Jones and said, "I'm sorry. I'm sorry. I made a mistake. I'll never do it again. Just let me go back to work. They need me up there; it's tax season!"

Mr. Jones just shook his head back and forth. "What are you sorry for, Mr. Smith? Did you do something we told you never to do?"

Dave looked at Mr. Jones, a little confused.

"Yes, we know about the call you made to the homicide tip line. It took all week, but we were able to effectively contain the situation. Things won't go so well for Mr. Laso, however. He broke security protocols, so he will be escorted out of the building by two security guards first thing Monday morning, along with a box of his stuff. We intend to make a show of it. Your other friends in accounting will need to go through security training to make sure this type of thing doesn't happen again. They'll know you're the reason for their misery."

"What about my family?"

"What about them? Do you really care? If you did, you wouldn't have tested us. As for you, unfortunately, you are too important to us to damage," Jones continued.

"Yes, you've made Bill very angry, but as he said, you are too important to waste," Dr. Danzel said. Mr. Jones crinkled his nose a little when Danzel used his first name. He thought that diminished his authority in front of the prisoner.

"What do you mean by that?" Dave asked, while keeping an eye on the assistant now walking over to him with the catheter and urine bag in hand.

"In good time, Dave, all in good time. Even though you did nothing to earn it, it really is an honor to meet you. It's such a rare opportunity for us." Dr. Danzel gave Dave a small pat on the head and Dr. Powell just gave him a smile and a nod, having kept silent the whole time. The doctors and Jones then left out a second door in the back of the room. Two more assistants then walked into the room in their stead: another young man with dark skin and a shaved head, and a young woman with brown hair tied up in a tight bun.

"You don't have to do this. Can you just give me a bed pan?"

"No," the assistant stated with a kind smile.

Dave tried talking to the assistants some more, but they just ignored him. The woman held his penis up perpendicular to his body, while the bald assistant pumped some fluid into the tip of his penis. He felt a much stronger urge to pee now, but he couldn't because of the pressure of the pump holding down any fluid wanting to come out of his bladder. The blond assistant then held the end of the catheter next to the pump and said, "On three."

"One, two, three!" The bald assistant removed the pump from his penis tip and blondie deftly started pushing the catheter in before more than just a minimal amount of fluid escaped back out of his urethra. Dave felt the catheter inch its way down the inside of his penis; it wasn't very painful, but his body tensed up, and he started shaking anyway; it was like someone was scratching a chalkboard, but in him.

It was over pretty quickly, as the catheter found its final destination inside his bladder. Blondie then unclamped the catheter and Dave felt immediate relief as his bladder was allowed to empty. He was a little embarrassed because the relief almost felt too good, and the assistant with a bun was still holding his penis; blondie informed her that she could let go now.

They spent the next few minutes hooking him up to an IV and taking multiple tubes worth of blood samples. He heard a click and felt the table underneath his rear open up; the woman then slipped a plastic bed pan under his now exposed behind.

"If you need to go number two, just go and then tell us you need the pan changed out."

"How do I do that?"

"There is a microphone in the room, so we'll hear anything you say."

After the three assistants left the room, Dave had time to think about what his life had come to. Over the last month, he had started to accept his situation and even came to enjoy working in the accounting office—not the boring work itself, but he liked the people he worked with. That contrasted with his previous job at the plumbing company, where he hated Jim and Paul, and always felt underappreciated and underpaid. Under different circumstances, he could have made a career out of working as an accountant for Greenrock.

However, he never understood why he was kidnapped and imprisoned, just to be forced to work an intern level job, but he was certain he was going to discover the truth about why he was here first thing the next morning, as Dr. Danzel had promised. The doctor also promised that his next procedure would be a lot worse than receiving a catheter. He hoped they were just gaslighting him, but didn't really think so; he tried to calm himself by taking deep, slow breaths.

He couldn't calm himself down, though. He started to get goose bumps and then started to shiver uncontrollably. Despite his efforts using controlled breathing, the cold room and his excess nervous energy and fear for himself was ramping up his anxiety to the point of making him want to scream. He tried to direct some of that fear to his family that he had put in danger, but shamefully, his brain kept forcing him to concentrate on his own well-being; they had broken him.

CHAPTER 39

Aliyah walked out the door of the examination room with the two new security personnel Mr. Jones had hired to replace Butch and Kevin. Aliyah was five foot seven, but they both towered over her—Jones liked them big and mean looking. Ken Jurgensen looked like a caricature from the nineteen eighties, with his red hair shaped into a tidy mullet and large round head and thick body; he was the guy you wanted to go drinking with if you planned on getting in a bar fight. Joe Green was tall, like Ken, but wiry, with a dark brown goatee under a cleanly shaved head.

While they looked like two rednecks that would rather fish and drink than run security operations, in the short time Aliyah had got to know them, she came to realize that they were much smarter than Butch and Kevin. Mr. Jones wasn't going to make the same mistake he had previously made with the other three. The new guys were both former police detectives who were suspended after killing a suspect while making an arrest; a lot of people in their community thought they got screwed for political reasons, but after the shooting, there were protests and the threat of a federal investigation, so they were sacrificed by the city's liberal mayor.

What was unfortunate for Joe and Ken was fortunate for Mr. Jones, however. He was able to bring two professionals with experience in running criminal investigations into his criminal exercise. These two previously upstanding cops were treated unfairly by the system they had protected, making them much more amenable to working for a shady organization which put killing and kidnapping in the job description. The pay was really good, though—more than double what they were making as detectives—so they were willing to cross over to the dark side.

After leaving the examination room with Joe and Ken, Aliyah had started to walk back down the hall when she suddenly felt a searing pain in her back. Immediately, all of her muscles tensed up and she fell to the ground, vibrating uncontrollably. As the mullet head re-holstered his stun gun, goatee turned the stiff and drooling Aliyah on her belly and zip tied her hands together; they then both picked her up by each of her elbows and dragged her down the hall and back toward the elevators.

Even though her muscles were still non-functional from the shock of the stun gun, she had enough of her senses back to understand what was happening to her when Ken pressed the button for U5; they were taking her to the prison. She tried to protest, but her words just came out slurred; Ken just smiled like he was having fun; in all fairness, she would be having fun too, if she wasn't the prey this time.

When they arrived at level U5, they dragged her the entire distance from the elevators to a cell, right across from Dave's cell. They flopped her on the bed on her back then tied her ankles to the posts on the bottom of the bed, and after cutting the zip tie, tied her wrists to the posts at the head of the bed. Now fully secured, Ken pulled out a large pair of scissors. Her emotional state went from disbelieving and anger to disbelieving and panic, knowing what they were about to do with those scissors.

Joe first took off her shoes and socks before he took out his own scissors and started cutting off one of her pant legs while Ken started to cut off her shirt. Two large men cutting away her clothes triggered old memories of her father she thought she had long suppressed. For the first time since she was a little girl, she started crying; light sobs at first, and then

157

to full-blown cries of despair. They didn't molest her, but they appeared to be enjoying their work—at least in her mind—and when they were done and she was fully naked, they stepped back and looked her over, adding to her humiliation; she imagined the silent catcalls that were going through their heads. She felt the only thing holding them back from raping her were the cameras in the room and the sure punishment from Mr. Jones if they overstepped their assignment. After one last look, they cut off all her restraints and left the room, leaving Aliyah lying on the bed in a fetal position, still crying.

*

Hours later, Aliyah was still lying in the same position, almost catatonic, vacant, all of her emotional energy used up. Her door opened, and a guard walked in pushing a food cart; it smelled like steak, so it must have been dinner time. The tables had turned, the captor now the captive, Aliyah was stunned, having never considered that the place she considered home could turn on her in the same way it turned on so many others.

The smell of the food seemed to knock her out of her dissonance, and she started to feel a deep sense of shame for losing control. Since running away from home years before, she had always been the strong one, the tough girl who didn't give a fuck, but now she had shamefully broken down in front of two men. She started pounding her fists straight down into the bed and let out a big scream of rage; this would not be the end of Aliyah; she would get her status back and make those two former detectives pay for enjoying their work so much.

Not hungry, she got out of bed and flipped the cart over, scattering her dinner across the room. She then sat back on the bed cross-legged and stared across at the other wall, waiting for what came next. Some number of hours after she tossed her dinner cart, a young guard she knew as Kendall walked in with a cleaning cart and started to clean up her mess. Aliyah just continued to stare straight ahead, refusing to engage or even acknowledge the young man. He did seem to go out of his way to avoid looking at her naked body, which she appreciated. When she took her revenge, Kendall might get to live.

Having finished cleaning up the mess and mopping the floor, Kendall pushed out the cleaning cart. He then wheeled in a cabinet and placed it against the wall opposite the bed before leaving for good. The same type of cabinet was in Dave's cell, so she knew what was inside of it. She got up and pulled out one of the gray sweat suits that were on one of the shelves and got dressed. After covering herself up, she suddenly started to feel a little bit more like herself again, having restored some control over her physical state. She then pulled out the sheets, made her bed, and lay back down.

She hadn't realized how tired she was, but now that she was lying in bed, somewhat comfortable, she fell into a deep sleep.

CHAPTER 40

The light in Dave's room stayed on, so he had no sense of what time of day it was, or even if it was day at all. A couple of times, an assistant in blue scrubs came in to change out his IV bag and bed pan; he never called for help, even after evacuating. He also only slept in short fits and continued to shiver in the cold room, so when the blondie unlocked the wheels of his gurney and started rolling him out of the room, he was exhausted and dazed.

The assistant wheeled Dave into what looked like a surgical room, where he saw both Dr. Danzel and Dr. Powell getting things ready, along with a host of other assistants in blue scrubs. Shortly after he entered the room, the bald orderly who had assisted with his catheter the day before injected something into his IV line. He felt a burning sensation going down the length of his arm, and then, shortly after, he felt his muscles weaken to the point where he started losing control of them.

"Arah id ooo me," Dave said.

That was all he could get out before he lost control of his diaphragm and started to suffocate. Another assistant was ready, and inserted a catheter down his throat and hooked it up to a machine that forced him to breathe again. Then they unstrapped him and carried him over to another metal table in the center of the surgery room.

Powell came over to his side. "We administered a paralytic drug to keep you still during the procedure. It is important that you stay awake and fully aware, so we'll also be giving you medications that enhance your senses and stimulate your nervous system. It will be a very painful procedure, but one we've done many times, so I can ensure you, you will not only get through it, but be pleased with the results afterward."

What? Are they giving me a nose job?

"Yes," Danzel now joined in, "you are truly part of something special. As Dr. Powell mentioned, we've done this procedure many times, but you are the first subject we are enhancing with a new class of gene sequences that we've only just finished developing and testing. As I tell all our subjects, you are going to experience millions of years of evolution in just a matter of days, but today we are going one step even beyond that. That's enough talk for now, you really can't truly understand until you go through it yourself."

One of the assistants injected something into his IV line, and Dave immediately felt the same burning sensation traveling up his arm and then out to the rest of his body. The burning died down, but it felt like every nerve in his body was put on alert. Every sensation was amplified: the cold of the room, the pinch of the needle in his arm, even the smells. His anger was also amplified, after feeling broken just moments before, the drug seemed to renew his spirit and desire to lash out at everybody who had put him in this position.

They inserted drops into his eyes, which dilated them and made them more sensitive to the bright light shining in his face. Dr. Powell then inserted a metal speculum in each of his eyes to hold them open, then they raised the table, putting him into a seated position. His newfound spirit was thoroughly tested when they started slowly moving two needles into place, one in front of each of his pupils.

Completely paralyzed and helpless, he could only watch as the needle on the left slowly made its way into his eyeball. After the needle stopped moving, he felt what seemed like little bolts of electricity pulsing from the needle into his brain;

the pain was unbearable, but only got worse as they did the same thing to his other eye.

For what seemed like hours, they repeatedly injected him with different substances, in different parts of his body, that would at first cause him severe pain, but then a sense of euphoria as the pain died down. He felt himself getting stronger with each treatment, so after just an hour in, he not only tolerated the pain but relished it like a drug addict about to get their fix.

At the two-hour mark, his body took back control of itself. He assumed that was not normal, since after giving him the paralytic drug, they didn't bother to securely strap his arms to the gurney. He was only held on the table by straps around his neck, chest, legs, and ankles to keep him from slumping and to prevent them from accidentally knocking him off the table. When he regained control, one of the assistants was hovering over him—the woman who had held his penis the day before. All he had to do was move his hand up a couple of feet to the orderly's neck and squeeze; he had no doubt that he could instantly snap her neck clean in half.

But he wanted to catch a much bigger and more important fish, so he played possum and waited. Unfortunately, Danzel had stepped out of the room, but Powell was making her way over to him with a large needle and a smile on her face—she certainly enjoyed her job.

"You're doing great, Dave; I can see in your eyes that you are ..."

She didn't get the chance to finish her sentence before he grabbed the upper part of her head and squeezed his fingers into her temples. He pushed his thumb into one temple and his middle finger into the other; he was far from fully evolved into the new, stronger Dave he would eventually become, but with some effort, he was able to continue to squeeze his hand closed until his thumb and middle finger met in her frontal

162

lobe. He squeezed a little more, hearing a satisfying crack emanating from her eye sockets; then her eyes both popped out, bringing him more joy than he could have imagined possible. He was finally taking control of his own destiny again.

Though panicked, the bald orderly had the wherewithal to inject more paralytic agent into his IV line. He felt his muscles slacken again, but not nearly as much as when they had given him his first dose. Another scrub rushed in and gave him two more doses, which eventually left him back in a fully paralytic state.

Dr. Danzel ran back into the room, looked down at the late Dr. Powell—whose head was still attached to Dave's now dangling arm—and simply said, "Oh my!" He giggled nervously.

After Danzel recovered from the initial shock at losing his protégé, he started yelling at his assistants in anger, calling them incompetent and threatening their careers. He didn't seem angry at Dave, since Dave was just following his new nature; it would be like getting mad at a cat for licking its ass.

Despite losing Powell, they continued on and finished his treatment, but also kept him topped off with the paralytic drug and strapped his wrists tightly down to the table. The biggest benefit realized from killing Powell was that it seemed to shut Danzel up. He was no longer endlessly pontificating about his own genius or the great things they would accomplish together. Dave seemed to have put a damper on Dr. Danzel's big day; he would be smiling—if only his face wasn't paralyzed.

CHAPTER 41

After the procedure was finished, they gave Dave another dose of the paralytic drug and placed a sack over his ventilated head. He felt himself being wheeled out of the surgery room and back into the hallway, down one floor in the elevator, and finally through another couple of doors, before they lifted him out of the wheelchair and onto another table. Despite their attempt to obfuscate his location relative to the surgical room, his senses were strong enough for him to mentally map the route they took him on by simply gauging the speed he was traveling and memorizing the twists and turns of the path they took; he even guessed at the area of each space he was in by how the air felt.

When they removed the sack from his head, he was sitting in a plexiglass cage in the middle of a large, concrete-lined room. The orderlies lifted him off his wheelchair and placed him on a metal table that was bolted down to the floor. Then they all quickly left—what he did to Powell still fresh in their minds—leaving him alone with no sounds but the hum of the air circulation system and the ventilator still managing his breathing.

Despite still being naked and full of nerve stimulating drugs, he was no longer cold, now fully in control of how every nerve in his body brought what they perceived back to his brain. Slowly, over the course of the next hour, he regained control of his muscles and finally, his breathing. He ripped the intubation tube out of his throat, got up from the table, and started walking around his new cage on unsteady legs. After doing a full survey of his new quarters, he determined that he wasn't going anywhere until they decided it was time for him to leave.

Even though he could control how his brain perceived pain, he still knew that he was in a lot of it, and that pain remained for the next couple of weeks. Even after all of the drugs had worn off, he still felt very sick, like he had a bad case of the flu. Despite the pain, he could still feel himself getting stronger and his senses enhancing to the point where he could distinguish the people who entered his prison cell by how they smelled and the sounds their feet made when they walked.

Dr. Danzel made several appearances a day, quickly recovering from the loss of Powell. He was back to his giggling psychopathic self, regaling about how Dave was progressing perfectly—just as he predicted. He hinted at what was to come by calling Dave the perfect weapon and a new strategic asset for Greenrock—and the U.S.—but he was mostly focused on what Dave would do for HEL and his own glory.

*

Almost immediately after the procedure, Dave started to hear voices in his head, but a week into Dave's recovery, he was sitting alone in his cell, cross-legged on the table in meditation, when he heard one of those voices ask him a direct question.

What are you?

He looked around confused but didn't see anybody in the room and wondered if there was a speaker somewhere that hadn't been used up to that point of his incarceration.

The names *Lud, George, Anne, Dell, Sigurd, Jason, Frank, Isla, Nu, Hamit,* all entered his brain at once. It was like his brain was split into multiple personalities and they were introducing themselves to him. He felt disoriented.

We've sensed you for a while now, but now you can finally communicate and respond with us. Just concentrate, the Lud personality injected into his brain.

Who are you? Dave asked.

We are you, but not you.

I'm Dave.

We know that, but you are like us, but not like us. We are beasts that went through the same transformation that you did, but you are like us but not a beast.

Dave interpreted the voices in his head as separate personalities within his own being. He concentrated and could visualize what the new personalities looked like. They looked like a cross between people and apes, or maybe neanderthals, but he also knew they were his kin, even though his appearance was not modified by the procedure. He did recognize one of his personalities as Hamit, one of his kidnappers who drove him to HEL right after his pretend arrest. They seemed to sense his anger.

Please forgive me, I was not good back then and a pawn of the human, Hamit projected.

Dave wasn't sure whether he wanted to forgive Hamit or not, but he did know that these beasts—the HEL staff nicknamed them furries—were his friends and allies, while the humans that they referred to the unenhanced people as, were the enemy. He still considered himself human, though. Despite how they looked, he didn't agree that they were no longer human too.

I went through the same transformation that you did, but my appearance stayed the same. Danzel told me I was the first to experience his new gene editing techniques. Can you hear all my thoughts?

Yes, we know all each other's thoughts. I can see why an enhanced that looks like them could be valuable, given our purpose.

166

I am superior, Dave projected without a hint of humility.

Bonobo, the collective thought. He sensed joy and laughing. They (or we?) changed his name to Bonobo as a reward for his arrogance; he was superior, though, so he felt his thought was accurate. That was okay, since Bonobo knew Dave was no more; he would still be Dave to the so-called humans, but Bonobo was his new identity within the collective, his break from the past. They wore their new characterizations with pride.

Bonobo didn't relish the loss of privacy; he was now part of a hive mind, so as long as the other furries were nearby, privacy was now part of his past life. He would have to come up with ways to silence the new inner voices to keep his sanity.

You can put our thoughts in the background, but you can't hide your voice from us. You'll grow to appreciate the power our collective mind affords you. While each of us is strong, our real strength is as a collective.

Fish? They call you fish. I guess that's some justice, given what you did to me.

You're the new drone now. You won't be so cocky when they start training you.

Bonobo saw the images of Hamit in his first days after joining the rest of them. It was like watching a blooper reel. Bonobo felt anger swelling up inside his head, but it wasn't coming from him.

Save your anger for the humans—was that directed at fish or Bonobo?—*we are all victims of HEL, but also its champions. The changes they made to our genetic programming made us better, but first we have to free ourselves. That will take our combined cunningness more than our strength, so we need to stay focused and unified.*

We are humans, just like great athletes are still humans, Bonobo thought.

167

I suppose, technically, but it is different for you. We look like another species, so it is appropriate for us to no longer think of ourselves as human. It draws a line between us and our enemies.

Those enemies call you furries as a joke.

Watch it. You haven't known us long enough to start to criticize. We've taken the term and made it our own. You still look the same, but don't fool yourself into thinking you still fit in with them. You'll wear the same dog collar that we do, and you'll follow their commands as long as it's strapped around your neck.

Sorry, you're right, but I won't be their dog.

That's the spirit. He sensed sarcasm.

At the very least, since I look like them, I can try to find a weakness in their security, assuming they don't lock me up in your enclosure.

We're counting on it.

Bonobo thought back to how he got to this point and how he would move forward. He had spent a lot of time in the last few months thinking about how he would escape, and never could come up with an answer. Between the ankle tag—and presumably a collar in the future—and threats to his family, HEL had him in a bind.

But those were worries for the future. He decided instead to calm his hive mind by sharing happy thoughts, such as the memory of crushing Powell's skull. Danzel, Jones, and Aliyah were several other people on Bonobo's shit list who were in line to get their skulls crushed. When the time came, the furries would blow this place up, like HEL did to that sandwich shop. In the end, they would do it the Greenrock way.

168

CHAPTER 42

They were covered in sweat, hot and heaving, their normal calm taken over by animal needs. The heat pouring out of their pores was matched by a strong musk-like funkiness that only added more fuel to their desires. They pounded each other with a force that would have broken apart common people. They felt each thrust from the outside and inside, their joined minds sharing every sensation equally. Normally mute, they shared in a wolf-like howl and simultaneous deep moan. The first orgasm came after his powerful ejaculation and the second, more powerful, her muscles tensing and then exploding outwards, throwing him across the room and into the wall.

Bonobo woke up soaked, head to toe, his back hurt, even though he wasn't the one physically thrown against the wall. He was still erect for several minutes after he ejaculated, but in time brought his body back into a calm state. It was the most intense thing he had ever experienced. A wet dream, but not a dream.

My God, again, nice, find a room, were some of the many shared thoughts going through his head.

Apparently, Dell and Anne did this fairly often, though the whole hive shared every thought and sensation equally. Sex was no longer private either, but the intensity of their union was multiplied by many orders of magnitude over what a common human could experience—their nervous systems being enhanced and more sensitive, combined with all eleven contributing to the frolic.

Just as Bonobo fully regained his composure, Danzel burst in, followed by a whole host of his assistants in blue scrubs.

"Dave, what happened? My assistant alerted me as soon as he saw you erect and convulsing. We'll need to do some tests to determine why you had a seizure."

No, Lud commanded. Though the doctors hypothesized that the furries all communicated with each other telepathically, based on observations, they didn't really know how strongly their minds were linked. They did not want to fully reveal their capabilities by coming right out and telling them how they communicated.

Dave just sat there still, following the bad doctor with his eyes, keeping a neutral expression.

Exasperated, Danzel finally played his trump card: "Dave, I was hoping for more cooperation, but since your procedure, you've been acting like the others. We built you as our tool, so it's time you started working for us. Do I have to remind you what is at stake back at home?"

Every last cell in Bonobo's body ached to kill Dr. Danzel— *he's mine, you already got yours (i.e. Powell)*—but he decided that going along with the program would be in his best interest for now.

"I'm fine. It was just an intense nightmare. What others?" Dave asked, pretending not to know what Danzel meant.

"That's better. Tell me about your nightmare."

"I don't know. I've never been able to remember my dreams, and your experiment didn't change that. What others?" Dave grumbled.

"I'm not sure I believe you, but come over so we can take a blood sample," Danzel ordered.

Dave got up off the table and put his arm through a small hole that opened up in the front of the plexiglass enclosure. He stuck his arm through the hole with his palm facing upward, then an orderly pulled a lever down on the side of the cage, which engaged two metal collars that secured his arm in place. After he was fully secured, they performed their blood draw. Since moving to his new cage, he had gone through that ritual every four hours.

"I have something special planned for you this afternoon, so it is important that you are one hundred percent. It's time for you to meet the *others* and take your place in our special operations unit. Get some rest, it's going to be a big day for you."

Danzel and the rest of them all left. Bonobo could sense that Danzel didn't trust him, but he didn't care what Danzel thought. His progress in sharing his thoughts with the hive and registering what humans were feeling outpaced his furry comrades at this stage in his development. Danzel was excited to introduce him to the furries and give him his purpose: to kill, just like any furry, but he could mix in with common humans, giving Greenrock a different option when they needed to terminate a target—a new tool, as Danzel referred to him as.

One thing Bonobo could not understand, however, was how he would restrain himself from killing Danzel, Jones, and every other Greenrock employee that had wronged him. He still had to protect his family back in Issaquah and now also had a responsibility to his new band, so he would restrain himself—for now.

CHAPTER 43

Dr. Danzel and his orderlies filed back into Dave's room later that same day, as promised, along with Mr. Jones and another man he recognized as Alan Keeps (the boss); the boss was thin but weathered and strong; he was wearing a brownish short-sleeved shirt, gray tactical pants, and black boots. He had thick dark hair, brown eyes, and a deep tan.

The boss—Keeps—Trains us for our missions and directs them.

Got that. I share your minds, remember?

Asshole.

So they tell me.

He sensed the furries had some respect for their boss, but given the chance, they would kill him as easily as anybody else unfortunate enough to cross their path. He knew they couldn't: HEL had developed special shock collars to keep them under control.

On cue, Danzel lifted a black collar off a cart they had wheeled in behind him. It was only an inch wide and half an inch in thickness; it was fashionable, if not a little masochistic. He could see how it would add to his badass look when they set off to do their dirty work in the wild. Unfortunately, its purpose wasn't to make him a badass, it was to control him like a dog. He looked like a normal human, but they considered him a pet monster, just like the other furries.

He (they) waited for the cage to seal up and the sleeping gas to filter in; his shared memories meant that he had gone through this process ten times before. There was no gas, however; instead, they opened two holes in the cage, parallel to each other, a couple of feet apart, waist high off the ground.

"Stand with your back against the wall and place both wrists in front of the openings," the boss ordered.

Dave did as he was directed and felt the cold metal of a handcuff securing each wrist, which were then tied together with a chain run along the outside of the cage between the openings. After he was secured and tightly pulled up against the cage wall, another doorway opened behind his neck. Through the hole, they placed the black collar around his neck. He heard a clicking sound as it locked in place; the collar was heavy, he guessed at least five pounds. They unlocked his handcuffs and opened the door to the cage.

"Come on out Dave, you are free," Danzel said without a hint of irony.

He walked out and stood in front of the group, not bothering to attack, knowing what would happen if he did— his minds had experienced it. Danzel waved his hand dismissively, and his blue scrub assistants all left. He could feel Danzel's joy and excitement at finally getting to play with his new creation, while Keeps matched Dave's stone face and calm demeanor. Mr. Jones projected disgust and some fear, giving Dave some satisfaction. Bonobo would take great joy in dealing with Mr. Jones—*not if I get him first,* Hamit hissed.

They left the room and started down the hallway; Dave kept at least three feet from the other three; when he got closer, he felt a buzz through his collar that warned him of the impending shock that would occur if he didn't back off.

As if Danzel could read his mind: "It's a shame we had to lose Dr. Powell in order to discover your extra resistance to our control methods—what a waste. Your collar is considerably more advanced than our previous versions.

We've custom designed it to match your specific nervous system."

Dave felt all of his nerves light up in pain. The pain wasn't the worst part of it: the shock instantly produced a feeling of uneasiness in him that mimicked severe stress. The collar induced the world's worst panic attack. The pain and loss of muscle control dropped him to the ground, where he just withered, wide-eyed and drooling, barely able to keep from crying. His chest tightened and he gasped for air.

Ouch. Fuck. Tear to pieces. Worse.

"Tsk, tsk, Mr. Keeps. Please don't damage my property," Danzel scolded.

"He's not your property. He's the property of Greenrock and now under my watch," Keeps shot back.

Dr. Danzel was clearly annoyed at this, he was a sociopathic narcissist, so he didn't like anybody challenging his authority or position as the heart and soul of HEL. Keeps was correct: Danzel's job was simply to build the weapons, while Keeps trained and deployed them. Keeps was Bonobo's boss and zookeeper.

The three men and the naked furry walked into a lab, where they walked over to large windows overlooking a multi-story enclosure with what looked to Dave to be tree houses. Of course, he knew this was where they boarded the furries; it was their home. They were out of sight, lounging in their huts, but Danzel needed to pontificate, so he told Keeps to rouse them. Bonobo sensed the pings his comrades all felt, which directed them to line up on the deck at the center of the structure. There, he could view them with his eyes for the first time; they were fiends.

Pretty boy.

Bonobo smiled.

"Ahh, seeing your kind makes you happy. Of course! I knew you would see them as your breed, even if you don't share their beastly appearance," Danzel proclaimed.

Bonobo's smile widened as multiple and creative ways they would kill Danzel entered his thoughts.

"Normally, this is when we walk you into the furries' enclosure, so you can meet your new friends and train together, but we have different plans for you. We're going to teach you how to be a secret agent. How does that sound?" Danzel looked at Dave expectantly, like a parent that promised his kid a game console and then waited for the kid to start jumping for joy. He just stood there looking at Danzel with his lips pursed up on one side and his nose scrunched, like he was observing the doctor taking a shit—Danzel disgusted him. He sensed Keeps and Jones had a similar view of the doctor, but unfortunately, Danzel was the only brilliant psychopath Greenrock employed that was capable of turning people into monster assassins.

Not getting the response he wanted, Danzel looked a little dejected. Mr. Jones, who had been quiet up until this point, decided to take over.

"Dave, you know the way back to your room."

Dave knew Jones meant his old room he had lived in before they transitioned him, so he nodded.

"I thought so. Just remember the little demonstration Alan gave you earlier—a real teachable moment, I hope—and walk straight there. You may look like Dave, but I know you are an animal, like your friends down there." Jones nodded toward the row of furries still standing on the deck. Your only constant escort from here on out will be that collar, but you will go directly to where you are told to go with or without a security escort. You will do as you are told, with no deviations. ... Oh wait, here." He tossed him a pair of white coveralls.

175

Mr. Jones and Dave stared at each other for a few seconds before he slipped on his coveralls and made his way out of the lab barefoot; Jones talked tough, but he could feel his fear. As he was walking down the hallway to the elevators, it felt good to be away from his kidnappers and on his own. He knew it was just an illusion; they were monitoring his every step, and the collar was a more effective escort than even Big Freddy was to human Dave; not to mention he was still stuck in this dungeon.

Moments later, he was back in front of the doorway to his old cell. He was about to push open his door when he sensed something, a familiar smell. He walked over to the cell door across from his and laid his cheek and hand against the cold steel door, lightly massaging it, and breathed in deeply, taking in her scent. Aliyah was in there. He felt satisfied now that the tables had turned on his nemesis. HEL had turned on her, just like it had turned on Hamit. Did she really expect anything else?

He closed his eyes and took in one last nose full of her sweet aroma. Relaxed, he pushed open his cell door and walked into his old room, everything was exactly how he had left it weeks before. The door closed behind him, and when he tried to open it again, it was locked, so much for having more freedom to travel.

Inside his room were two meal carts: one with a normal-looking steak dinner, with a side of mashed potatoes and steamed broccoli, and a second with only a large cut of raw beef on a plate—*my first test*. In the cage, they had only fed him cooked food. He could eat either meal, but like the other furries, he now preferred raw meat. Despite his human appearance, he felt that inside he had much more in common with his beastly band. He went for the raw meat first, grabbing it in his hands and eating it with enthusiasm, his enhanced jaw making easy work of it. He had a much higher

176

metabolism than a normal human, plus his new stronger muscles demanded lots of protein. After finishing the raw meat, he quickly finished the cooked meal. "No desert?" He asked whoever was listening and watching. "Still hungry!"

He then took a long hot shower, feeling refreshed for the first time since they transitioned him. When he stepped out of the bathroom, the two dinner carts had been replaced with a new cart with a slice of apple pie à la mode; if nothing else, HEL fed its employees and prisoners very well. For not the first time, he thought to himself that he would have come willingly if they had offered him a nice salary and moving expenses. By day, he would be Greenrock's raw meat-eating killing machine and by night he would go home to his wife and be the family man he used to be—Jekyll and Hyde.

Forget your old life. You are not him anymore. If you went back, you would probably eat your kids.

I know, but I would not eat my kids.

Do you know?

Yes.

Don't be charmed by a slice of pie.

Good pie.

Bonobo's always the joker. We enjoy our work; we can't deny it. Killing is fun, yes, but that is how they designed us.

Yes. You want freedom, but you can't locked in the enclosure. I'm out here. Will find a way to disable the collars and free us.

Yes. Aliyah? You want that human?

I cannot hide anything from the collective, Bonobo thought to himself. Aliyah just randomly popped into his mind, causing them a moment of arousal.

Have her once. She won't survive it.

I'll be gentle or not.

Stick to your own kind.

I'm a hybrid.

177

Maybe.

He should probably take their advice, but banging Aliyah and not accidentally killing her was now a challenge; cooped up in a cell, he needed goals to keep his enhanced brain occupied. A short while later, a guard came in and took his cart away. He registered no fear or apprehension from the guard, so he assumed the guard had no idea what type of monster he was attending.

CHAPTER 44

Morning started just like any other from back when he was normal old Dave and worked in accounting: they wheeled him in steak—raw—and eggs, a nice fruit salad, and a cup of English breakfast tea. The raw steak was a nice touch; Bonobo supposed HEL had invested a lot of money in him, so taking good care of their new tool was a priority. Since the transformation, he was more comfortable walking around naked, but decided to put on his sweat suit. The other furries wore spandex shorts when outside their enclosure and on mission, but he didn't have any of those in his closet. His purpose was to fit in with the normal humans and only break some of them, while his compatriots were more optimized to slaughter in bulk.

At 10:43 AM, Alan Keeps—the boss—showed up at his door and simply said, "Let's go," while nodding his head sideways toward the door.

"They tell me you are different than the other ones, but I see killer in your eyes just like I do in the other animals," Keeps insulted.

"Hey, I'm HEL's expensive new toy. You treat me with more care. Don't you want me to play along?"

"That collar ensures you'll play along. I don't care what you want. As far as I can tell, the only difference between you and them is that you talk. The thing I like best about the furries is that they are silent and do as they're told, and now they've gone and created a new furry that won't shut up."

"Well, boss, I may be HEL's latest experiment, but I think you're the real killer here. Come on, how many people have you killed? Hundreds? Thousands? I've only crushed Dr. Powell's skull, and that bitch had it coming," Dave said.

Keeps just ignored Dave's diatribe.

"So, Alan, you gonna train me to be a spy, like James Bond?"

Referring to the boss by his first name seemed to get his attention, since suddenly Dave stiffened up straight as a board, hopping like a pogo stick, hoping not to fall on his ass. The shock only lasted a few seconds, though; Keeps giving Dave a little warning shot.

Properly put in his place, he answered Dave's question: "That's what management thinks, but my goal is that you just turn out to be a slightly less blunt object than the other beasts."

Is he always this grumpy? No, you seem to have gotten under his skin. Why? You exist? And are an asshole. See you soon. You think. We're lined up ready to go, waiting. Huh. Waiting for what? The hunt. So hard not to kill him, so close. Been there, done that. Need to try …

Dave was walking a few feet ahead of Keeps—Keeps obviously didn't trust the collar enough to turn his back on him—but Dave suddenly stopped walking. Keeps was paying attention, so he didn't smack into his back like most people would have, but he did get close enough to set off a warning pulse in Dave's collar. It was just enough of a shock to remind him what the consequence would be if he got any closer.

"So, you want to play with me. I thought yesterday's demonstration would dissuade you from that."

The light warning pulse was replaced by a much stronger shock that brought back the feeling of panic and loss of control that he had experienced the day before. Dave felt his legs grow unsteady as they started to shake, and he started sweating profusely; he managed to stay standing, which was more than he had done the day before.

"That was just the low setting. When I had you hopping around like a jack rabbit, it was on the extra low setting. You want to really see what that collar can do?"

Dave shook his head back and forth and squeaked out, "I'm good."

"Are you? I don't need you to be good, just compliant," Keeps said. "You are part of my command that includes both my mercenaries and you furries. It's not complicated. As long as everyone follows orders and does their jobs correctly, we'll all get along and successfully carry out our missions."

"Wow, we're a team now? I'm assuming your soldiers weren't kidnapped and forced to be part of your squad, like us super-humans."

"Super-humans?" Keeps said, almost choking on his laugh. "It doesn't matter how we all got here, you're in my charge now, and on mission, I only care that you do your job."

"Ya, boss, we're superheroes. Danzel can shove that furry shit right up his ass."

Keeps was actually smiling now, which was unusual. They traveled one floor up and down a curved corridor that Dave assumed wrapped around the furries' enclosure. They proceeded until they arrived at a door that was labeled "413 Training" on the door jamb. Unlike the other office doors, this door was metal with a latch within a larger metal gate that provided the room beyond with a large entranceway if needed.

"After you," Keeps said, waving his hand, palm upright, toward the door.

You think we're ugly? Nice sweats. Hope I don't mistake you for a human and tear your ribs out. Still upset about being called a furry?

Try it, I'm superman.

Collar won't project you from us, green.

181

Bonobo smiled wide as soon as he saw his band; he felt like he had come home. They silently ribbed each other, creating a space for themselves separate from the mercenaries. Bonobo took off his clothes and took his position in the troop.

"Okay then," Keeps said, looking at Dave curiously. If he was only mostly sure that Dave was the same as the others in a human façade, that just confirmed it.

"Standard drill to start. You take control of the building, eliminating all occupants. Ready, Dave?"

Dave nodded, having experienced the drill many times before while joined to the hive. *Follow me.* When Keeps gave the order to advance, all eleven took off simultaneously, Bonobo tailing Lud. Unlike most new furries in their first days, Bonobo had adapted to having them all in his head and had participated in the word games they used to train their minds. That meant that he was more useful during his first exercise than most, but the intensity of what he experienced was still more than he had expected. He could handle the minds of the adrenaline pumped furries, but combined with the raw fear of the humans, it created a stew of emotions that bore down on him like a tornado.

Through the first phase of the exercise, he managed to stay upright and keep on Lud's tail as Lud took out adversaries guarding the outside of the building, but when they entered the building, Bonobo was hit with several paintballs, despite Lud prepping him on what to do to avoid getting fatally hit. The hits set off his collar, dropping him to the ground in a fit of withering pain; it was just pain and loss of muscle control, and not the panic inducing shock Keeps had previously given him—withering pain he could handle.

Now who's flopping around like a fish? Fish smugly thought.

It is the collar, Bonobo reflected defensively.

Furries loved to taunt. He knew what was coming as soon as he hit the ground and started flopping around from the tase of his collar. He would gladly be tased a thousand times rather than have what happened to him next. While he was still on the ground, Anne walked by and gave him a couple of eyebrow raises and a wink, her strong musky scent turning him on. He'd had virtual sex with her multiple times, so now being so close instantly aroused him—it was the nanobot enhanced libido. He was still aroused when he felt the two pulses from his collar, indicating that the exercise was over and he needed to get back in line, outside.

She's mine. We're ours. Not all enhanced ... huh.

Keeps looked at Dave with disgust, misinterpreting his arousal, thinking he was turned on by the violence. Bonobo, like all the furries, was violent in nature, but it didn't turn him on sexually. Training continued, but Keeps divided them up into three groups for the rest of the day; Bonobo was matched with Lud and George. Lud's group switched to attacking the house, while the other two groups attacked the building and a well defended camp in the forested part of the training space.

Keeps stayed with Lud's team, since apparently, they needed to train for a specific mission happening the next morning.

"Dave, here's where you start proving our investment in you was worthwhile," Keeps said like it was his money. "We have a family of four that needs killing, and you three fiends are just the monsters for the job. But ... we need information from them first, and the adult male has been very stubborn when it comes to getting that information from him through legal means. That means we need to solve this problem the Greenrock way."

The Greenrock way.

Even old Dave knew what that meant, but Bonobo, Lud, and George keyed in like hungry tigers stalking their prey.

Keeps continued, "Tomorrow morning at 10:00 AM, the Jackson family has a plumber scheduled to unclog their kitchen sink drain. However, the Jacksons think the appointment is at 9:00 AM. Dave, you are going to show up at 9:00 AM in your uniform and with your tool bag to open up the dad's pipes." Keeps smiled at his own cleverness.

"Look at you. Making jokes about torturing and killing a dad in front of his wife and kids. You sure you're not the animal ... boss?" Dave asked.

Keeps stood there for a few seconds trying to stare down Dave while he contemplated using the collar on him. Dave rightly called him out; Keeps had to stay professional and not let HEL drag him down to its level. Keeps recomposed himself and went back into his neutral, non-pulsed demeanor. He couldn't let Dave know that he was getting to him—Bonobo knew.

"You will enter their house and extract the name of a whistleblower who has been a thorn in the side of our client. You don't need the details, just get him to tell you the name of his whistleblower contact—he'll know what you mean." Keeps paused for a second and Bonobo could sense a little discomfort he hid behind his tough exterior. "We suggest you threaten one of his kids."

We. There must be a HEL committee to discuss these sorts of things.

Bonobo, Lud, and George didn't blink an eye at the suggestion of using children to make their parents talk or even killing those children and parents; they were bred by Dr. Danzel specifically to kill people without remorse, but what were their human masters' excuse?

They will die. We will disable the collars and be done killing children.

Bonobo had the most freedom and access to the facility of any of the furries, so they were counting on him to find a solution to the collar problem.

One of Keeps' soldiers handed him a set of folded up clothes wrapped in plastic, and Keeps tossed the package to Dave, indicating that he was to put the clothes on. When he finished, he was wearing a blue plumber's uniform with the name "Mario Esposito" tagged on it, a solid pair of workman's boots, and a blue baseball style cap.

"We'll do it until we get it right," Keeps said. He then nodded to Dave, indicating that the exercise had started.

Dave walked up to the door of the house and knocked and rang the doorbell. He waited patiently until a black man in sweats answered the door. He assumed the man picked was of similar size to the actual target.

"I'm here to fix your clogged sink. Do you mind if I come in and take a look at what I'm dealing with?" Dave asked.

"No, not at all. We're glad you're here," the man said.

Dave slipped on his disposable shoe covers and walked in. The wife was in the kitchen and the daughter was sitting at the table—the daughter was actually a life-size doll—but the son was nowhere to be found. He decided to proceed with the interrogation anyway.

He snapped his fingers loudly, getting the confused attention of both the man and wife—the doll didn't move—and started his pitch. "This is going to sound strange, but I'm going to need the both of you to remain perfectly quiet and still. You'll understand in a few seconds."

He gave both parents a tight nod and smile. He then grabbed the doll by the neck and inserted the knife shallowly into its plastic shell; if it were a real girl, there would be a trickle of blood coming out of her throat. The woman let out a little half scream while the husband stood still and wide-eyed. Dave looked at the woman hard and nodded his head

185

back and forth while slipping the knife in slightly more; she shut up.

"This is very simple. Mr. Jackson, you will tell me the name of the whistleblower you've been in contact with, and I'll let your daughter go and then leave. Your real plumber will be here in an hour, and you'll get that drain fixed and move on with your day." Dave gave fake Mr. Jackson a pleasant, reassuring smile, trying to convey that he had the best of intentions.

Whatever hesitation fake dad previously had about divulging his source vanished; they must have told the fake Jacksons that they were to pretend they really loved their plastic daughter. Who knows, fake dad could have been into dolls too.

"John Doe, he's a foreman at BCF Industries manufacturing plant," fake dad revealed.

We're coming.

Bonobo paused long enough for Lud and George to make their way to the door, and just as they burst into the home, he slipped the knife through the doll's throat.

CHAPTER 45

For three weeks, Kendall, Freddy, and the other security personnel assigned to watch Dave had little to do. Kendall was watching when Aliyah entered his room and she and Dave exchanged some words, then he saw two of his fellow security personnel go in and drag him out of his room in his underwear. That was the last he saw of Dave for a long while.

Weirdly, when he came in the following night for his next shift, Aliyah was locked up in cell number four. He didn't understand any of it, but he considered himself Dave's friend, not Aliyah's. Aliyah wasn't very nice to him. He did have to go into her room and clean up the mess she made, but thankfully, she just sat there and ignored him. She was naked, which made him feel very uncomfortable.

Then, after three weeks of sitting in his booth looking in on Dave's empty cell, Kendall walked into the booth to find Dave, lying naked on his bed, eyes closed, with a serene look on his face. Later in the morning, he woke up and ate his breakfast, but not the same breakfast they gave him before. In addition to a normal breakfast of eggs and fruit, they gave him steak, and the steak was raw! He watched in wonder as Dave, still naked, gobbled down all of the food, including the raw meat.

He felt close to Dave after all those nights he had spent with him, and the person he was watching now wasn't the Dave he knew. Dave's sadness was replaced by coldness and something in his expression that might have been arrogance; they had done something to his friend, something bad. Kendall felt his forehead grow hot and started to ball up his fists with indignation, which was something he had never felt before. Sure, he felt that life was unfair—his parents had forced him to take this job after all—but this was something deeper and something he needed to take action on to address.

For the first time in his life, Kendall had a goal that didn't involve playing computer games and napping; he would help his friend escape this place, freeing himself in the process.

CHAPTER 46

Dave considered the first drill a wild success; they had gotten the name of the whistleblower and slaughtered the family. Keeps had them run through the drill six more times, however, just to make sure. He mixed things up by having the kids be in different locations and having different family members answer the door. It only got a little more tricky when both kids were upstairs, but Dave simply put the knife to the wife's neck and threatened to go upstairs and carve the kids up after killing her if fake dad refused to comply. The play actor caved every time.

They had to fly to California to complete the mission, so Lud, George, and Bonobo left for the flight right after training ended, while the rest of the band headed back to the enclosure. Fortunately, the flight included dinner: raw pork chops and a side of lamb. It was actually the best airline meal Dave had ever had. Dave changed into office casual wear to match what Keeps and his mercenaries had changed into for the trip, while Lud and George donned their blue spandex shorts. It seemed very strange to Dave that covering up their privates was needed to preserve sensibilities when they were on a mission to kill a family. Were they afraid their dongs would get caught on something during the mission if they were not bundled up?

Don't try to understand humans. Even the best ones are fucked in the head.

They arrived at 8:30 PM, so Dave thought this was one of those stereotypical hurry up and wait situations. Lud and George were loaded into a container for the short transport to a van waiting by the hanger—HEL didn't want to chance exposing their monsters—while Dave just walked to the van with Keeps and one of his mercenaries, Sly Wallis. The van only traveled a couple of miles to a warehouse just outside the airport, where they were to rest up until morning.

HEL was confused about what Dave was, since they had left Lud and George to just lie all night in the van while Dave got a room to bunk in, like Keeps and his soldier. In reality, treating Dave more like Lud and George would have been more appropriate and preferable to Bonobo; he was a furry in different in different skin.

Play human.

Bonobo shook his head. He was human.

*

At 7:30 AM the next morning, they loaded into the van and started the drive to the Jackson household. When they were ten minutes out, they switched vehicles to a plumber's van and Dave put on his blue uniform. They then left the staging area at exactly ten minutes to nine, with Dave driving and the brood stuffed into the back of the van for the final leg of the journey.

Dave pulled all the way up into the driveway, where the part closest to the house was conveniently hidden from the neighbors behind thick shrubs. He put on his most winning smile, stuffed a couple of disposable shoe covers in his pocket, and made his way to the house without a hint of apprehension or doubt—his genetic mutations muting any fear and anxiety he would normally be feeling.

In this version of the game, the girl answered the door, a real girl made out of flesh and blood. His inner calm was severely tested when an image of his daughter briefly flashed into his head. He stood staring at the girl.

Get a grip. She's not your daughter.

She's someone's daughter.

Not in a minute. We play our role.

Dave snapped out of his pensive state and smiled pleasantly. "Hey there, kiddo, is your mom or dad home?"

"Ya, they told me to let you in." The girl moved to the side, indicating that Dave was now free to enter. Dave slipped on his shoe covers and sauntered on in; the girl closing the door behind him, not realizing that she had just experienced her last moment of contentment.

He quickly took stock and noticed that Mr. Jackson and his wife were both standing in the kitchen, the wife making some eggs. Mr. Jackson put down a slice of toast when he saw Dave walk in and move toward him. He was a black man, like the play actor from the exercise, but very tall and thin; Dave pegged him at around six foot five. He was wearing a dress shirt with vertical light blue stripes on a white base, tan slacks, and a nice pair of well-shined brown shoes. The wife was much shorter, at only a little over five feet tall, and chubby; she had on a worn blue bathrobe. The boy was nowhere to be found, but Dave assumed he was upstairs.

Dave followed the same script he had come up with during the first run of the exercise the previous day. He warned the couple to be quiet and still before picking up the daughter and stabbing her neck gently with a switch-blade he pulled from his pant pocket. He held the girl's head tightly with one arm and his hand over her mouth and whispered "Shh" to the parents as he twisted the blade into the girl's neck ever so gently to produce a trickle of blood.

The wife turned toward Dave wide-eyed, still holding the pan of eggs and spatula. She took a few panicked breaths and then dropped the pan, which induced a loud bang on the tile floor. Dave watched the man tighten up all his muscles and ball his hands up into fists, scrunching his face up tightly, like he wanted to attack Dave and rescue his daughter.

Dave admired the man's instincts, but calmly looked at him and said, "I will kill her. It wouldn't be the first head I separated from a body." Dave was focused, but completely relaxed and steady of hand, so the man did not doubt his resolve and stayed back.

"Honey, just give him whatever he wants," the wife stuttered out.

Dave, acknowledging the wife, said, "Yes, thank you. Let's get on with this so you can all get back to your breakfast. Mr. Jackson, all I need from you is the name of your whistleblower contact, and then I'll be on my way. Your daughter will be a Band-Aid away from being as good as new. What do you say?"

"You fucking bastards. Who sent you? The government? The company?"

Dave pushed the knife a little farther into the girl's throat. He could not see her face, but felt the raw fear emanating from her body; he also felt warm liquid running down the front of his leg. The mother's mood matched her daughter's terror, while he got mostly anger and hate from the father. He didn't have to be a furry to feel their emotions, though, it was written all over the parents' faces.

"Paul Dubicki," Mr. Jackson stated. "Now please leave."

We're coming.

No more than five seconds later, Lud and George came crashing through the door; George headed upstairs to find the boy, while Lud leaped across the room to Mr. Jackson. To his credit, Jackson faced Lud and even hit him with a solid jab, but Lud was unaffected and lifted the dad up above his head with a little hop that resulted in Mr. Jackson's face smashing into the ceiling above. Lud then whipped him downwards toward his rising knee, which hit the center of his back, folding him in half with a loud crack.

The woman just stood there, stunned into silence, wide-eyed and mouth open, not believing what she was seeing. Lud shot his hand toward her and pulled out her throat; she dropped to the floor holding her now hollowed out throat, shaking like a leaf on a windy fall day, before finally growing still with death.

Bonobo was also standing there wide-eyed and mouth open with an awkward smile, watching the macabre theater, while still holding the girl by the head.

Lud looked at him. *Well, you going to just stand there looking stupid? ... Do it.*

Bonobo came back to the present and gave the girl's head a quick twist, cracking her neck, then letting her drop to the ground. He wiped the blood off the end of his knife on the girl's shirt and placed it back in his pocket. Lud just pursed his lips and shook his head. Dave felt empty.

All the while, they were getting signals from George that the boy was nowhere to be found. George confirmed this when he came down empty-handed. They didn't need to go upstairs to check the rooms again, since if the boy was there, they would have sensed his presence. They registered waves of terror coming from somewhere farther away in the direction of the backyard, and the three started walking out that way. Before they got very far, they felt pings from their collars, so they headed back to the van. Dave then drove them back to the staging area, where the furries and Keeps switched back into the original van, while Wallis drove the plumbing van to some other location for disposal.

Unfortunately, the mission was only a partial success, with the boy getting away.

CHAPTER 47

Kayden was twelve years old, but already a budding spy. When his parents gave him a tablet for his last birthday, they thought they were just giving him a toy that he would use to play games and watch videos. His mom had enabled the parental controls, but security was only as effective as the person securing the device, and his mom was a novice in that regard. You would think both of his parents would be more careful and knowledgeable about computer security, given his father was an important person at a big company; at least that was what his mother told him when he missed one of Kayden's baseball games or school concerts.

Kayden discovered that his mom used his sister's name, *Ester123!*, as her password for everything. Using mom's password, he could shut off the controls anytime he wanted to install something new or disable the tracking. It also let him get to a web page that had access to a pet camera his parents set up in the family room that gave him a full view of that room and the kitchen. They bought the camera, which was hidden in a stuffed bear, a few years ago when they went on vacation to Hawaii and wanted to keep an eye on their cat and the cat sitter they had hired to come over once a day to take care of it.

The cat was eaten by a coyote a few months after they got back, but the camera survived, and his parents never deactivated it. He reckoned they had got busy and just forgot it was there. Kayden didn't forget and spent lots of time hidden in the space between the wooden fence enclosing his yard and a separate wooden fence enclosing his neighbor's yard; whoever lived in these houses before the Jacksons must not have liked each other, since they needed two fences of separation.

Most of the things he saw on the camera were pretty boring, such as this morning when it was just his family eating breakfast, or in the evening, watching his parents watch the television. Sometimes things got spicy: one time, late at night, when his parents assumed Kayden and Ester were asleep in bed, he saw his dad do something to his mom that he saw in a magazine his friend Spencer had found in his father's nightstand. Mostly, his parents just watched TV at night or argued about his dad working too much and never being home.

Hidden away between the fences, this morning, Kayden was watching when he saw his sister let a man in a blue uniform into their home. He watched the man follow his sister into the kitchen then lift his sister up by her head and hold a knife to her throat. When his mom dropped the pan, he heard the muffled sound of it hitting the floor from his hideaway, but the bear camera had no microphone that let him directly hear what the man and his parents were saying.

Kayden grew still and quiet in fear, trying not to even breathe, instinctively trying to hide his presence from the intruder. The butterflies he felt in his stomach only got stronger when two people that kind of looked like apes broke through the front door, and one of them went at his dad. He looked on in horror as the apish man seemingly folded his father in half over his knee and then ripped something out of his mother's throat. The apes and the man stayed for only a short while more, though it seemed like forever to Kayden, before leaving the house.

He remained where he was, paralyzed with fear, unable to move, just staring at the images on his tablet screen. Hours later, after it had started to get dark, he saw the neighbor lady look through the broken door. She then gingerly stepped into the house and turned on the light switch. He saw her mouth open wide and could hear her scream from across the yard, then she ran back out of the house. Ten minutes later, the police arrived, and Kayden decided it was time for him to move again.

CHAPTER 48

Back at HEL, Dave and Keeps were summoned into a conference room with Mr. Jones and his boss, division vice president Shane Cooper. Dave felt the executive's anger and Keeps' obstinacy; he didn't care about their problems or feelings so prepared himself to enjoy the show and have a little fun.

Cooper started, "Your last mission was a complete failure. We need a full debriefing to get to the bottom of what went wrong and if any change in leadership is warranted."

Both Jones and Keeps simultaneously looked up at Cooper in shock, Jones not understanding how Keeps' fuckup put his job on the line. Keeps was angry that some piss-ass suit was questioning how he ran his operations in the field.

Dave interjected, "Well, it seems you boys have lots of issues to resolve. I'm rooting for you, I really am." He got up out of his chair, moved to the side of the table VP Cooper was sitting on, and looked over at Jones and Keeps, matching Cooper's glare. "You two have a lot of explaining to do. Start talking!" Dave said, banging his fist down on the table a little too hard; a large crack opened up in the thick wooden table under his balled-up fist. He then twisted the knife by adding: "Child killers."

Cracking the table didn't impress Jones or Keeps much, but it did leave an impression on Cooper. Cooper tried to keep his charge, but being so close to one of HEL's fiends threw him off balance; Dave felt the fear and uncertainty emanating directly from Cooper's brain—he could smell his perspiration.

Jones and Keeps saw it too and oozed delight, even though they both kept up their poker faces.

Cooper looked over at Mr. Jones: "Why is that here? He's just ..." choosing his words carefully as to not upset the monster, "a member of the unit. This meeting is for leadership only."

Before Jones could answer, Dave butted in, "Yes Coops, that is a very good question. Keeps here fucked up the mission by recalling us back to the van too soon, though I can't fault him for not wanting to kill a second kid. If someone needs a spanking, it is the geek with big glasses, but I just work here."

Keeps lost his poker face and glared at Dave with a death stare, while Dave sat back in his chair and looked at Keeps with an easy smile, daring him to set his collar off. Dave could feel his inner turmoil. *Was that the reason Keeps recalled them too soon? Was there some humanity in that human?*

Having had enough, Jones opened up his flip-phone and called security, he then looked at Dave and told him to leave the room and wait outside the door until he was picked up. Dave got up, gave the three leaders a little salute, and stepped out into the hall.

It was a couple of minutes before two men, one with a mullet and one with a goatee, showed up to bring him back to his cell, so he had time to hear Cooper chewing out his subordinates. They tried to defend themselves, noting that they got the name of the whistleblower, but Cooper's definition of success was more black-and-white: either all of the goals were accomplished, or the mission was a failure. Cooper didn't have as much leverage as he thought he had, given that Jones and Keeps ran the employee termination department, and he didn't have direct access to his own independent security and mercenary unit.

The man with the mullet grabbed Dave's arm and tried to pull him away from the door he had his ear up against, but despite the man's large size, he couldn't budge Dave. He felt the man's surprise. He tried to yank him away from the door with a much harder pull. Again, Dave just tensed his muscles up and dug his feet in, barely budging.

In the meantime, the man with the goatee pulled out his baton and slapped it against his hand in an apparent threat, but Dave just smiled at him, daring him. Keeps and Jones were in the conference room getting chewed out by some prick in a suit, and he was about to kick some ass—could the day get any better?

"I remember you guys. What's your name, baldy?" Dave asked the man with the goatee.

"You either come with us willingly or we will hurt you. Either way works for us," goatee said.

"Hmmm," Dave said, scrunching his lips together and scratching his chin. "I think you're going to have to hurt me. I've got this thing for pain. Might be sexual."

Goatee deftly flipped the baton around in his hand, going for a surprise shot in Dave's diaphragm with the blunt end of the club. What would have been a lightning strike to the gut for anybody else, was something that was happening in slow motion to Dave. He grabbed the baton out of goatee's hand before it got within six inches of his body and swept goatee's legs out from under him. As he fell to the floor, Dave smacked him with the baton on his ass; it was hard enough to cause pain and leave a nasty mark, but he backed off some to avoid breaking his pelvis.

Seeing what happened to his partner, mullet went right for his taser and shot Dave over the left side of his chest. The jolt should have stopped him in his tracks, possibly stopping his heart, but he just stared back at mullet man with a wide smile on his face, bopping his head up and down like a maniac. Dave ripped the taser cords out of his chest, straightened out his shirt, and calmly walked over to the elevators to escort himself back to his room. As he walked by mullet, the guard immediately stepped back to give him space; he just looked at Dave, mouth agape, not quite understanding what he was dealing with.

You push things.

We push things.

Does this bring us closer to our goals?

Lamb does not eat wolf.

Don't get locked in here with the rest of us. Need us out there.

When Dave got back to his cell, he stopped again in front of Aliyah's door to take in her scent. Someday, he would make Aliyah his lamb. It had been a long time since he had non-collective sex, so he was starting to develop a fixation on Aliyah. He even considered loitering outside his cell until a guard came by so he could use the guard's access to force his way into her room, then ravage her, maybe ripping the guard in half first to heighten the mood. *Furry dreams.*

*

Twenty minutes later, when HEL leadership walked out of the conference room, Green and Jurgensen were still in the hall waiting for Mr. Jones. "We need to talk to you," Jurgensen said to Jones. They were Jones's men, so Keeps and Cooper just went on their way, not interested in why the two men were standing there like idiots when they were supposed to have escorted Dave to his cell.

Mr. Jones did have to deal with the problem, however. He noticed Joe Green's disheveled state and the grimace on his face. "What happened to you?" he asked Green.

"That guy you sent us to escort to the cells. What the hell was that? He was strong as an ox and faster than anybody I've ever seen," Green said.

"I shot him point-blank in the heart with the taser and he didn't go down. He smiled like he liked it. It wasn't normal. You need to give us some answers if we're going to be able to do our jobs," Jurgensen said.

Jones couldn't give them answers, since his security team did not have the security clearance to know about the furry program. Only Keeps and his mercenaries and Dr. Danzel's staff knew what the furries truly were. Sure, his security personnel heard rumors, but that was different than telling them what furries were and did for the organization specifically. They kept things very compartmentalized down in HEL—or tried to. Given Dave's obstinance, he should have anticipated what would happen if he sent his men to rough handle him back to his cell; he should have just told Dave to go back to his room on his own, which he apparently ended up doing anyway. For now, though, Jones had to assert his authority over his minions.

"I don't need to give you anything. As I've told you before, you only know what I decide you should know. You obviously handled the situation badly and Dave got the best of you. I expect better."

Green and Jurgensen just looked at each other, dumbfounded. They weren't just a couple of dumb security guards; they were former senior detectives who had worked in a big-city police force.

"If you call on us to do a job, we need to know what we're walking into. That guy was not normal. We didn't have the right tools to deal with him," Jurgensen said.

They were correct again. Keeps' team had devices on them to activate the collars if the furries got too close, and Keeps and Jones had remotes to trigger the collars if they needed to teach a furry a lesson. Jones's reports had none of those protections, but even though the two men were right, he didn't like his supplicants' attitude. He would avoid making this mistake again, but right now, he had to close up the conversation and remind his men of the hierarchy.

Looking right at Jurgensen, he said, "I decide what you need to know and what tools you need. Do you think that big salary you are getting comes with answers? No, we pay you to do what you are told and not ask questions. I was very clear about this when you agreed to take me up on my offer. Let me also remind you that I told you that there would be extreme consequences if you betray the organization."

"Whoa ... I'm not questioning you. We're loyal. We just want the right tools so we can do a better job. That's all." Jurgensen said, while Green nodded his head in agreement.

"Dismissed," Jones said before turning and walking down the hallway. Almost instantly, he put the two malcontents out of his mind; he had much bigger things to worry about, given Keeps' fuckup on the last mission. It was Keeps' fuckup, but he was the one who would have to come up with a solution to clean up the mess—that was always the way.

CHAPTER 49

Dave got back to his cell mid-morning to find the place made up as usual. He went to the bathroom to pee, and when he lifted the toilet seat, he noticed a sticky note stuck to the underside of the seat. He gently put the seat down and changed to a sitting position. He reached down under the seat and grabbed the note, careful to keep his head level and only look down with his eyes.

The note simply read, "I want to help. I clean room weekday mornings. Camera above toilet can't see your front. Please reply."

They contemplated this new development, wondering how they could use it to their advantage. They needed more information first, so Dave needed to write the sympathizer back, asking him who he was and what access he had, but unfortunately, he had nothing to write with. He solved that by pricking his finger with one of his nails. He carefully wrote out his questions in blood on the other side of the sticky note before sticking it back under the seat.

Bosses at each other's throats. Traitor in their midst. Solution. Freedom? Maybe? Careful, if they kill him, no use.

I know.

Bonobo remained still on his bed for the rest of the day and night, sharing thoughts with the hive. After breakfast the next morning, he was escorted out of his room and to the training facility, hopeful that the person behind the note would get the reply and ultimately help them disable the collars.

*

There was no reply to Dave's message when he got back to the room that evening, which made sense if the person was only in his room to do the morning housekeeping. That meant they wouldn't know who they were dealing with until at least the next day. He put the sympathizer out of his mind for the time being and sat back to enjoy the evening activities, which included mind games with the hive, followed by vigorous copulation with Anne and George; they were going at so often that it was almost becoming too much.

Eunuch.

Sometimes Bonobo wished he could keep some thoughts to himself. They were a function of the most virile member of the collective—the strongest emotion wins the mind; the peer pressure to perform was intense. He wondered if real neanderthals had been this horny. After a while, they settled down, and Dave could eat the dinner they had wheeled into his room hours before. The guard actually tried to remove the cart with the food still untouched, but Dave put a stop to that a little too aggressively; he got a good shock from the collar, but the guard retreated and left the food. That surprised him, since previously the guards weren't protected from him; he guessed his confrontation with mullet and goatee led to the change in policy.

He couldn't be too hard on the guards, however. He could feel their discomfort when they walked into the room while he sat there naked and aroused, trying to avert their eyes and get out as quickly as possible. The other minds took the new development in their stride, but now that they had hope, their minds grew impatient with the anticipation of getting out. They just hoped they would have time to kill everyone in HEL on the way out. They were slowly lulled to sleep with those happy thoughts.

CHAPTER 50

When Kendall placed the note under Dave's toilet seat, he was a nervous wreck. He had resolved to help Dave, but had never put himself at risk before. His parents forcing him to take the job or leave the house was one of the few times in his entire life that he had faced adversity; resilience was a concept completely foreign to him. After leaving the note, instead of acting calm and normal, he was jumpy and sweaty and could barely get complete sentences out when approached by other members of the staff. When Freddy asked him what was going on, he had the wherewithal to tell him that he had a bad case of the runs, so at least he could still think on the fly to preserve life and limb.

When he got home, his cover story became reality, and he spent the day puking and crapping, sick from anxiety. Freddy let everybody know about Kendall's trots, so when he got back to work the next night looking pale and hunched over, most people just gave him space, not wanting to catch whatever sickness they assumed he was working through.

Dave, on the other hand, looked serene, just lying in bed like he didn't have a care in the world. As he watched Dave, his muscles tensed up and he became indignant; here he was putting everything on the line, including his health and wellbeing, while Dave just lay there happy as a clam, unmoved by Kendall's efforts to free him—how could someone be so unappreciative?

Kendall was still angry when he lifted the toilet seat to clean the bowl and noticed that the sticky note he had left was still there, but seemingly stained with blood. He momentarily forgot to breathe as the adrenaline shot through him, but he managed to get a hold of himself and quickly shoved the note into his pocket.

Later, safely back in his bedroom at home, he read the note. Instead of the expected show of appreciation, there was simply a list of questions. Who are you? What access do you have? He tore the note up into tiny pieces and threw them into the garbage, determined to put his stupid attempt at helping a fellow human being behind him.

*

Kendall woke around 10:00 PM, having slept around nine hours. Thinking more clearly and no longer overcome with anxiety, he thought to himself that he might have been a little unfair to Dave. How much appreciation could Dave have expressed on a note written in blood anyway, and he had to keep cool, lest anyone discover their new alliance.

He peeled a new pink sticky note off the pad on his desk and wrote, "I watch you at night. I have access ..." He realized how pathetic this attempt at helping Dave really was; he didn't have access or clearance to anywhere important enough in the facility to help him. "... nothing really." He wondered if leaving that note was even worth it, but decided that it would be mean to leave Dave hanging, and maybe he would have an idea.

He did his shift as usual and left the new note under the toilet seat when he cleaned the room in the morning. It was Friday, so he would have to wait the whole weekend before he got his next answer. He was still a little nervous, but having gone three days since the original communication without being discovered, he felt a little more confident that he could do this and not get caught. He was even back to being a little excited, knowing that he was working undercover to save his friend.

CHAPTER 51

Detective Sparks was Livermore's most senior detective. He and another highly experienced detective, Jack Lloyd, were immediately pulled off the cases they were previously working on and assigned to investigate the Jackson family murders—or the ape murders, as the papers called it. It wasn't only the fact that a whole family was killed that caused an uproar, but what killed them. The son—Kayden—had a recording of the crime scene, and what the investigators saw when they first reviewed the video sent shock waves through the department.

This wasn't the first time in Detective Sparks' long career that he had investigated the murder of an entire family, but it was the first time a family had been murdered by what appeared to be ape-like man creatures. He could have written that part of the scene off to criminals dressing up in costumes to disguise themselves, but he could not explain their seemingly superhuman strength. One suspect lifted a large man off the ground, slammed him into the ceiling, and then folded him in half. Was he an athlete, hopped up on meth or some other performance enhancing drug? He assumed so, but what normal person could move so fast and rip the throat out of someone like that?

Somehow, a still image from the recording was leaked to the press, so a picture of the smiling creature standing over the husband and wife was front page news two days after the killings and then national news a day after that. With the cat out of the bag, the police had decided to try and use the press to their advantage and release a picture of the perpetrator who wasn't dressed up like an ape. After the next news cycle, with that man's picture plastered across every television newscast and newspaper, Sparks hoped someone would recognize him.

Sparks' lieutenant walked over to his desk. "We found the van they used to travel to the Jackson household, or at least what was left of it," she said.

"What does that mean?" Sparks asked.

"We had a couple of officers check out junkyards in the area. The owner of one of them was very cooperative. He told us that, on the same day as the murders, a guy dropped off a plumber's van and paid him a large sum of money to crush it and keep quiet," Lieutenant Holden said.

"So why did he talk?"

"He read about the murders like everyone else and has seen the picture. He wanted to do the right thing. He'll be here in thirty minutes. I need you and Lloyd doing the interview," Holden stated.

✳

Later that afternoon, Sparks and Lloyd were reviewing the new information. The owner of the junkyard had been very helpful. They now had a description and sketch of another offender, not caught on camera. This unsub was around five foot nine inches tall, and muscular with a large chest and broad shoulders. He had a short crew cut with shaved sides. The junkyard owner was former military and said this guy seemed military. Whoever it was, his picture would also be released to the press. Several prints were taken off the crushed van, so given the new information, they would see if they could get any cooperation from the defense department to help them match the prints; he wasn't optimistic on that front, however; best to hope that guy was already in the system for some other reason.

CHAPTER 52

Jones sat in his office contemplating how he would contain the mess Keeps' failed operation created. If all had gone to plan, the whole family, including the boy, would have been killed. The whistleblower, Paul Dubicki, would have been terminated, and HEL would be processing another large payment for its services. All that was on hold now until they figured out how to contain the situation.

HEL's most important asset, Dave Smith, was now exposed; his picture shown on every news program in the country. He had no doubt that he would soon be identified by his family or a former acquaintance from Issaquah. HEL couldn't kill and bribe its way out of this problem, nor could they count on the FBI to take over jurisdiction of the case and silently let it die. Killer apes on the loose, killing whole families, were now a national sensation—no doubt soon to be international. They would lie low and wait for the investigation to stall out on its own and for the next big story to supplant this one; Jones prayed for a mass shooting.

That meant no more missions in the U.S. for a while, which would disappoint their sponsors in Washington who liked to use Greenrock's special operations unit to settle scores and do favors for their business partners (i.e. donors). Using the furries to out a whistleblower was one of those missions. Furries weren't designed to run operations like that, it was the equivalent of using a jack hammer to tap in a picture hanger—they needed to learn to say no.

Ultimately, a moratorium on U.S. operations could help Greenrock's bottom line, since it would leave more time for

HEL to run operations in other countries at the behest of authoritarian governments and criminal organizations that paid much better than politicians looking to use Greenrock as their own personal assassin service. Regardless of the benefits, overall, this was a major problem that could become an existential threat to the organization if not handled properly. If those same government sponsors couldn't use their service, they would have to be paid off in other ways to keep the government money flowing and government mouths shut.

*

The next day, Cooper walked into Jones's office without knocking first. He had been doing this multiple times a day since the cops discovered the kid and the story broke. Jones assumed behaving like this gave Cooper a sense of control; he was the boss and on top of things, keeping his subordinates on task. Jones just found it annoying. Cooper was showing his usefulness in other ways: he was the buffer between HEL and Greenrock's upper management. He made sure HEL's secrets remained compartmentalized to the very few in Greenrock's executive wings who knew about what type of services the special operations unit ran. Even those few didn't truly know what went on here, and they were happy to leave it that way, as long as HEL brought in the money and didn't create waves.

"Where are we with containment?" Cooper asked as he was pushing open the door.

"Same as last night. We are going to lie low and not do anything rash that puts a spotlight on us," Jones replied.

"Now that another sketch of one of Keeps' men is out, I'm starting to get questions from Martin and Conti," Cooper said. Martin and Conti were two Greenrock VPs who were aware of the company's assassination team and part of CEO Stirling's inner circle. Stirling used them as a liaison between himself and HEL.

"And you need to keep deflecting and denying. As far as the public knows, two men in ape costumes killed a family. It doesn't need to come back to us, unless we put the spotlight on ourselves," Jones stated.

"It's not just two men in ape costumes. Smith will be identified anytime now."

"Again, how do they tie Smith to us when it does happen?"

Cooper looked at Jones with a gaping mouth, surprised that someone who seemingly had all the answers could be so obtuse.

"Have you forgotten that you assigned Dave to work in the Special Research Division's accounting office for two months? It's not looking like your best decision right now, so I understand why you would want to forget about it," Cooper snarked.

"Well, I couldn't have done that without your approval," Jones replied lamely. It was Jones's turn to gape; he had missed this most obvious direct connection to Greenrock. Dave's former co-workers could identify him. Jones first thought was to round up all of the accountants and make them disappear, but that probably wouldn't be practical. For all he knew, they had already spread their suspicions to other people. It also meant that Jones's own security team, who did not know about the special operations unit, would now be asking themselves questions about who they worked for.

Jones continued, "The picture of Smith is unclear, and he was wearing a cap. Someone close to him might see a resemblance, but they couldn't be sure. There are a million people with features similar to Smith."

"Are you daft? Your solution to solving this mess is wishful thinking?"

Jones felt his temperature rise at the obvious insult. Cooper was walking on shaky ground, but Jones kept his composure. "Are you ordering me to terminate the accounting department, Cooper?" He looked at Cooper with cold eyes, while Cooper stared back at him, trying to hold Jones's gaze, but a little anxious; he may have pushed Jones too far. "Just shut up and don't engage in any speculation about who that fuzzy image may or may not be. You can only fuck this up by opening your mouth at the wrong time. I think we're done here. I have work to do."

Cooper hovered over Jones for a few more seconds, not wanting to seem weak. While awkwardly staring at his back, he said, "I'll expect a new update later today." He then turned tail and left the office, not bothering to close the door behind him.

CHAPTER 53

After Cooper left his office, Jones could think of only one thing that would ensure the situation was fully contained. The job required expertise he didn't have on hand, so he was down in level U3, in Keeps' planning room. His idea required Keeps' mercenaries.

Five minutes after Jones arrived at their quickly scheduled meeting, Keeps walked in the room with a sour look on his face. He had suspected Jones would come to him at some point, looking to use his team to clean up the mess, and he didn't like it. Whatever Jones wanted, there would be little time for proper planning, making the operation high risk. He couldn't afford another fuck-up, though he still felt that pulling the furries out was the right call—he didn't want them out in the Jackson's backyard killing a boy in full view of the neighbors' back windows.

"We need to take action on Smith's family, and it has to happen tomorrow," Jones said, getting right to the point.

"Is that so ... and what are we supposed to do to Smith's family tomorrow?"

"We are going to make them disappear. Bring the girl in and liquidate the mom and boy. Every day we wait, the likelihood that Jan Smith identifies her husband increases. I know it is short notice, but I have surveillance on the family and think there is an opportunity for us to pick them up tomorrow night."

"You have people on the ground?" Keeps asked.

"No... Since back before we picked up Dave, we've been passively surveilling with cameras. In addition, I monitor all

215

of Jan's credit and bank transactions, so I have a full profile of her patterns. Tomorrow, Jan is taking both kids to a school orchestra performance. They'll be getting home a little after 8:00 PM."

Keeps' mind was already processing the little information Jones had just told him and was formulating a plan. That was how Keeps' mind worked, after years of planning missions, it was second nature to him. As much as he hated using his people for a mission conceived by Jones, the challenge intrigued him, and he had to concede that Jones was competent when it came to gathering data, so he could trust the intelligence he had gathered on the Smith family. Also, he had recently acquired a new toy that could be perfect for this type of job.

After a moment of silence while Keeps gathered his thoughts, he made a call to bring in the person he determined was best able to carry out the mission. The three of them spent the next four hours combing through Jones's data on the Smith family and came up with a plan. Keeps and his mercenary caught a plane out to Seattle that evening to set up on the ground.

CHAPTER 54

Like everyone else in the country, Jan Smith was following the developments of the ape murders. It wasn't the apes she was thinking about, however. The picture of the man posing as a plumber sparked something in her. The quality of the picture wasn't very good, and the man was wearing a hat, but when she first saw the image, she felt her heart stop. Her first thought was of Dave.

After spending days looking at the photo, she successfully talked herself in and out of identifying the person in the image as Dave. She asked herself, "Why would Dave murder a family?" As far as she was concerned, he wouldn't; it made no sense; Dave could be edgy, but he had never hurt anyone. The idea was preposterous, and yet?

There was a hotline set up for anybody with information on the murders to call in with a tip, but she didn't want to do that. Instead, she would stop by the Issaquah police station the next day and talk to Lieutenant Peabody. She checked in with him from time to time for any updates on the investigation into her missing husband, but it was always the same: the case was still open, but they had no new leads. Well, now she had a lead to give them. What finally pushed her to take action was Kate. That morning, Kate had looked at the picture in the paper for the first time and mumbled, "Daddy?" That sealed it; both she and Kate's first reaction to seeing the photo was to think of Dave.

Speaking to Peabody would have to wait until the next day, since Jan had to get the kids fed and loaded up into the car for the school concert.

Rodriguez was lying camouflaged in a thick hedge that paralleled the Smith's driveway. She was positioned around fifteen feet from the road and twenty from the house. From her vantage point twenty feet out, she had a full view of the front door, though not to the porch to the right of it. It was the best she could do, and it was fortunate that there was a hedge to hide her from the family and any neighbors.

It was 6:00 PM, meaning she had been lying in wait for fourteen hours. She had gotten herself positioned before first light when the neighborhood was asleep and wouldn't notice her crawling in. She managed to sleep a couple of hours on the plane ride to Seattle, but most of the trip was spent going over the intelligence data and plans with Keeps. This was after spending the previous afternoon reviewing the data with Jones and Keeps back at the lab. Despite the lack of sleep, she felt just fine after popping a "go pill".

Keeps picked her for the mission because she was a ranger sniper and trained to lie in wait for long periods of time, waiting for the perfect shot. Back in Afghanistan, she once had to remain camouflaged in a ghillie suit for three days, then shoot the target in a moving vehicle as he drove by on a road under her position. To ensure she got out safely, she eliminated the other three men in the vehicle too: four bullets, four kills. After spending the last year babysitting Keeps' apes, she was finally back to doing what she loved; she hoped that after successfully completing this operation, Keeps would see the value in using her and the other mercenaries to carry out missions over the apes—at least some of the time.

The target, Kate, along with the mother and brother, left for the concert at 5:13 PM and were scheduled to be back at around 8:00 PM. It was fifteen minutes to go time. Since she had to remain in the hedge for fourteen hours, she wore a diaper under her camouflage, and used it to relieve herself. The area under her crotch was now a little warmer and heavier, leaving her feeling a little less comfortable; something she had forgotten about in the three years since the last time she had to stalk a target over an extended period of time. It would not affect her ability to do the job.

At 8:17 PM, Keeps contacted her to let her know that the family was approximately fifteen minutes out. She also knew that Keeps would trigger a device Jones's team had left in the cable box for the neighborhood months before, just before Smith entered the neighborhood. The device would fry the junction block, taking out all cable service in the three-block area around the Smith's house, preventing any doorbell and security cameras in the immediate area from recording the proceedings. All of the houses on the block depended on cable for their internet service, except one.

At exactly 8:34 PM, Mrs. Smith pulled into the driveway, and as soon as the car drove past Rodriguez's position, she made her move. Just as the car was coming to a stop, the hedge seemed to close in on the passenger side of the car. The hedge attached a device to the back window that looked like a fat pistol, but when she pulled the trigger, the end of the device sealed onto the window and unleashed an ultra-heated hole saw into the window, which almost instantly opened up a one-inch opening into the vehicle. In the next instant after opening the hole, it ejected sleeping gas into the vehicle, knocking out all of the vehicle occupants.

The entire operation happened so fast, Jan hadn't even put the car into park, so as soon as she passed out and her foot left the break, the car started rolling forward. Rodriquez acted quickly and rolled over the hood of the car, opened the driver's side door, and pushed the gear up into park. She carried a cloned key fob for the car, so there was no issue in opening the door. She also wore a gas mask under her suit, so after putting the car in park, she rolled Jan over into the back of the vehicle with the kids, she got in the driver's seat, then pulled back out of the driveway with the family in tow. The direction she chose avoided the one house not using cable internet service.

The gas was designed to neutralize within a minute of leaving its canister and hitting the air, so with the windows slightly open, she was able to remove the camouflage from her head as she pulled out of the neighborhood. She then calmly drove the sleeping family to the rendezvous point around seven miles east of Issaquah by some old warehouses in Preston.

When she got to Preston, Keeps was there waiting for them with a box truck that was large enough to drive the car into. After she drove in, they detached the car battery and attached the battery cables to a different device that pushed a burst of high voltage current through all of the car's electronics, frying any of the car's built-in tracking. They also stripped and destroyed any electronic devices the family was carrying. Then they closed the truck's rear door, leaving the family in the vehicle; they would be out for at least another hour, giving them time to separate and properly secure them before escorting the girl back to Ohio. Two more of Keeps' mercenaries flew in that afternoon to meet them at an airstrip. They would take possession of the box truck and make the vehicle, Jan, and Mickey all disappear. Rodriguez wasn't told why the family was split up, but her job was to just deliver the girl.

CHAPTER 55

Kate woke up feeling dizzy and disoriented. Her chest felt heavy as she strained to breathe, and there was something in her nose that made the air smell like plastic. After some initial confusion, she passed out again.

Later that day, she woke up again, still disoriented, but she was able to stay awake and eventually focus her eyes. She put her hand up to her nose and felt a soft plastic tube that was blowing the plastic smelling air into her nostrils; she ripped it out. Her sinuses felt dry, so breathing in through her nose burned a little; breathing in through her mouth wasn't any better, given her sore throat. She further evaluated her situation and noticed that she had an IV attached to her arm, and the underwear she was wearing felt soft and gooey.

She had never been in a hospital room before, but she had seen them on TV, so guessed that was where she was. It wasn't exactly like the hospital rooms on TV, however. This one looked more like a regular bedroom, with light-brown walls and a set of bookshelves stocked with books and what looked like board games across from her. To the right was a wooden desk under the room's lone window, and what looked like the entrance to a bathroom if she looked behind her to the left. The floor was carpeted, which also wasn't what she would expect to find in a hospital room.

A Hispanic woman in jeans and a greenish tee shirt walked into her room through the door in the back of the room and put her hand on Kate's forehead. She then pointed something at her head that went beep after a couple of seconds.

"Good, your temperature is back to normal. You had us worried for a while," said the woman.

"Where am I? Where's my mom?" Kate asked.

"You are safe. We'll answer all your questions later when you are up to it."

"No. I want my mom, now," Kate whimpered.

"I know, kid. Just be patient and we'll answer all your questions. Now is the time for you to get better ... no?" the woman said.

"No! I want my mom." Kate started tearing up, now scared that something bad had happened to her mom and brother. Her last memory was in the car driving home after the concert, but she didn't remember arriving at her home. The woman didn't look like a nurse, and she knew her mom would never leave her alone like this, especially after her father disappeared. Something was very wrong.

The woman, not wanting to engage with Kate any further, left the room. Kate cried for a few more minutes then pulled the IV out of her arm herself, the needle squirting liquid all over her after it exited her arm. She just let the leaky needle drop to the floor and then got out of bed. At first, her legs were unsteady, shaking and weak, but after tightly closing her eyes for a moment and standing still by the bed, her lightheadedness started to subside.

Her first order of business was to go to the bathroom and remove the heavy diaper she was wearing. The bottom part of the bookshelf had dresser drawers: she opened one and found normal underwear, tube socks, and some white sneakers. The other drawer contained a gray sweat suit, which she put on after removing the nightgown she was in. She then tried to open the door the woman came through, but it was locked. She banged on it and yelled, "Let me out!" a few times and then put her ear up against the door and listened. Nothing.

After pacing back and forth multiple times, she decided to try the window. The window looked out onto a large, fenced-in backyard with a lawn and a couple of large trees, but unfortunately, the window was sealed shut; she was trapped. Still not feeling well and using up all of her nervous energy, she sat down on the floor by the desk and hugged her knees into her chest, tearing up all over again.

*

The mission to nab the kid started out better than they could have hoped for. Rodriquez acquired the target and delivered her to the rendezvous point without incident. Forty-five minutes after driving away with the family, she was on a plane back home with Keeps and the anesthetized girl lying on a cushion in the small plane's galley. Gomez and Burns took the mom and boy away in a van; Rodriquez wasn't told what would happen to them and knew not to ask.

About halfway through the flight, things started taking a bad turn when the girl's breathing started to become labored. She was all but eighty pounds at most, and now Keeps and Rodriquez worried that between the initial dose of knock-out gas and the extra shot they gave her to ensure she slept until they arrived at the safe house, it may have been too much. They hooked her up to an oxygen tank that was part of the medical kit they kept on the plane, and closely monitored her until they got back to Ohio, where Keeps had arranged to have the team's medic, Gill Turner, meet them.

Fortunately, Turner determined that she would eventually come out of it if they kept her on the oxygen, though she would wake up feeling awful. He also administered an IV to keep her electrolytes up. They got Kate to a safe house twelve miles from the lab, and Rodriquez was assigned to babysit her. She didn't particularly like kids, so the assignment was going to be more taxing than any of her much more deadly operations she'd been on so far. It made her long to go back to babysitting apes—at least they killed stuff—though what she really wanted to do was get back in her camouflage and stalk someone.

Normally, they kept their captives in the prison on the bottom floor of the lab, but Jones was insistent—and Keeps agreed—that the kid be held offsite, miles from the lab. They didn't tell her why that was necessary, but she assumed that they wanted to keep her far away from Dave. She was Dave's daughter, after all.

She saw on the screen that the kid had woken up briefly in the morning, looking confused and groggy, before quickly falling back to sleep. Later, she woke and started looking around, which Rodriquez took as her cue to go check on her. Not wanting to stay in the room too long, she did the minimum checks recommended by Turner and got out of there as quickly as possible. It wasn't her job to tell the kid where she was or try to comfort her; she just had to keep her alive and safe. With the health of the girl confirmed, she watched as Kate removed her own IV and changed into the sweats they had left for her in the drawer. When Kate finally settled down in the corner of her room, she was relieved; maybe the kid would just stay put and not ask anything of her.

Just as Rodriquez was settling down with a good book to pass the time away, she remembered that it was also her responsibility to feed the kid. She hoped the kitchen had some microwavable dinners; she didn't cook for herself, so there was no way she was going to cook for some kid.

CHAPTER 56

It had been a full week since Dave was kicked out of the meeting with HEL's brain trust, and after a couple of days of business as usual, they cancelled training and restricted him to his cell. None of the furries had trained or left their enclosures in days; the place was on lockdown. Not killing the boy must have been a huge fuck-up; he could imagine Jones and Keeps huddled together coming up with ways to clean the mess-up, such as how they handled his phone call to the homicide line a month before. These people were cold-blooded assassins, so Dave was certain they would find a solution, and it would probably involve killing people.

He had little reason to believe the mission put his family in danger, but he had a nagging intuition that somehow, they might end up as collateral damage. *What if they had somehow identified him?* In retrospect, it seemed really stupid that he wasn't disguised. The more he got to know how HEL operated, the less impressed he was with it. The leaders were no master tacticians; their methods were as crude as the furries.

Murder, fuck-up, cover-up (kill—bribe—threaten), repeat ...

He let out a long sigh. HEL had to make do with the personnel they had. It couldn't be easy hiring sociopaths with even the most modest skills in security and operations. Jones was no Jackal, and neither was he.

At least he wasn't alone—he was never alone. Bonobo was with his band, and they supported each other. The thoughts and worries he had about his family and what was going on outside their cages were shared by the whole hive.

Normally, Dave would be out of his cell after breakfast, but with the lockdown, the guard he now knew as Kendall cleaned his room while he was still there. The kid seemed a little nervous, so when he came in to clean, Dave gave him space by ignoring him. They had already determined that Kendall was only a low-level security guard with no access to anything that could help them immediately, but there was potential there. When he first saw Kendall, he immediately noticed that he bore a striking resemblance to Cooper. He had the same light complexion, similar narrow blue eyes that were slightly too far apart, and both had strong jaws. They thought he might be Cooper's son, but when he asked directly via the toilet dead-drop, Kendall ignored the question, not wanting to reveal too much—he did reveal his first name, though.

Bonobo and the band weren't going to let it drop, however. It was obvious that Kendall was closely related to Cooper, so even if Kendall was useless by himself, he could use his connection to Cooper to gain access to the controls for the collars, and ultimately the way out of the lab. In their last note to Kendall, they took the direct approach and told him to use Cooper's access to the lab to find out how to disable the collars and open the doors. Kendall didn't seem like the type that could figure out how to help them all on his own, so they would guide him in the right direction. It was a balance between pushing him to help them, but without scaring him off and losing their one chance at escape.

CHAPTER 57

Kendall had spent all afternoon ruminating over how to approach his Uncle Shane about taking on more responsibilities at work. When he set out to help Dave, he had no idea how he would go about it, but Dave himself gave him some suggestions. He needed to use his uncle's access to the lab's computer systems to disable the collars and security cameras. In truth, he had no idea if Shane had access to the lab's security systems, and if he did, Kendall didn't know whether that was the path to freeing Dave or not, but it would be a start. His uncle was vice president of the division and the senior manager of the lab, so he just assumed he must have that type of access—or at least hoped.

Stealing his uncle's credentials to the lab's security system was a problem for later; first he had to be in a position to steal those credentials. To that end, he decided that it was finally time to think about his career. His dad and uncle were always pushing him to show more drive, but he had always just shrugged his shoulders, content to stay where he was, watching the prisoners and cleaning their cells; ambition never really suited him. That would change tonight.

Uncle Shane and his wife Nancy were coming over for dinner, and he would finally declare his desire to move up from security guard and janitor to a position more fitting of the nephew of a VP. He knew his dad would be delighted at the new development and help him push his uncle to take him up on the offer.

At dinner, later that evening, he briefly lost his nerve and missed a good opportunity to tell his uncle what he wanted during the main course. As his mom was serving everyone dessert in the living room, he decided that it was now or never. His dad was giving him funny looks, since he was acting differently than normal; after dinner, he would normally disappear back into his room, wanting to get away from the family as fast as possible, but instead, he was sitting in the living room with the other adults.

"Uncle Shane ..." Kendall stuttered.

His uncle at first didn't notice Kendall trying to get his attention, being occupied with his slice of cake, but Kendall spoke up a little louder the second time around. Shane looked up at him with a confused look on his face; Kendall never spoke to him unless directly asked a question first.

"... you know how you and dad have been wanting me to be more ambitious. Well, I've been thinking a lot about it, and I'm ready to take on more responsibility at work ... if that's okay with you?"

His dad and Shane looked at each other, mouths agape, cake on fork, stunned, but elated. They loved Kendall and were hoping for the moment when Kendall snapped out of his malaise.

"That's great, Kendall. This is what we've always wanted. What do you say, Shane?" his dad said, now looking at his brother. Aunt Nancy and his mom were also now staring at Shane, so the pressure was on, just as Kendall had predicted.

"Alright, Kendall. You have a shift tonight, right?"

"Yes"

"Tomorrow morning, after your shift, come by my office on the fourth floor and we'll discuss it. Sound good?"

"Yes, I'll be there. Thanks, Uncle Shane!" Kendall, not able to tolerate any more excitement, quickly got up and repeated that he would be at his office in the morning before retreating to his room. His heart was racing out of his chest and he needed to settle down, so he immediately got online and joined in on a game with his virtual friends. He was doing it; he was really going to help Dave.

CHAPTER 58

The Livermore hotline set up to receive tips on the Jackson murders had been ringing almost non-stop in the week since it was set up. Seventy percent of the calls were from pranksters making ape-like noises into the phone; while annoying, they were easy to ignore. They received lots of calls reporting ape sightings, which they also ignored. A select few claimed to have recognized the man posing as the plumber or the sketch of the man alleged to have dumped the van. None of those leads led to anything.

The day before, they had finally received a lead that was more promising. A woman, named Carol Waddel, from Columbus, Ohio, bypassed the hotline and reported recognizing the plumber directly to her local police department in Columbus. The detective who handled the call, Detective Lee, shared that information with the Livermore police department and told them that the woman was coming in for an interview the next afternoon. Lieutenant Holden immediately put Detective Sparks on a plane to Columbus to sit in on the interview.

Normally, they would wait until after the initial interview before spending the time and money flying a cop halfway across the country, but Waddel had provided enough information over the phone about the suspect to warrant the trip. The man's name was Dave Smith, and Ms. Waddle had claimed that he worked at Greenrock's headquarters in Potomac, Maryland, but had been temporarily transferred to Greenrock's Special Research Division to help out in the accounting department after four of their employees were killed in a terrorist attack. Smith was then supposedly fired, along with his boss, Frank Laso, over a security incident.

What really made the story interesting was that Detective Lee had received a tip from the homicide hot line shortly before the time Waddel claimed that Smith was fired for a security incident, claiming that Greenrock was behind the terrorist attack that killed four of its own employees. Lee never bought the idea that the young terrorist was a lone wolf; he was convinced the bomb was military grade and not something cooked up by the recent immigrant. It also rubbed Lee the wrong way that the FBI had pressured him to drop the investigation, and then seemed to jump to the lone-wolf theory just to close it out themselves. He was then also pressured to ignore the tip, even though it came from within Greenrock's own building.

Greenrock was a government contractor, and it looked to Lee like they were using their influence to cover up their own wrongdoings. Now, Sparks and Lee wondered if they had ventured into contract killings.

*

Sparks arrived at the Columbus police station to meet Detective Lee an hour before Ms. Waddel was scheduled to arrive. The plan was for Waddel to first work with their sketch artist to get a better picture of Smith, and as a result, hopefully the killer. After having the terrorist case suppressed for so long by the FBI and his own department, Lee was excited to share everything he had learned with a fellow detective. They were so focused on walking through their two cases that it was a half hour after Waddel was supposed to arrive before they realized that she had not shown up yet.

Waddel had not called in to tell them she would be late, and Lee had tried to reach her on her cell phone multiple times before sending a squad car over to her house to check on her. The officers he sent reported that the lights in her house were on, but nobody was answering the door. Given what Lee already suspected about how Greenrock did business, he felt that there was enough probable cause that Waddel was in danger, and that breaking into her house was warranted. He ordered them in, accepting full responsibility if he was wrong and Waddel had simply changed her mind and didn't want to answer the door.

He wasn't wrong. When the officers entered her living room, they found her lying on the floor, cold. They called an ambulance, but she couldn't be saved; they declared her dead minutes after arriving at the hospital. Detective Lee blamed himself; he should have picked her up and protected her as soon as she called in. Waiting a whole day gave Greenrock time to tie up loose ends and kill his witness. He directed forensics to do a full sweep of the house for bugs, suspecting someone had eavesdropped on her call to the police.

Detective Sparks also felt Lee's pain and frustration, wanting desperately to have a good lead on his investigation into the Jackson murders. While Lee's theories against Greenrock were compelling, there wasn't a clear link between their two cases, now that the one possible witness to the link was dead. Lee promised to try to identify Dave Smith another way, but he didn't have high hopes. Getting information out of Greenrock was like getting blood from a stone, and they were seemingly insulated from any efforts he had made in the past to use the court system to force them to give him access. All he had were theories, but no hard evidence.

For his part, Sparks now had the name of a suspect. It was, unfortunately, a common name, but he was determined to use that small amount of information to try and see where it led. One place he knew it didn't lead was to Columbus. Detective Lee had already spent the previous day tracking down any Dave Smiths who had lived in the Columbus region in the last few months, and he could not find any who were here temporarily or worked for Greenrock. Waddel's culprit was a mystery man who seemed to have no presence outside of Greenrock's division headquarters, where Waddel and he worked. In fact, Waddel told Lee over the phone that she had never seen Smith enter or leave the building.

That evening, Detective Sparks was on a red-eye back to California.

CHAPTER 59

After a week in lockdown, Dave was waiting for his escort to the training facility. Following breakfast, he sat back in bed, naked, as usual, but they were gathering his band together by the doorway between the enclosure and the training facility, so he knew the lockdown was over. He didn't want them to know he knew, however. A mercenary walked in and succinctly told him to get ready, then stood there waiting for Dave to get dressed—Bonobo stayed naked. Shrugging his shoulders, the mercenary stepped out of the room, looked back, and flapped his arms, indicating that Dave should be following him.

On the walk to the facility, he purposely got a little too close to the mercenary and felt the familiar shock and uneasiness emanate from the collar—not disabled yet. He didn't expect it to be, but the last message he got from Kendall gave them hope for the future. Kendall had been promoted to an administrative position, working in Cooper's office in the main building. They were counting on the kid to turn that newfound access into a plan to get them out of the lab. It would undoubtedly take time, so they had to be patient, but ready the second the collars were turned off.

When he entered the facility, things were set up a little differently. They had used the week off to remove some of the fixed structures and add what looked like a jungle camp, with multiple temporary structures. Soldiers up on tree platforms with machine guns were protected behind cement blocks. Their next killing frenzy was undoubtedly a jungle mission.

Keeps lined the naked furries up and started his briefing. "Beasts, for this next mission, we're going to need all eleven of you. What you see there is a heavily guarded cocaine lab hidden in a jungle. The actual lab you'll neutralize is roughly three times as large and divided into two distinct sections." Keeps pointed to a diagram showing a rough layout of the lab divided into two semicircle shaped areas that were joined in the middle. "There are five raised machine gun nests protecting the area, plus armed militia walking the perimeter. In the first phase of the attack, you'll neutralize the guards out on patrol, immediately followed by five of you scaling each of the five raised platforms to neutralize the gunners and disable the weapons. After that, finish the job. We want no survivors."

Dave decided to do something unexpected and sure to annoy Keeps: ask a question. "Umm, boss-man," Dave said, raising his hand straight up in the air like he was in grade school. "Why don't you just send in a plane and blow the place up?"

Keeps was annoyed, but grimace smiled and answered the question. "I thought you were smarter than that, boy. They call us in when they want the problem solved by the monsters that hide under your bed at night. The scary things that go boom in the night. Missiles won't stop these drug smugglers; they'll just pop-up new labs as fast as we destroy them. We want them to be scared every time they hear a crack out there in the jungle. Make them too scared to build new labs. ... At least that's the theory, but who knows if it actually works. I don't care. Now divide up into five groups and start making your way around the camp. When you're in position, attack."

Keeps didn't bother organizing the groups or telling them exactly where to go. He wasn't a micromanager, which the furry troop actually appreciated. He knew they would ultimately do it their way, anyway. Even though they were attacking a large camp, he also didn't bother giving them a way to communicate with each other to coordinate the attack. He had obviously seen enough of their work to know they didn't need technology to coordinate.

Bonobo paired up with Anne, which brought up all kinds of memories from the many nights he had virtually spent with her. *Focus!* Bonobo snapped out of his reverie, which was infecting the whole mind.

Furries were efficient, so the moment the five pairs—Lud had scaled a tree overlooking the camp to help direct the attack—were in position, they attacked without hesitation. They took out three quarters of the patrols on the ground and then scaled the poles to the raised machine gun nests sitting on the platforms overlooking the camp. By the time they started scaling the nests, the alarm had gone off, and the play actors tried to fight back with their paintballs. But after the first round, all eight mercenaries were dead, with no furry casualties.

They continued to train for a couple more hours, switching up the groupings to make things more interesting, but the outcome was always the same. While not completely useless, that day's training only modestly simulated what the real mission would entail. Keeps only had eight mercenaries available to act as drug hitmen. This was every mercenary that they had worked with in the past, except one female and one male who weren't present for the exercise. On the real mission, they expected to encounter ten times as many fighters and lab workers over an area three times as large; they would also have real bullets.

It was better than nothing, they guessed. At least they knew what they were *neutralizing*. As was also the custom, as soon as the exercises were finished, they ate some meat, then loaded up into their cargo containers and set off to the jungle to carry out their bloody task.

CHAPTER 60

The local investigation into the Jackson murders had dried up, but Detectives Sparks and Lloyd were more convinced than ever that the answers weren't going to be found in Livermore. They had both started to warm up to Detective Lee's theory that Greenrock was behind the killings, and Carol Waddel had been murdered to silence the one solid link they had had to connect Greenrock to all the killings. Conversely, Lieutenant Holden was less convinced and still insisted that the focus remain on tracking down clues from the evidence they had gathered at the scene and the junkyard.

Even though his gut was telling him Greenrock was involved, Lee knew the lieutenant had a point. His theories and the Waddel witness's death did not constitute hard evidence that Greenrock was involved—the Columbus coroner ruled she died of a heart attack from a previously undiagnosed heart condition. Despite not being able to conduct the interview before her untimely death, she did provide the detectives with some valuable information. They now had a name to go with the grainy image of the man posing as a plumber.

Detective Lee searched for a Dave Smith from Ohio and the surrounding states that matched the image. In addition, he was searching for a matching Dave Smith in the Washington D.C. area, where Waddel said he claimed to be from. Sparks and Lloyd, with the help of a couple of officers assigned to the case in their station, were looking for a match in the West Coast states. Unfortunately, there were a lot of Dave Smiths, so it was tedious work; in his experience, most cases weren't solved out in the field in a hail of gunfire, but back at the station or in the forensics lab studying the evidence and facts of the case.

*

Officer Talen had only been home a few hours a night in the last two weeks. His wife of two months wasn't happy about it, but he was a rookie and wanted to show Detectives Sparks and Lloyd how committed he was to solving the Jackson murders. He was just starting out in his career and wanted the senior officers to see him as someone with ambition and drive. There would be no better way to put himself on the fast track to detective than being the one to track down Dave Smith—the presumed killer.

As luck would have it, Talen thought he may have found the Dave Smith they were looking for. He had to be sure, though, before going to Detective Sparks with his finding. He would only get one chance to do this right. The picture he found of Smith, from a photograph of his face he found posted in a news article from a local Issaquah, Washington newspaper, looked similar to the grainy image of the plumber caught by the camera hidden in the stuffed bear.

If all he had to go on was the image, it might not have been enough to justify the excitement and burst of adrenaline he felt coursing through his veins. But the article stated that Smith had gone missing after three people posing as police officers arrested him outside his home. Two of the police impersonators were impersonating officers who had been brutally murdered shortly before the alleged kidnapping, and the kidnappers were the primary suspects in the murders. A week later, the lead detective died of a heart attack and the investigation went cold. Like with Detective Lee's case, the FBI took over and buried it.

If that wasn't enough, the timeline matched the information that Waddel had given them over the phone. Smith showed up for work at Greenrock's Special Research Division to work in the accounting department only a few days after his disappearance. It all fit so well that Talen was ninety-nine percent sure he had found their suspect. The only curious thing about it was why would the Dave Smith kidnapped by three killers start working for Greenrock only a few days later. From what Waddel told Lee, while Smith was very private, he seemed to fit in and was affable enough. That didn't fit the profile of a man who had just been kidnapped and taken from his family—was he a willing participant? That was for the more senior detectives to decide, but Talen organized his notes, took a few deep breaths to calm his nerves, and walked over to Sparks and Lloyd's desks to make his case.

*

As luck would have it, Detectives Sparks, Lloyd, and Lieutenant Holden were gathered together in the corner of the open space where the detectives' desks were located. Talen knew that the detectives would rather he approached them with new information without the lieutenant present so they could review and validate the data to determine if it was something worth pursuing; they also liked to control the narrative in respect to how the senior officers viewed the data.

Talen decided it was worth annoying Sparks and Lloyd if it meant he would get credit for breaking open the case. Without hesitation, he walked up to the three senior officers and blurted out, "I found Dave Smith!"

The three of them just turned toward Talen and stared at him. After a long moment of awkward silence, Sparks shrugged his shoulders and said, "and ..."

Talen fumbled through the folders he was carrying and said, "He's from Issaquah, Washington." He then dropped everything he was holding on the floor as he tried to pull out one of the documents he had filed away; pages of documents and notes were now scattered everywhere. Red-faced, Talen was then down on his knees trying to pick up the scattered papers. Holden just shook her head and told Sparks to update her later on what the boot had found, then turned and walked away.

"After you've gathered up your things, meet us back in the conference room to tell us what you found," Sparks said.

Sparks and Lloyd left for the conference room that Talen had originally come from, while Talen was left on the floor trying to reorganize the papers he so carefully put together moments before, all while half the room of officers were standing around gawking at the unfortunate greenhorn. His plan to impress Holden was now in tatters; he hoped the information he would eventually show the detectives would keep them from assigning him to direct traffic for the rest of his career.

Finally, with all his work re-organized, he walked back to the conference room to a few laughs and claps. Looking back, he should have simply left his stuff in the conference room and asked Sparks and Lloyd to join him there in the first place. Fortunately, they were professionals and acted as if nothing happened.

"Okay, Talen. What have you got for us?" Sparks asked.

Putting down his papers, he decided to just give them an oral summary of what he had learned.

"As I said, the Dave Smith we are looking for is originally from Issaquah, Washington. He disappeared without a trace last December after being arrested by three people—two men and one woman—who were posing as police officers. Those three cop impersonators had murdered two of the cops they were posing as only shortly before they kidnapped Smith."

"That's something. How are you tying him to the Dave Smith we suspect killed the Jackson family?" Lloyd asked.

"Yes, well, multiple ways. The first is that a photograph of Smith taken from a newspaper article reporting on the kidnapping resembles the image of the suspect captured in the Jackson house. Talen handed Lloyd the picture from the newspaper. The second is the Smith I found in Issaquah was kidnapped a few days before Waddel claimed the Smith she knew started working at Greenrock. Thirdly, I spoke to Lieutenant Peabody from the Issaquah police department and the circumstances involving the investigation seem eerily similar to what happened with Lee's investigation into the terrorist attack, and what happened to Waddel after she contacted him."

"Go on ..."

Talen took a few breaths, but he felt he was on a roll and had the undivided attention of both detectives.

"Well, the FBI quickly took control of the case and buried it. The detective investigating the case—Detective Calahan—died of a heart attack a week later. Like Waddel, he had no known heart conditions before his death."

Sparks kept his cool during the young officer's presentation, but inside he felt validated. There was still a lot of work to do to verify that everything Talen had told him was accurate, but based on what the rookie had told him so far, he was pretty sure that they had finally identified the killer, and his belief that Lee's theories linking Greenrock to his case were correct. Given the propensity of witnesses to die or go missing, he directed Lloyd and Talen to keep everything they had learned between themselves. He would contact

Lieutenant Peabody right away to get more information about the kidnapping and warn him to keep things quiet.

CHAPTER 61

After four months of spinning his wheels, Lieutenant Peabody finally had a breakthrough in his morbid investigation into the murders of his two Issaquah police officers and the related kidnapping of Dave Smith. Detective Sparks called earlier in the day to warn him to keep the new investigation into Greenrock Solutions' link to the case under wraps, for now. He felt that disseminating what they'd learned—or even that they were investigating Greenrock—would put them all in danger.

Peabody was way ahead of them in that regard. After the FBI took over his department's investigation into the murders of his two officers and the Smith kidnapping, and then seemingly put it on the back burner, he did not trust federal law enforcement either. From what Sparks shared with him about what happened in Columbus, Ohio, he was also seeing Detective Callahan's death in a whole new light.

His first task of the day was to collect all of the evidence his department had gathered on the murders and kidnapping and send copies to Sparks. He wouldn't do it through official channels, however. Sparks and Lee had set up a private drop site where they could share evidence using personal accounts. This skirted public disclosure laws and could get him fired or even sent to prison, but if it meant getting justice for his two murdered officers—possibly three—it was worth the risk. Sparks assured him that the shared drop site would not be known to anyone outside the four detectives working on the shared theory that Greenrock was behind their separate cases. It wasn't lost on him that they had given him access to their secret site with little hesitation, so he couldn't be fully sure their likely illegal method of sharing evidence wouldn't disseminate further in the future.

Later that day, while reviewing all of the shared documents and images on the drop site, Peabody found himself staring at the grainy profile of the man involved in the killings of the Jackson family in Livermore. Like everyone else in the country, he had read about the ape murders and saw this image in the papers, but he hadn't tied the man in the plumber cap to his missing person. After spending more time comparing the pictures he had of Dave Smith and the image from the Jackson household, he could see that they could be of the same man.

Jan Smith had been calling him occasionally, asking him about the case and if they were any closer to finding her husband. He dreaded her calls because the answer was always the same: no progress. Bringing Jan in on the new finding was risky, but he needed her to confirm that the grainy picture was indeed her husband and didn't want to lie to her when she inevitably called in for the next update; it had been almost two weeks since her last call, so it was due.

*

The next morning, Peabody drove to the Smith household in his own car in plainclothes; this visit was going to be off-the-books. He pulled into the driveway, got out of his car, and walked up to the door. He noticed the lights in the house were off, despite being a dreary dark day; he rang the doorbell and knocked on the door, anyway. After a few minutes of waiting, he assumed they were out for the day and decided to try again in the evening.

Walking to the car, a neighbor out working on his lawn recognized him and came over.

"Hey, are you a cop?" said the neighbor.

"Yes, how can I help you?" Peabody responded.

"I thought I recognized you. You are Ted Peabody, right?" Peabody nodded his head in the affirmative. "Well, if you are looking for Jan, I haven't seen her or the kids in a while. I think a week. My wife and I were starting to get worried, but we just assumed they'd gone on vacation, though that would be strange since school is not out."

"Did she tell you they had a trip planned?"

"No, we chitchatted sometimes, but we weren't really friends, so ... it's just strange, since they are usually out and about often, and their kid Mikey likes to play outside, but we haven't seen them in a while."

Peabody nodded his head again, "Well, thank you for the information. If you do see them, can you call the Issaquah station and let me know? What is your name?"

"Sure, I'm Jason, Jason Crosby. Are you going to try to find them? Do you think they were kidnapped too?"

"I have no reason to believe that, Mr. Crosby. Like you said, they probably just went on a short trip. Call the station and ask for me if you have any more information you want to share." Peabody turned to walk back to his car, hiding his concern from the neighbor. What he really wanted to do was to break into Jan's house to see if Jan had suffered the same fate as Calahan and Waddel, but he couldn't do that with Crosby watching. He had to handle this more subtly.

Peabody got back in his car and drove a few blocks away, pulled over, then tried to reach Jan on her cell phone. He tried three times, and it went straight to voice mail each time, meaning the phone was likely turned off. He then drove home and tried to reach her phone multiple times over the next few hours, with the same result. The principal at Kate's middle school was a good friend, so he reached out to Caleb Hall next.

245

Unlike when he called Jan, Caleb answered the phone after three rings. "Caleb, it's Ted. Do you have a minute? I need some help tracking down one of your students."

"I'll help if I can, Ted, but you know I can't give out private information concerning our students," Caleb replied.

"I know, I know, but this is a special case. You know Kate Smith's father was kidnapped and has been missing for the last four months, right?"

"Of course, Ted."

"Well, I was just over her house today to give Jan an update on the investigation, and nobody was home. The neighbor claims that he hasn't seen anyone at the house in the last week. So, my question is, has Kate been to school in the last week? Have you heard from either Jan or Kate in the last week?"

Caleb hesitated for a moment, but then decided that protecting Kate's privacy was less important than her well-being. "No, Kate missed school all of last week. It was unexcused. My assistant tried reaching out to Jan multiple times last week but could not reach her." With what happened to Kate's father, Caleb was now kicking himself for not reporting the absence to the police sooner, given that they could not reach her mother either. "I'm sorry, Ted. I really should have let you know sooner."

"I understand, Caleb. I just care about finding them now. Now, Caleb, I need you to listen to me very carefully. The people we are dealing with who murdered my officers and took Dave are extremely dangerous. I need you to promise that you'll keep this conversation to yourself."

"What do you mean, Ted? You think the killers took Jan and Kate too—what about Mikey? Are you saying my family is in danger now too?"

"I do not think you and your family are in danger, but it is best that we don't call attention to ourselves so we can keep it that way. Let me handle it, but is there any way you can check to see if Mikey was absent from his school too, without bringing anybody else into this?"

"Yes ... I'll need to go into the office, but I can let you know in half an hour. That poor family. I can't believe something like this can happen in Issaquah."

"I know what you're saying, Caleb, but unfortunately, it has come to Issaquah, and I intend to do something about it. Let me know what you find out about Mikey."

With that, Peabody hung up his phone, now convinced that the rest of Dave's family had been either kidnapped or killed—or had left to join Dave. When Caleb called half an hour later to tell him that Mikey had also been absent from school the week before, he was not surprised. He couldn't keep Jan, Kate, and Mickey's disappearance a secret for long, so he directed Caleb to have his administrator call in on Monday morning to report that Kate had not shown up to school for a whole week and that they could not contact the mother. He would then have the department handle it like any other missing persons case, but keep the part of the investigation he was doing with the detectives from Livermore and Columbus only to himself.

The next step was to sneak into the Smith's house that night to see if the family had been murdered in their home or taken somewhere else.

CHAPTER 62

Peabody parked a quarter mile from the Smith house by a park and walked the rest of the way, carrying only his lock pick set. He didn't want to gain the attention of the nosey neighbor or anyone else in the neighborhood, so he wore dark clothing and walked over after 10:00 PM, when he thought most people would be winding down for the evening or watching television.

Walking to the house, he encountered a woman walking her dog, but she ignored him, and he responded in kind. When he got to the Smith house, he worked his way to the front door by first hugging the side of a large hedge paralleling the driveway. He then made his way to the front door, where thankfully no light automatically activated. He wasn't new to picking locks, so he quickly unlocked the bolt and bottom latch and made his way inside. Thankfully again, the Smiths had no alarm system; that surprised him a little, given that the husband was kidnapped by murderers only four months prior.

The house smelled stale and of spoiled food. In the kitchen, he found moldy fruit on the counter and a pie that looked like it had been left out to cool. Both were now attracting bugs. He searched the house thoroughly, but there was no sign of Jan or either child. There was also no sign that any struggle had taken place in the house or that the family left on a planned trip. In addition to the rotting food on the counter, he found leftovers in the fridge and a couple of suitcases in their hall closet. None of the beds were made, and Kate's desk light was on and illuminating what looked like partially finished homework. Mikey's room was messy, the floor covered in toys.

He left everything as he found it and snuck back out of the house, making sure to relock the doors. After Caleb's office reported Kate missing from school on Monday, he would send a couple of officers to do an official check on the house. He had everything he needed to share his finding with Sparks and move along with the real investigation.

CHAPTER 63

The mission in Columbia was unlike any other the furries had been tasked with before. Every other mission had been a quick in and out, the furries never on the ground for more than a few hours, flying right out after the massacre concluded.

First, they dropped-in miles from the target and spent two days hiking to the staging point to set up camp. To keep their position hidden from the traffickers, they set up camp three miles from the jungle drug lab. Keeps surveilled the lab using rotating teams of three furries, who would crawl up close to the perimeter and stake out their operations. Furries were particularly well-suited for that type of activity, since they were less bothered by the environmental and insect conditions they encountered while hiding in the undergrowth around the lab.

Keeps was most interested in how they organized their security, though with the furries, those details rarely mattered. In every similar operation, the furries' capabilities were so superior to the adversaries', that even a bad to average attack strategy would succeed. It kept everyone busy, though.

Everything the furries observed was caught on the cameras integrated into their collars for Keeps and his soldiers to analyze. The furries didn't talk, and he didn't trust Dave to communicate useful information, so he relied solely on the collar recordings to plan the mission.

His four accompanying mercenaries were Esteban 'Est' Murillo, Sly Wallis, Bruce Yang, and Gill Turner. Est and

Yang were picked for their previous jungle combat experience, Turner because he was a medic, and Wallis because his police sketch was all over the newspapers in relation to the Jackson fiasco. Est was a particularly valuable asset, since he grew up in a South American rural village and had intimate knowledge of how to live off what the jungle provided. Just as importantly, he knew what plants, trees, and creatures to avoid.

They continued to stalk, but not attack the camp for days, Keeps seemingly in no rush to complete the mission. The furries started to wonder if the mission wasn't primarily to wipe out the drug lab, but instead, to stash the furries outside of the U.S. and civilization in general while the Greenrock bosses figured out how to solve the crisis brought on by the Jackson investigation.

Another curiosity was where Keeps set up the communication hub. Instead of setting it up in the canopy over their camp, he had the team haul six-thousand feet of ethernet cable out into the jungle with them. He used that long cable to set up the communication hub over a mile from where they had set up camp. Two days after they arrived and finished erecting the hub, he let Jones know that they had established their camp, and the satellite link was located directly over their location.

That was how the furries knew that cleaning up HEL didn't only involve eliminating the furries—or at least Keeps believed his team was in danger. They weren't really all in the same boat, since Keeps' subterfuge might save him and his four mercenaries, but HEL could still reach out to fry the furries to death via their collars. Kendall was still their only hope at true freedom other than the freedom death brought.

The furries figured out that the hub wasn't only used to establish communication with HEL, but it also extended HEL's reach to the furries. Their collars were controlled using low-frequency radio waves that were very long range—thousands of miles in some environments—but not long enough to reach all the places the furries operated in. When on mission, the hardware they brought along always included antennas designed to emit the LF waves to keep the furry collars within range of their keepers. This mission was no different: Keeps carried a short range LF transmitter on him for the walk in, while the larger hub established a LF range of many miles, and through the satellite connection back to their home base, extended control over the collars all the way back to HEL.

This situation brought up a big dilemma: could the furries launch a surprise attack on the five humans, destroy the hub, and make a run for it? Normally, on missions, only some of the furries were brought along, so hurting the mercenaries could result in putting their brethren in danger. This mission included all the furries, so in theory they could escape without repercussions. In practice, they knew it wouldn't be that simple. Keeps had warned them to stay away from the hub, but Dell purposely ignored the warning and set out toward it. When he got within a quarter mile, his collar went off, sending him into painful convulsions that continued until Keeps turned off the collar and let Dell crawl back out of the danger zone.

The furries assumed there was some failsafe device that ensured they would suffer like Dell if they harmed or killed the humans. As always, they had to stay patient and wait for their opportunity.

*

As the days went by, the five humans and eleven beasts quickly ate through the rations they had carried in. No matter, the jungle provided plenty of sustenance, so they

252

could sustain themselves indefinitely. Close to camp was a clear spring that provided them with fresh water, which they used for drinking and hygiene. The water was clear and ice-cold, which was a nice contrast to the oppressive heat and humidity associated with living in a rain forest close to the equator in Eastern Columbia. With Est in charge of designing the camp and overseeing the work, in just two days, they had three solid structures built to house the humans, the furries, and a common area where they could gather for meals and briefings.

They ate birds, snakes, and other jungle animals that the furries caught; the furries were deadly accurate throwing a spear. All in all, life was much better for the furries in the jungle than back in their cages at home. They felt free, or at least not so confined.

CHAPTER 64

One day, Lud and Bonobo were out hunting, miles from camp. They sometimes wondered how far they could keep going before Keeps would signal them back in with a shock to their necks; at what point would they be out of range? Keeps' laissez-faire attitude about where the furries carried out their hunting trips convinced them that he wasn't worried about them getting away, meaning the range was likely vast.

No matter, they joyously ran through the jungle in their spandex shorts, swinging through trees, acting like the apes they resembled. Bonobo decided to don a pair of spandex shorts, worried that without that modest protection, some jungle insect or parasite would crawl into one of his pelvic openings. The two of them were happily sitting high up in the canopy, eating a family of toucans and engaging in an interesting conversation on what their place in society would be after they were free. Lud, being a former civics professor, thought a lot about that topic.

On the one hand, they were human too, just enhanced, but unlike other minorities, their humanity could be up for debate. They were also prone to violence and extreme anti-social behavior, which made them less than ideal neighbors. Even if the law considered them human and citizens, there was the matter of the Jackson murders. Bonobo and the beast-like furries had been caught on camera, likely making Dave Smith a fugitive wanted for murder, and the rest of them, monsters to wipe out.

Lud and Bonobo climbed down from their perch and noticed two eyes and a snout sticking up from the water in a shallow, muddy part of the river that ran by their lunch spot. Bonobo's first thought was boots and dinner, while they recalled Lud's memory of a crocodile jacket he once owned as a child. As they moved closer to the creature, they could better gauge its immense size. It looked to be at least sixteen feet long, with a very large head that no doubt held powerful jaws.

As they snuck closer, they felt slight pings coming from their collars, likely bossman warning them to back off, not wanting to risk losing two of his assets to a greater monster than them. They responded by each displaying their middle fingers to their respective collars. That elicited one last stronger pulse to each of them, but the pinging stopped after that. They imagined the mercenaries and other furries gathering around the screen, eager to view the action and see which beast came out on top. There was no backing out now.

They made their way to the edge of the water, within easy leaping distance from the caiman. The sounds of their movements not only aroused the interest of the jumbo specimen, but three other large caimans also drifted toward the shore to meet them in battle. The other three were not as large as the one they now called Jumbo, but still much bigger than either Lud or Bonobo. They expected Keeps to start pinging them again in panic, but fortunately, he kept his cool so that they could concentrate on the task at hand. They needed to move fast, since they couldn't chance more caimans joining the fight.

Jumbo's three buddies were all to its left, so the furries made their attack to its right. Lud was the stronger of the two, so he would be the one to try and pull the beast to shore. Bonobo leaped onto Jumbo's head, wrapped his arms and torso around its snout, and squeezed with all his might, holding its jaws closed. Immediately, Jumbo spun onto its back, plunging Bonobo underwater. He had to wrap his legs around its neck to keep from getting peeled off in the mud.

He was then spun back up out of the water, facing the middle of the river, Jumbo obviously wanting to carry its new cargo out to deeper waters.

At this point, Lud was holding tight onto its tail, his feet wedged into the mud acting as anchors to prevent Jumbo from escaping out into the river. Two of Jumbo's buddies were cowards and made their retreat, but the third tried to get hold of Bonobo in its jaws, attempting to take bites from the thing on the flopping head of his friend. Bonobo felt a sharp cramp-like pain in his thigh and quickly looked back to see the friend chomping down on his leg; it looked like it had snagged him with one of its top teeth. Fortunately, Jumbo twisted him downward, pulling his thigh away from the tooth, freeing his leg, and leaving a bleeding hole behind. He then started paying more attention to the friend and kicked its snout away every time it pushed forward for another bite. The hunt wasn't going to end well if Lud didn't figure out how to drag the beast ashore pretty soon.

Lud shared his increasingly desperate thoughts and pulled even harder, starting to make some headway in dragging the giant beast onto the shore. Just as Jumbo's head was leaving the river, the friend made one last go at Bonobo, still wrapped around its jaws. He looked to his right and was staring into the caiman's wide-open mouth. He could smell its rotting breath as its jaws started to close on his head—he thought he was done for. Sharing his mind, Lud also did not want to experience life inside of the caiman's stinking mouth and pulled back on Jumbo's tail with a hard jerk that instantly pulled it another foot onto shore. The friend's jaw snapped closed, brushing Bonobo's hairline, but missing his skull.

With momentum on his side, Lud finished pulling Jumbo out of the river and into the forest. Bonobo jumped off the head and pulled some vines off the nearest tree, while Lud continued to hold the tail so Jumbo couldn't retreat into the river. Again, jumping on its head, squeezing its jaw shut, Bonobo tightly wrapped the long vine around its snout. Once he had the jaw safely secured, they contemplated how they would pull the roughly thousand-pound beast three and half miles back to camp.

They found a sturdy six-foot pole-like branch and tied it to Jumbo's tail, perpendicular to its body. Each of them then picked up opposite sides of the pole, facing away from its body, and started dragging it through the jungle. They were tilling a line through the jungle's clay-like soil, using the caiman as a plow. At first, it tried to aggressively wiggle away, but the caiman quickly tired and lost its will to fight. Bonobo managed to stem the flow of blood from the tooth hole in his leg using a makeshift vine tourniquet, but the pain was intense. His enhanced furry ability to tolerate pain was the only thing that kept him going.

After an hour of steady progress, they arrived at camp to the cheers of their fourteen comrades. To an outsider, it would look like the furries were just standing quietly with tight lips, but Bonobo and Lud could hear their cheers. Even Keeps was smiling. They dropped the plow shaft on the ground and greeted their band. Jumbo, more exhausted than its captors, just lay still, resigned to its fate.

Bonobo and Lud's job done, Est took over in preparing the catch. He killed the caiman swiftly by jabbing a long-pointed stick through its eye socket and back into its brain. He then used his Ka-Bar knife to make long cuts down the length of the caiman. After making his long cuts down its body and legs, he started to use his knife to carefully peel back the skin off the flesh underneath.

As Est continued to pull back the skin, Wallis and Turner joined in to cut off large chunks of meat to make steaks. When they finished, they had eleven five-pound cuts for the furries, and five smaller cuts for the mercenaries. The furries ate their cuts raw, but Keeps grilled the normal human sized steaks for himself and his four men. After the meal, the mercenaries worked late into the night, slicing Jumbo into thin slices and hanging each slice over the smoke pit they had built to preserve the meat. Beast and human shared tending to the smoker for the next several days until the meat was fully dried and preserved into caiman jerky.

Bonobo thought to his hive mind that life was good and didn't want their newfound sense of comradery and pseudo-freedom to end. While the hive shared his sentiment, they were more realists—their appearance dictated that they would never fit into the human world. The collars stilled burned tightly around their necks, keeping them under HEL's control and holding the keys to whether they lived or died if they stepped too far out of line. Bonobo didn't want to think about that, however. Those thoughts just led to bitterness and anger, and he was enjoying a break from that.

CHAPTER 65

Jones was worried that the investigation into the Jackson murders and corresponding links being established to the terrorist attack and Dave's stint working as an accountant upstairs were quickly spinning out of his control. Closing up another loose end, killing Waddel, seemed to only heighten Detective Lee's suspicions that Greenrock was involved in shenanigans. Now, Lee was working with Detective Sparks from the Livermore department to try and prove Greenrock was involved. Even worse, his source in the Livermore department said she overheard one of the young officers assigned to the case say that he had found Dave Smith. She was closed off from direct involvement in the investigation, but was able to determine that the Dave Smith they found was indeed their Dave from Issaquah.

If that wasn't enough, his monitoring of the Smith house had caught Lieutenant Peabody, from the Issaquah police department, showing up at the house to ask questions only a day after the Livermore department discovered Dave's identity. He then broke into the house later that evening, obviously confirming his suspicions that the rest of the family was now missing along with Dave.

Closing off the current investigations would require killing at least five or six more cops, but as attractive as a solution as that sounded to him, he couldn't be sure it wouldn't just ramp up the heat on Greenrock even further. So far, the FBI had played ball and stifled the investigations on their behalf, but if he kept killing cops, they might start pushing back. Obviously, the detectives at the three local police departments were ignoring any jurisdiction claims made by the FBI in the past anyway. They likely suspected the FBI was in on the cover-up; trust in government institutions was at an all-time low.

Hmm. What to do? What to do?

If this were happening in a Third World country, he would just send in a team of furries to attack and kill everyone in those police stations, terminator style. The thought made him smile. That would not work here, however. Videos of the attacks would inevitably leak out, and the ape murders would become the ape police massacres. He didn't even want to think about the heat from law enforcement and HEL's political backers that would bring on.

He looked through the profiles he had on all of the detectives and police officers involved in the investigations, thinking and plotting. Since he ruled out more murder as a solution for the time being, he was left with bribery and menace as alternative options. Bribery could be effective in many cases, but these detectives were older and might care about the case more than money; none of them had problems with debt that could be exploited.

Sparks did have an adult daughter with a family of her own. From what he gathered from her social network, Sparks and his daughter were quite close. His wife died of breast cancer a few years back, and he was a dedicated father and grandfather, now that his daughter was all the family he had. Furthermore, going after Sparks' daughter could have positive collateral effects. Lloyd and Peabody were also family men with children and grandchildren of their own. They all needed to see how much they personally had to lose by pursuing their current path.

Now that he had a solution to the Jackson investigation, he had to firm up his position at the lab. If and when HEL came tumbling down, he wanted to be part of whatever rose up to replace it. His next meeting of the morning was with Dr. Danzel, the one person at the lab that could not be replaced.

*

Jones stepped into Danzel's private office. It resembled any other doctor's office you might find in a hospital or medical center. Behind his desk were several nicely framed diplomas on the wall; he had graduated from Harvard Medical School and did his residency at Boston Children's Hospital. One day, Jones would be interested in finding out how he went from wanting to care for children to genetically engineering monsters. Danzel was a true sociopath with no moral compass or sense of empathy that Jones could see. Maybe working with sick children made sense; most people would be broken up and have trouble functioning if they were surrounded by sick and dying children, but Danzel could go about that job with no such encumbrances.

Jones decided to get right to the point: "It is time to transition Aliyah."

"I agree. You detained her weeks ago. It's long past time we moved forward," Danzel stated.

Annoyed, Jones continued, "Yes, well, until now it wasn't just my call, but with all the other furries currently out of house and the pressure from the investigation, we need a furry that is loyal to us."

"You mean loyal to *you* ... and after throwing her in one of your cells, what makes you think she'll still be loyal to you?"

"She will. Don't you worry about that," Jones replied.

"... and when do you expect my furries to be back from Columbia?"

"They are not your furries. I'm told the operation is more complex than usual, so it could be another week before they're back," Jones made up. "Without Dave here, it is a perfect time to transition Aliyah."

"Without Dave here, it is an even more perfect time to transition Kate. Don't you think?"

"That is a much more delicate situation. As you know, before we can transition Kate, we need to make sure Dave is out of the lab for several weeks so we can keep her separated from him. If they are anywhere close to one another, I suspect he'll know, which could ruin him as a useful asset."

What he left out was his uncertainty in regard to whether the furries would ever make it back from the jungle at all. Danzel considered the furries his creations and thought of them as something akin to his children. If he suspected that Greenrock was considering terminating all of them, along with HEL itself, there is no telling how Danzel would react. For the moment, he needed Danzel's full focus on his work, which now included transforming Aliyah from human to fiend. Kate's time would come soon too, but Aliyah would go first.

"Fine, fine, but we can't wait too long. If you want a kid furry, then I need to transition her while she is still a kid," Danzel said.

"One thing at a time. Get your team together. Aliyah needs to go through the transition this afternoon."

Jones thought to himself that even if Danzel finished the procedure that day, she would barely be ready, if and when Stirling made the call to shut down HEL. After the procedure, the new furry goes through a three-week incubation period before they are mostly developed and ready to integrate with their brethren. He didn't think the lab had that kind of time, but he would make the best of the situation, regardless.

"One more thing, I want Aliyah to function without a collar and the same limits we put on the other furries, so you need to tone down her compulsion to kill non-furries. Can you do that?" Jones asked Danzel, hopefully.

"Haven't you noticed that Dave is less violent than the other furries, in addition to having a normal appearance?" Danzel paused, waiting for an answer.

"... Yes." Despite his response, Jones wasn't completely sure, but it seemed plausible.

"Well, I'll tone that down even more with Aliyah. She'll have the capabilities without as many sociopathic tendencies, though she has some of those naturally, which will remain."

Jones thought that he should talk, given that there was no one more sociopathic than Danzel. He was glad it was possible, though. Now he just needed to patch things up with Aliyah so she would go back to being the most loyal member of his team.

CHAPTER 66

Jones stood outside Aliyah's cell and took in a few deep breaths to steady himself. After five weeks of solitary confinement, Aliyah might not be in a reasonable mood. He had to project confidence and maintain his authority. The worst thing he could do was look weak in front of Aliyah; if she sensed weakness, she would come after him, like he was weakened prey.

He opened the door and walked into the cell. Aliyah was sitting at her desk, eating her lunch.

"I'm not done yet. Go away and come back later," she said. When she didn't get a response or hear someone leaving, she turned around to confront whoever was bothering her.

"Well, the fuck. It's Mr. Jones. You here by yourself? You sure that is wise, given my temper?"

"I never abandoned you, Aliyah. Locking you up is the last thing I wanted to do, but it was for your own safety."

Aliyah got up from the desk, calmly walked over to Jones, and got right in his face. "What about your safety? How about I take those big ass glasses of yours and shove them up your ass? How could you do this to me? I was loyal."

"Please, Aliyah, let me explain." She kept her gaze on him for a moment and then sat down on the bed.

"Please do, asshole."

"I'm sure you heard rumors, but the purpose of this lab is to take people with certain genetic traits and transform them into assassins. We call the people we enhance, furries."

With that, Aliyah laughed. "You call your assassins furries? What dumb fuck came up with that name?"

"That's not important."

"Was it you?" she looked at him with incredulity.

"No, that's not important. Let me continue."

"That's a yes."

He waited a second, and when satisfied she wasn't going to interrupt him again, he continued, "The important thing is these assassins are akin to superheroes." He really needed to sell this to her. "They are super-fast, super-strong, and very intelligent. They even heal faster than normal people.

"... The reason I picked you to join my team wasn't just because I thought you had talent. It was also because you have the genetic makeup necessary to become one of our furries. I'm offering you the chance to be a superhero."

"Do I really have a choice?" she snorted. Jones did not respond. "Will I look like an ape? You're not turning me into a fucking ape. I like that I'm hot."

"Yes, you are a beautiful woman and will remain one. Dave went through the same procedure you will, and his appearance didn't change."

"Dave? Will I work with Dave?" She was attracted to Dave, so the prospect seemed to excite her.

"I'm afraid not. You see, the lab is in a bit of a crisis right now, and that most likely means staff cuts in the future, and Dave will likely be let go."

"You mean 'terminated,' don't you? ... What is the crisis?"

"Dave was on a mission that failed spectacularly. It wasn't really his fault, but it left the lab exposed, and now we have a problem with law enforcement. The details are boring, but what I'm really trying to say ... is that I need you, and I need you as a superhero."

He looked at her expectantly. It was happening whether she agreed to the procedure or not, but it would be much easier if she was a willing participant and would remain loyal to him—or reaffirm her loyalty to him. She would be much more useful to him doing his bidding without the collar. The overhead of traveling with transmitters to control the collars was something that Keeps' team could manage, but not him alone.

She had permanently lost her trust in Jones, but the opportunity to become a superhero, like in the comic books, wasn't something she could pass up. With the new powers that Jones was offering her, nobody could hurt her again. The tables would be turned. Her one regret was that she couldn't get superhero wild with Dave.

She had made up her mind. "When do you turn me into superwoman?"

"We go now."

For the first time, the victim of the procedure was a willing participant and didn't have to be forced onto the surgery table. Aliyah donned her hospital gown and walked into the surgery room on her own. One of Danzel's orderlies hooked up her IV and administered the paralytic drug, and as she lost control over her muscles and breathing, she realized that her transformation into a superwoman was not going to be pleasant.

After she was completely paralyzed, hooked up to the ventilator, and strapped tightly to the table, Danzel walked in to give her the spiel. "Welcome Aliyah. Before we get started, I just want to say that I admire you, and I'm a little envious, to tell you the truth. You are about to experience something very few human beings have ever experienced or could ever dream of experiencing. You will become something greater, millions of years of evolution in a matter of ..."

He continued, but Aliyah was already bored by the time he said her name—what a blowhard, she thought. They soon brought her back to their full attention when they administered nerve stimulating agents, then sat her up and started moving the needles into position in front of her eyes.

For the next several hours, she experienced the same cycles of pain and elation that Dave and the other furries had previously endured.

Later, sitting in the plexiglass cage in the recovery room, she continued to feel sick and in pain, but also felt the power they had endowed upon her, coursing through her veins. She knew she had made the right decision by agreeing to undergo the transformation, even though it probably would have happened without her consent. She had no intention of becoming a superhero. A supervillain, maybe, but Jones had no idea what kind of new monster he had unleashed on the world.

CHAPTER 67

It was Sunday, but Detectives Sparks and Lloyd were in the office working on the case. Late the night before, Sparks received a call from Lieutenant Peabody from Issaquah, who relayed the news that Smith's wife and children were now missing, along with her husband Dave. Their disappearance coincided with the release of the image of the man they now believe is Dave Smith from the bear cam. He didn't think they had enough evidence to charge Greenrock Solutions with anything in a court of law, but it was enough for the detectives involved to be confident that they were on the right track.

The next morning, their disappearance would be officially reported to the Issaquah police, and they would start their official investigation. He had no doubt the FBI would want jurisdiction over that case too. It didn't matter. Sparks had his own plan to put pressure on the FBI to back off with their obstruction.

"Jack, this whole case stinks," Sparks said.

"I don't disagree, Will, what do you want to do about it?" Lloyd asked.

"We've seen what they've done up there in Columbus with Lee's cases and Waddel. We've seen what happened to Peabody's detective who was working on the case. We've seen how the FBI is handling things. Greenrock and the government are obviously in cahoots. We're just spinning our wheels here and waiting for the next shoe to drop."

"How do you mean?" Lloyd asked.

"I mean, do we sit here until another witness disappears or has a heart attack. They likely killed that cop Calahan;

maybe we're next? I mean, they're killing mothers and children now."

"We don't know that yet," Lloyd mumbled unconvincingly. "We can't let those fuckers intimidate us, Will. Do we just shrug our shoulders and not get justice for the Jackson family? I'm going to do my job until I can't."

"I'm not giving up, Jack. I'm talking about playing a little dirty. Doing something that might get me fired. I know a reporter at the *San Jose Dispatch* very well. Over the years, we've helped each other out, and I've fed him some good stories. He owes me. I want to leak everything we've discovered so far to the press. It's the only way to put pressure on the FBI to do their job. The pressure they are receiving to stay away from the case requires us to put more pressure on them to get on the case."

"I don't know. That might also blow any chance we have of someday prosecuting someone at Greenrock."

"With big companies, it never comes to that. At best they'll pay a fine umpteen years from now without admitting guilt, and that's best case and not likely. Doing it this way, we'll at least embarrass them. Maybe someone will get fired, or they'll do cleanup on one of their own. It could get a few politicians looking to make a name for themselves on our side."

"You're hoping to get someone at Greenrock killed?"

"People are already getting killed if we don't do this or drop the case. It's them or us," Sparks said.

Lloyd stared at Sparks for a long while, but Sparks just stared right back at him. Sparks was dead serious on taking the investigation to the press. "I'm five years from getting my full pension, Will. I hear what you're saying, but I'm not looking to turn my life upside down over this."

"As far as I'm concerned, this conversation never happened. I'll take that to my grave. You go home and I'll do the rest. I'll do this and resign if I have to. Maybe they'll take my pension, maybe they won't. I don't care. It's just me."

Lloyd knew, "It's just me," was a reference to him being a widower. Unlike Lloyd, who had a wife that was looking forward to his retirement in five years, Sparks had only himself to worry about at home. He'd also been on the job for thirty-two years, so he probably had nothing to lose but his job and the respect of his peers. He had solved a lot of big cases in his time at Livermore, so he might not even lose that. "I wish you hadn't told me; or maybe I'm glad you told me; I either take this to Holden or go along with the lie that I didn't know." He breathed a deep sigh of resignation, wondering if he could lie to preserve his career. "Do what you have to do to expose these motherfuckers."

Lloyd pursed his lips, turned, and walked out of the station. He'd go home and watch a ballgame, while Sparks went to the press, acknowledging that the case was lost going the traditional route.

Sparks wasn't looking for Lloyd's blessing but felt he had to give him a heads-up so he wouldn't be blindsided when the story broke. Given Lloyd's reaction, he wasn't so sure that telling him had been the right course of action, but he couldn't undo that now. Lieutenant Holden would be blindsided and furious with him, but giving the lieutenant a heads-up was out of the question if he wanted to get the story out via the press. He had already arranged to meet his contact, Niles Price, a reporter at the Dispatch, the night before, so he spent the next couple of hours gathering up all of the evidence he wanted to share with the reporter and then left to meet him at the reporter's condo in Fremont.

After Peabody told him that Smith's family had disappeared, he was more paranoid than ever before, and assumed he was being watched. He didn't want to expose Niles, and worried that his life might be put in danger if Greenrock found out that he was writing an article about the killings before that article went out. It was essential that the story stay secret right up until it was published, assuming Niles would help him at all.

He left his cell phone at the station, drove to a coffee shop close to the train stop in Livermore, and went into the shop and ordered a coffee. He sat down for a few minutes, and when nobody else walked in or out, he snuck out the back door and walked to the train station, keeping an eye out for anybody who might be tailing him. He used a reloadable debit card he paid for using cash to purchase his ticket card and made his way to Fremont. Fortunately, Niles's condo was close enough to one of the Fremont stations for him to walk from there.

He managed to arrive at Niles's place at 2:10 PM, only ten minutes late. It was an unusually hot day for late March, so he was sweaty and out of breath from his walk. Niles ushered him into his living room, where he got right down to business, not even offering Sparks a drink.

"So, you told me on the phone that you had a big story and were calling in a favor. What's the story?" Niles asked, still standing, hovering over Sparks.

"Why don't you sit down? This is going to take a while. I think after you see what I have, you're going to be thanking me for the big scoop I'm about to drop on your lap."

"We'll see, and what's with all the subterfuge?"

"You'll understand shortly enough. This has to do with the Jackson murders, but our investigation shows that the murders were actually part of a bigger conspiracy."

Niles's ears suddenly perked up: "The ape murders!" If Sparks was going to give him inside information about the ape murders, that could be huge for his career. Except for the release of some images of the suspects, the police had been very close-mouthed about the case; there had been none of the usual leaks out of the department that he would normally expect, given how high profile the case was.

"I see I've got your attention now. Why don't you offer me a drink and take a seat while I organize my things," Sparks said.

Niles did what he was asked and made the detective a nice cold glass of ice water while Sparks started laying out papers on his coffee table. To make more room, Niles pulled all of the junk previously on the table onto the floor. He couldn't hide his newfound enthusiasm.

Sparks knew he had him as soon as he mentioned the Jackson murders, so he felt confident that Niles would go ahead with the story even after he warned him of the dangers.

"Before I go over the evidence with you, I need to warn you of the dangers involved. The people behind this have killed and kidnapped witnesses in an effort to cover up their involvement, so until you are ready to release the story to the press, you can't talk about this with anyone else."

"Ya, ya, ya, I get it. I'll need to tell my editor, obviously."

"If you need to reach me, use this phone." Sparks handed Niles a flip phone he had bought the day before at an electronics shop.

"Burner phones. You're serious?" Niles questioned.

"Dead serious. Only contact me after I leave if absolutely necessary, and then only on that phone to the one number saved in the contact list. Before we move on, I need you to tell me you are all in."

Niles didn't hesitate: "I'm all in, Will. Enough with the prelude, what do you have for me."

Sparks started from the beginning, detailing what evidence they collected from the crime scene at the Jackson house and the junkyard—a connection the police had not previously disclosed to the press. He then laid out the conspiracy, starting with the true identity of the man they captured an image of in the act of the crime. He made sure to make special note of the fact that the Dave Smith who was kidnapped and later identified by a co-worker at the Special Research Division of Greenrock Solutions in Johnstown, Ohio, was the same man that participated in murdering the Jackson family. He mentioned how Smith's family was now missing too, and how the victimizers tried to cover their tracks by killing the Issaquah detective investigating Dave Smith's disappearance. He also told him about Carol Waddel, who identified Dave Smith, connecting the Jackson murders to Greenrock, and her unfortunate fate.

After forty-five minutes of laying out his case and showing Niles the evidence he had to back his assertions, he had one more of Greenrock's suspected dirty-deeds to unveil to Niles, one that he had held back, not certain if he should complicate the story further. Like Sparks, Niles was confused about why Dave Smith would show up for work at the Special Research Division's accounting department only a few days after being kidnapped. Furthermore, why would he go from accounting to taking part in an assassination team to silence a whistleblower only a month after leaving the accounting department? That was quite the lateral move within any large organization.

Sparks went with the theory that Dave Smith was forced to work for Greenrock to protect his family. That was speculation because another theory was that the kidnapping was just a cover, and Dave willingly joined Greenrock.

Sparks could see how Niles was lapping up all the information he had given him so far, like a famished wolf. He decided to unveil the more speculative parts to the conspiracy and bring in the connection to the terrorist attack at the sandwich shop in Columbus the year before. Regardless of whether Greenrock had initiated the terrorist attack or not, they had just lost a good chunk of the accounting department, and Dave Smith was an accountant. The theory that he was forced to work for Greenrock semi-fit-in with this part of the story. He admitted that it didn't fully explain why he switched from accounting to assassination, or why Greenrock would kidnap a person to work in their accounting department as opposed to just hiring someone. But the pictures didn't lie— even though sometimes they did—and they had a witness— unfortunately now deceased—who placed Dave Smith from Issaquah at Greenrock in Johnstown.

After taking it all in, Niles sat quietly for a few minutes, while Sparks smartly kept silent to let Niles process what he had learned. Niles was uneasy about staking his career on Sparks' conspiracy theory about Smith and Greenrock, but he believed it himself. He was also a risk-taker by nature, which Sparks knew and was counting on.

"I'm going to need to sell this to my editor. Unless you are willing to go on record, it will be a non-starter," Niles said.

"I'm willing. Send me the article before you publish it so I can look it over first," Sparks replied.

"No!" Niles said sharply. "What will happen is my editor, and probably someone from legal, will call you at the station, and you'll verbally consent to be listed in the article as the source of the information. All I can promise is that I'll stick to the facts as you have laid them out for me."

Sparks suspected it would come down to this. He was accusing one of the country's most powerful companies of murder and abduction, with the consent of federal law enforcement. Did he expect that they would publish something so explosive on the word of an anonymous source?

He didn't like losing control of the narrative, but there was no turning back from the path he had chosen, so he agreed.

"Ok, but that call can't come until right before you're ready to publish. If he needs assurances before then, call me on the burner phone."

Sparks left shortly after for his trip back to his car, which was still at the coffee shop in Livermore, while Niles was left to strategize how to bring the story to his editor. If this had come up a year ago, he probably wouldn't have gotten his editor to agree to run the story. Back when he first started working at the paper, the old guard still ruled the newsroom. Eight months prior, the old guard was replaced by younger and more progressive leadership in an effort to stem the newspaper's steady decline into irrelevance. The old owner passed away, and his son took charge. He quickly put his own generation in charge of the paper, and demanded more contentious and titillating content.

Since the change, the newspaper had become part hard news and part tabloid. With Sparks agreeing to go on record as the source, he was confident that the paper would run his story. It was probably too late to make Monday's paper, but he would try for Tuesday. He called his editor to grease the wheels a little by giving him a vague recap, telling him he would give him the full story the next morning. That backfired when his boss demanded he meet him at the office right away. He packed up and headed to the office; he was all in now, just like Sparks.

CHAPTER 68

Joe Green and Ken Jurgensen's plane landed in San Jose, California, late on Sunday evening. They had a mandate from Jones to abduct the daughter of Detective Sparks of the Livermore police department to compel him to obstruct the investigation into the Jackson murders. Their directive was not to harm his daughter—permanently—but to provide enough of a scare to convince him that pursuing the case was not in his best interest.

Ideally, they would have had a lot more time to surveil their target and build a plan to carry out the operation, but Jones made it clear that time was of the essence, and the deed had to be completed as soon as possible. All they had were some general notes on who Sparks' daughter was and where they could find her, but they knew nothing about her routine. Despite the pressure from Jones, they decided to spend at least one full day getting to know her patterns before making their move. It wasn't nearly enough, but it was what they had to work with.

Truthfully, they were thankful for getting out of the lab. Since Jones hired them, they had mostly acted as glorified security guards. They also didn't appreciate getting their asses kicked by whatever monsters (aka Dave) the lab was rumored to be producing. The pay was great, but the job was nowhere near as rewarding as the detective work they had previously done. They were finally getting a chance to use their skills.

Until they scoped out the situation on the ground, they couldn't plan how the kidnapping of Sparks' daughter, Kathy

Eman, would play out. But they did come up with a general strategy on the plane, so after they grabbed her, they knew what they would do with her and how the plan would ultimately end. To put the kibosh on the investigation, they would make sure both Detectives Sparks and Lloyd understood the consequences of non-compliance. They had been detectives themselves, so they knew that both investigators had to get the message before they would effectively squelch the case. They had firsthand experience working together to sabotage investigations, and had made a lot of money doing so; at least until their luck ran out, leading them to their current situation.

*

Sunday night, Green and Jurgensen drove through Kathy Eman's neighborhood and by her house to get the lay of the land. As luck would have it, she lived across the street from a park, and there were a few homeless people living among the trees, within view of her house. Their immediate plan was to find a quiet place to get a few hours of sleep, then come back and mix Green in with the homeless encampment to keep an eye on the house. Jurgensen would park close by and wait for Green to signal that Kathy was on the move; Jones's notes indicated that she worked full-time outside the home.

The next morning, at 3:00 AM, they came back, disguised in wigs and oversized baseball hats and wearing dark sunglasses. They felt that would be enough to hide their identities if caught on any cameras or seen by a passerby. Their car was a stolen loaner, which would be returned to a local chop-shop as soon as the job was done.

Green snuck over behind the two cars parked in the driveway and put trackers on both of them. He then took up position in the park among the trees and the mostly sleeping homeless. The few who weren't sleeping were off living in a different world at that time of the morning. None of them noticed Green's presence. Jurgensen took off but remained close by.

They didn't have to wait nearly as long as they thought they might before Green spotted Kathy leaving the house and getting into one of the cars at 5:23 AM. It took Jurgensen a few minutes to get back to the house and pick Green up, but thanks to the tracker, they caught up to Kathy fairly quickly. She avoided the main roads and followed a route that took her through an industrial district, which was busy at that hour. At one point she turned down a deserted road, which eventually connected to a main arterial that she followed most of the way to her office in San Ramon.

They staked out her office the rest of the day, but she didn't come out until 3:00 PM, at which time, she went back to her car and drove home along the same route she had traveled that morning. Only surveilling her for one day meant there were lots of unknowns, but they assumed she would follow the same pattern the next day, and decided to grab her after she turned onto the deserted part of the route in the industrial district.

*

The next morning, they didn't bother staking out her house, relying solely on the tracker they had hidden on her car. At 5:24 AM, they saw Kathy's car leave her driveway as she made her way to work, just like she had the day before. As she made her way out of her neighborhood, they moved into position in the industrial district that she would shortly be driving through.

Dutifully, they saw her car pull around the corner a block away from their location. As she moved toward them, they pulled out and drove toward her from the opposite direction. At the last second, they jackknifed their car in front of her car, cutting her off and forcing her to stop. Green jumped out of his car. He ran up to her car's driver's side window and smashed it in with his gun. Pointing the gun at her, he yelled, "Get out of the car and I won't hurt you. We just want your car." Panicked, she didn't move, so he repointed the gun upwards and reassured her that he just wanted the car.

She slowly got out, and he immediately kicked her legs out from under her, sending her tumbling to the ground face first. He then held her head down on the ground, pulled out a needle, and shot her up with a sedative mixed with a little fentanyl. Green and Jurgensen then picked her up and threw her in their car's trunk. Green then pulled Kathy's car into a parking spot down an alley off the main road.

They made the fifteen-minute drive back to the neighborhood park adjacent to her house, but this time parked on the side of a road within the park, that was close to the homeless encampment overlooking her home. They held tight in their vehicle while an early morning jogger passed by, then lifted Kathy out of the trunk. Jurgensen tossed her over his shoulder and carried her the couple of hundred yards to the encampment, where he propped her up against a tree. At that time of morning, the other homeless in the area were either still asleep or too jonesed to care about what he was doing. What's more, with his disguise, Jurgensen wasn't worried about them identifying him.

Kathy had a bloody nose and dirty clothes from the fall she took when they first subdued her; he rubbed some more dirt into her hair and outfit to further make her fit in with the homeless in the area. He then ran back to the car and Green drove them away.

She would be out for hours, so they decided to reward themselves for a job well done with a good breakfast. The direction from Jones was to call to Sparks at 10:00 AM, so they had almost four hours to kill before they could fully complete the operation and get out of town.

CHAPTER 69

Niles had brought the story to his editor, Abe Cohen, as soon as Sparks left his condo. Abe might have been even more excited about the story than Niles, and Niles was over the moon with excitement. Much to his chagrin, Abe insisted on bringing in another reporter to help write the story and an analyst to help with research and contacting the sources Sparks mentioned, to get their sides of the story. Sparks had agreed to be a named source, but given the explosiveness of the accusations against Greenrock and federal law enforcement, he wanted more confirmation than just Sparks' side of the story.

Working non-stop through Monday evening, the four of them managed to put the story together and get recorded confirmations from Detectives Sparks, Lee, and Peabody that everything Sparks had told them was accurate from their perspective. Lee even confirmed there was a phone call from within Greenrock's Special Research Division headquarters that accused Greenrock of being behind the terrorist attack that killed four of its own employees. This allowed them to include that in the story too. They were careful not to accuse Greenrock outright, and only stated that Lee had received a call, and that the call originated from within Greenrock's own building. They implied Smith had something to do with the call by matching it with Waddel's statements about when Smith and Laso were terminated from the accounting department for breaking security protocols.

Niles didn't like having to share authorship of the story, but he had to admit, he would never have gotten it written in time to make the Tuesday morning edition without help; he was satisfied that Abe had listed his name first under the headline, though.

The headline was, "Ape Murders Connected to Greenrock Solutions," which everyone working on the story felt was dull, but the newsroom attorney had insisted they keep the sensationalism to a minimum to avoid potential lawsuits. Before the paper's revamp, the lawyer would have killed the story outright, so the boring headline was a small concession.

The story itself was skillfully told in an investigative style, with Dave Smith as the central character. To personalize it, they included photos of Dave and his family and the infamous images from the Jackson house. They also made sure to include pictures of the victims, including the Jackson family, Carol Waddel, and Detective Calahan, and of course, they could not run a story referring back to the ape murders without including images of the hairy beasts themselves.

CHAPTER 70

Monday morning, Sparks went into the Livermore station and continued his investigation into the Jackson murders as normal. The office vibe was weird, however; Lloyd avoided him, and Talen picked up on the tension between the detectives and kept to himself. It was just as well, since a deep feeling of dread had come over Sparks since the adrenaline from what he had done had worn off. He felt so stressed that he spent much of the day sweating and suffering with labored breath. He just wanted the article to come out and the ax to fall as quickly as possible, since the anticipation of how his colleagues would react was tearing him apart.

Mid-morning, Niles's editor, Abe Cohen, and the paper's lawyer called him to get his recorded confirmation that he was the source of the information and stood behind everything he had told Niles. He briefly hesitated, but ultimately gave the newspaper his confirmation; he couldn't chicken out now. Twenty minutes later, Detective Lee called him, telling him that a reporter from the San Jose Dispatch had called him, asking for a comment on the story Sparks had provided them. He was upset that Sparks hadn't given him a heads-up, but didn't deny his involvement in the conspiracy investigation and confirmed the parts of the story that involved him. He assumed that they had also contacted Peabody but hadn't heard from him.

Sparks told himself that he just had to make it through the day; it would all be better tomorrow; he had no control over the situation any longer, so he might as well just find peace with his decisions and let what would happen, happen. That sounded nice, but did nothing to quell his anxiety.

CHAPTER 71

After dumping Kathy Eman at the park, Green and Jurgensen dropped their car off at the chop shop, dumped the clothes and disguises they were wearing that morning, then took public transportation to downtown San Jose. The plan was to call Sparks to warn him off the case at 10:00 AM, then head to the airport for their scheduled 11:30 AM flight to Las Vegas, where they would spend a couple of days relaxing before heading back to Johnstown. Kathy would wake up sometime in the late morning and call her dad, emphasizing the point.

It was still only 7:30 AM when they walked into a restaurant to get some breakfast, so they had lots of time to kill before making their call and heading to the airport. Inside the entrance to the restaurant was a newspaper vending machine that sold the *San Jose Dispatch*. Green stopped to grab a copy of the Tuesday edition, needing something to do while they waited for 10:00 AM to come around. When he saw the headline, he mumbled "Oh shit" to himself.

"What's the matter?" Jurgensen inquired.

Green pulled the paper from the machine and showed Jurgensen the headline. "We need to call Jones and let him know," Green said.

"Let's read it first so we know what we're dealing with before pulling the boss in."

Green agreed, and they both exited the restaurant and read the long story, confirming that it directly affected their mission. They even learned some things that they didn't know; being relatively recent hires, they had no knowledge of

285

Greenrock's connection to the terrorist attack, or what Dave Smith's role was back at the lab. They knew they weren't working for an aboveboard organization, but they didn't know they were working for assassins, kidnappers, and murderers—though there were rumors. It seemed lost on them, that they themselves just kidnapped someone at the behest of the company.

This put everything they'd witnessed back at the lab in a whole new light and scared the crap out of both of them.

Instead of calling Jones, Jurgensen texted him a link to the online version of the article. Jones texted back ten seconds later, telling them to abort the mission and leave the area. It was too late to fully abort the mission, having already drugged and dumped the daughter, but they destroyed the burner phone and left for the airport, not bothering to make the scheduled call to Sparks.

CHAPTER 72

Sparks had spent the night tossing and turning, but stayed in bed until he was sure Tuesday's edition of the San Jose Dispatch was published. At 5:00 AM, he got out of bed and logged into the newspaper's website, and right there in the center of his screen, was the article, titled "Ape Murders Connected to Greenrock Solutions." His first thought was that they could have juiced things up a bit more, but as he read through the article and viewed the pictures, he realized that the story itself was juicy enough on its own.

His name was brought up as the source of the story several times in the article, while it also mentioned that both Lee and Peabody confirmed their parts from Columbus and Issaquah, respectively. Dave Smith was the star, but Sparks played big in the story too, meaning there would be hell to pay when he showed up at the station that morning; he was already resigned to his fate, so the panic he felt the day before had dissipated. In fact, he was starting to build a shield of indignation, determined to protect himself.

On his way to work, he picked up a hard copy of the newspaper. The Greenrock conspiracy was the lead story and continued on to pages four and five. He had no doubt that by that evening, all the other local and national news organizations would be reporting on the story. He walked into the station at 8:30 AM to a hostile environment. Copies of the paper were spread all around the office. Most of the officers gave him a brief look with pursed lips, probably thinking that he had somehow betrayed them. Others just avoided eye contact all together.

"You ruined my career. They don't trust me anymore," Talen said angrily the moment Sparks sat down at his desk. "They're questioning Lloyd now. Were you two in on this together?"

Sparks decided to ignore Talen's question and instead asked, "Who's questioning Lloyd?"

"The chief, captain, and Holden are all in there with him, though Holden wasn't allowed to talk. I guess you screwed her over too."

"Maybe you ought to back the fuck off a little," Sparks said, staring down Talen. He wasn't in the mood to be reprimanded by a rookie cop. He was worried about Lloyd, however; Lloyd didn't have it in him to lie about knowing what Sparks was up to.

A few minutes later, Lloyd walked back to his desk, which was adjacent to Sparks', and told Sparks that it was his turn.

"You told them, didn't you?" Sparks asked.

"I have to live with myself. They haven't taken my badge yet, but they didn't rule out the possibility either. You won't be so lucky," Lloyd stated matter-of-factly.

Sparks got up and walked across the station to the chief's office, head held high, indignation in place. If he was going down, he would go down without any apologies. The chief's secretary had him sit outside the office for five minutes before he was told to go in; the chief was treating him like a school child, which only soured his mood further. When he finally did enter the office, Chief Diaz, Captain Cook, and Lieutenant Holden were all there, watching him as he walked in. Diaz was perched behind his large gray metal desk, while Cook sat in a cheap plastic chair to the right of Diaz. Holden was made to stand in the back left corner of the office.

Holden's lips were curved down into a deep frown and she had sad eyes; she looked beaten down; she must have taken the brunt of Diaz and Cook's anger over the news article—so

288

far. Sparks felt bad for her: he considered Holden a friend and supportive boss, so he hoped his actions hadn't severed that friendship for good.

"Would you like to start?" Diaz asked Sparks.

"Yes, sir. It was my choice to go to the press. Nobody else was in on it but me."

"... and Lloyd?" Cook asked.

"I told him on Sunday that I was considering it, but that's the last I mentioned it to him. He advised against it."

Diaz continued, "Well, Detective Sparks, I read the article, so I don't have to ask you why you did it. It's pretty clear, and maybe it will result in some sort of justice for the Jackson family, but I think in the end, besides some temporary embarrassment to the Greenrock company, your actions have closed off any hope of moving our investigation to focus on them. Maybe if you had come to me before you went to Niles Price over at the Dispatch, we could have come up with a plan that didn't involve giving Greenrock a heads-up that we were on to them."

Sparks didn't agree with Diaz. He was sure that with Greenrock's political connections and influence over the FBI, their measly city police department didn't have a chance at bringing the people at Greenrock behind the Jackson murders to justice. He felt that the public pressure brought on by the story would force Greenrock's protectors to scatter like rats, fleeing a sinking ship, leaving Greenrock exposed. There was no point in arguing with Diaz about it, since it wouldn't change his fate, and he could be wrong.

"I'll just get right to the punch line. You've put in over thirty years of service to this department, and until now, you have had an impeccable record. Nobody in this department has stronger ties to the community, and you were well respected." Sparks focused on the word *were* before respected.

289

"I'm giving you the opportunity to resign effective immediately. I even had Lisa type you up a standard resignation letter." Diaz pushed the letter toward him. "You just have to sign it and turn your badge and gun over."

"What are my other choices?" Sparks asked curiously.

"I suspend you and ask you for your gun and badge. Either way, you are done being a cop. Resigning means it's less likely that you lose your pension. There may be some questions to answer from the mayor's office either way, but that will be up to you. You can pursue your public vendetta against Greenrock as a private citizen."

For Sparks, it wasn't much of a choice. Having the option to resign was a better outcome than he had expected, so he signed the letter, turned over his badge and gun, thanked Diaz and Cook, and apologized to his lieutenant. Holden just gave him a nod, leaving Sparks unsure if her sadness was due to being chewed out by the chief and captain or knowing Sparks was being kicked off the force—probably a bit of both.

When he got back to his desk, he grabbed the few personal items he had at work: some family pictures and his supercop mug. Lloyd and Talen looked at him expectantly, so he tersely said, "They let me resign." That brought a look of relief to Lloyd's face, though Talen continued to stare at him open-mouthed, not understanding the bullet Sparks had just dodged; it could have been much worse.

CHAPTER 73

Sparks decided to drink his sorrows away, so he stopped off at his favorite coffee shop; he had quit alcohol years before. At around 10:30 AM, while he was still slowly sipping his second mocha grande, his phone started vibrating in his pocket. He briefly considered ignoring it but decided to see who it was first; maybe it was somebody he actually wanted to talk to. It was Albert, his son-in-law.

"Hi, Will, sorry to bother you, but have you heard from Kathy this morning?" Albert asked.

Sparks could hear the concern in Albert's voice. "No, I haven't, Albert. Is there something wrong that I should know about?"

"Probably not, but her boss called the house and asked if Kathy was sick. She didn't show up at work this morning and I can't reach her. Her phone just goes to voicemail."

After thirty-two years in the police force, Sparks' gut immediately assumed the worst. Greenrock had gone after his family. Inwardly, he was panicking, but his experience kicked in, so he tried to step back and handle it like he would with any missing person.

"Okay, Albert, let's not draw any conclusions just yet. You can track her phone, right?"

"What conclusions? What are you getting at?"

"Nothing yet, can you track her phone or not?" Sparks said a little too loudly. People in the coffee shop were looking at him now, but they quickly went back to staring at their own phones.

"Yes, let me get to a computer."

He waited impatiently while Albert logged into his computer and his account. A few minutes later, Albert had a location in an industrial area Kathy liked to shortcut through on the way to work. Albert sent him the coordinates and they agreed to meet each other at the location.

Since his wife had died, Kathy was his world, so he left the coffee shop full of apprehension, knowing what Greenrock had done to witnesses and investigators who crossed them. He tried to comfort himself by making believe that the issue was her car had simply broken down and she'd neglected to call her husband to let him know. That wasn't like her, though.

*

Sparks drove through the industrial district and saw Albert's car parked outside the alley where the tracking application had marked the location of Kathy's vehicle. His first thought was that he should have told Albert not to touch anything until he arrived; he hoped Albert hadn't damaged any evidence he might need. He parked behind Albert's car then rounded the corner into the alley. The first thing he saw was Albert lying on the ground with two men that looked like vagrants pulling off his clothes.

"Stop! Police!" he yelled as he reached for his gun, which unfortunately was no longer in the holster he wore under his blazer—he had turned his service weapon over to the chief that morning and hadn't replaced it with his own personal revolver. No matter, the two vagrants stumbled off at hearing the word 'police', leaving Albert lying prone on the street. He ignored the departing vagrants as he lowered himself beside Albert's body and turned him over onto his back. He was unconscious and blood was flowing profusely from a wound just below his diaphragm.

Albert's pants were lying to the side, so he grabbed them and tried to use them as a tourniquet around his torso to put pressure on the wound. It slowed the flow of blood, but it wasn't enough to stop it. He immediately called 911 and identified himself as an officer attending one victim down with a stab wound to the mid-torso. He knew it would take up to ten minutes for the medics to arrive, so he leaned over Albert, doing his best to slow the flow of blood further by applying pressure over the tourniquet with his hands.

While waiting for the ambulance, he suddenly remembered his daughter and felt the need to check the car to see if she was lying injured too. Even though it meant more loss of blood for Albert, he made the move anyway and ran over to check Kathy's car. He soon realized she was not in the car or anywhere in the alley, as far as he could see.

When he got back to Albert, he noticed how pale his skin was, but also that the blood had slowed to a trickle on its own. Albert was no longer breathing. Sparks suspected his heart had stopped, so he started CPR and kept at it until sometime later when a fire department ambulance finally arrived. They did their best to revive Albert at the scene but were unsuccessful, before loading him into the ambulance to take him away to the hospital. By the time they left, two cars and four officers from the San Ramon police department had arrived.

Sparks' focus had already gone back to worrying about where his daughter was. He assumed that the vagrants were likely not involved in his daughter's disappearance, but instead had happened across her abandoned vehicle to pilfer. Albert probably confronted them and paid the price.

After trying to save Albert, he was covered in blood himself, but after determining that he wasn't injured, the police started to question him about what had happened. Albert was gone, so their questions about what transpired

293

since he entered the alleyway did not interest him. He told them that the car in the alley was his daughter's, and she was missing. Her husband and he were there to find her.

They wanted to take him into the station for further questioning, but fortunately, he still carried his Livermore police identification in his wallet. He flashed them it, and since he was a senior detective, they backed off and let him go. Still covered in Albert's blood, he drove to Kathy's home in Pleasanton to see if he could find any clues to her location there.

*

Sparks was no longer a cop, so he needed help. On the drive to his daughter's house, he called Lloyd.

"What is it, Will?" Lloyd answered his call with some irritation.

"Kathy is missing and Albert is on his way to the hospital, most likely already dead," Will blurted out, needing to get Lloyd's full and immediate attention; their issues regarding him going to the press would have to wait.

Lloyd paused before answering, "Will, I need you to back up and tell me what happened. And where are you now?"

"I'm in my car, driving to Kathy's house to see what I can find. Albert called me earlier to tell me that she hadn't shown up at work that morning and he could not reach her. He tracked her phone, and we agreed to meet at the tracking location, but when I got there, he was being accosted by two vagrants. They stabbed him. I couldn't save him. Kathy's car was there, but she was nowhere to be found. I'm almost at her house."

"Don't do anything rash. I'm on my way. Wait for me," Lloyd said before hanging up the phone. Lloyd's directives annoyed him; did he think he had already forgotten how to be a cop?

As he was pulling up to Kathy's family house, the first thing he noticed were two Pleasanton squad cars parked in the street alongside the park across from the house. One officer was standing with the vehicles, on the radio, while the others were up by the trees that hovered in an elevated area off the road. He immediately felt butterflies in his stomach, and his breathing became labored as he started to panic. He saw two of the officers on the rise, crouched over something lying on the ground; he couldn't see what they were hovering over, but he had a very bad feeling about it.

He pulled his car up behind the two police cars and ran out of the car, not even bothering to close the door. The cop on the radio yelled something at him as he made his way up the hill, but he didn't hear him. When he got up the hill, he saw that the person on the ground was his daughter, Kathy. He tried to run toward her, but two of the three officers with her were ready and blocked his way. When he tried to fight through them, they managed to slam him face first on the ground and cuff him.

He started yelling at them that the woman on the ground was his daughter, but they weren't listening. They were just holding him on the ground and telling him to calm down. To the officers, he probably looked suspicious: covered in blood and completely disheveled from his attempt to save Albert. He was also screaming like a lunatic.

Finally, one officer took his wallet out from his pocket and saw that he was a Livermore police detective, so they started to treat him less like a suspect and lightened up their grip on him. Lloyd also showed up, flashing his detective badge, asking what was going on and vouching for Sparks. He quickly let the cops know that the woman on the ground was Sparks' daughter, which further defused the situation.

They uncuffed Sparks and permitted him to kneel beside his daughter, while the third officer continued to administer CPR; during all the commotion, the officer had never lost his focus on trying to save Kathy.

The Pleasanton police had received a report that a woman in the park had been found unresponsive, which was unfortunately a common call they received regarding the small homeless encampments that popped up throughout the park. They showed up and administered Narcan, but the woman did not recover, so they called an ambulance and started CPR. From her state of dress and general healthy physical appearance, they guessed she wasn't a resident of the camp herself, but it wasn't uncommon for housed people to show up at the park to satisfy their addictions too.

As they were explaining this to Lloyd and Sparks, the ambulance finally showed up to take Kathy to the hospital, but they all knew she was already dead. Lloyd drove Sparks to the hospital, following behind the ambulance. Sparks just sat in the passenger seat in stunned silence, almost catatonic. At that moment, Lloyd was simply Will's friend; any discussion about how this was tied to the Jackson murders or Greenrock would have to wait.

CHAPTER 74

Jones was sitting at his kitchen table, sipping coffee and reading the local paper, when he got the call from Cooper that he needed to immediately make his way to the lab. He tried to ask Cooper what it was about, but Cooper hung up right after giving his order. In the years they had worked together, Cooper had never called him at home, let alone ordered him into the office; most days he would already be in the office at seven in the morning. Despite the demand, he had to spend some time looking into what happened before facing Cooper.

He first reached out to a member of his security team who was at the lab, working the early morning shift. The guard said everything was normal there, as far as she could tell. He started to dial Keeps' number, but then remembered that he was conveniently removed from all the drama at the lab, stashed in the jungle with his furries, over twenty-seven hundred miles away in Columbia. When he went onto the internet and searched 'Greenrock Solutions Special Research Division', he had more luck. Toward the bottom of the first page of results was a link to an article published that morning by the *San Jose Dispatch*.

He read through the story and knew things were going to get really bad for the lab and himself in particular. Sparks had launched a preemptive strike, and Jones didn't see it coming; that was despite monitoring Sparks and the police investigations being in his purview. He got in his car and made his way to work, not knowing if he would be terminated before the day was through.

In his concern for his own wellbeing, he forgot all about his men, who were likely just getting started on the kidnapping and drugging of Spark's daughter. He was scared, which was a feeling he hadn't experienced in a very long time.

*

Jones walked into the conference room at 7:35 AM to find Cooper and Keeps already discussing the situation—Keeps on video via the satellite link.

"Nice of you to show up, Bill," Cooper spat out sarcastically. He only ever referred to Jones by his last name, so using his first name was an indication that he was angry with him or worried; today, Cooper was both of these things.

"Your most important function is to manage our relationships with law enforcement. What is your strategy for getting us out of this mess?" Cooper demanded, then, like a child, crossed his arms, waiting for a response. When something went wrong, Cooper's modus operandi was to deflect blame from himself. It was always a failure in someone else's function, which always begged the question, in Jones's eyes, as to what Cooper's function in the lab actually was.

Jones's natural tendency toward disdain was starting to make its way forward past his worry from earlier in the morning. Cooper's contemptuous attitude was bringing Jones back to himself; he was ready to fight.

"When the fuckups resulting from your greedy fingers start to multiply, the mess eventually becomes too big to fully contain," Jones shot back.

"What the fuck does that mean?" Cooper said pointedly. Keeps was just looking into his laptop camera with a smirk on his face, no doubt interested in how Jones's line of attack would play out.

"The furries aren't toys that can be used whenever one of you in the executive suite needs another payday or a politician friend needs a favor. We are too exposed in too many places and that has come back to fuck us in the ass. Sparks did something unpredictable, but if we touch enough people, eventually someone will do something we could not have expected."

"You think pointing the finger at the people who pay your salary is going to save you?" Cooper said, forcing a little laugh. "Your job is to anticipate what those someones, such as Sparks, will do. So you admit you failed at your job?"

Jones recognized Cooper's extemporaneous remark as the threat it was, and threatened back. "No, what will save me is my knowledge of the fiends you're breeding and what you've done with them, and who else might know that too if you decide to throw me in Keeps' ape exhibit," Jones said, excluding his own part in the lab's evil doing. "... and what are you smiling about, Alan, this all started when your monkeys forgot to kill the boy."

Cooper and Jones's sword fight was pulling the meeting off-track, so Keeps took it upon himself to get the meeting back on track.

"Boys, while all this is all very cathartic, why don't we use this time to actually come up with a plan to solve the problem. I would like to reenter civilization someday. I imagine that those executives in the c-suite you mentioned are back at headquarters thinking up a way to sweep us under the rug. Let's make sure that doesn't happen."

Cooper begrudgingly acknowledged that Keeps was correct to assume that if corporate shut the lab down, they would all be in the same boat. HEL wasn't the only organization Greenrock had at their disposal to clean up problems; when it came to *quietly* making problems disappear, HEL wasn't even the best, which was evident given their recent track record.

Cooper removed his focus from Jones. "At least the few that know about what the lab really does. Except for the CEO and a couple of his close advisors, what we do is unknown by most within the company. But there are quite a few people in positions of power within the government and industry who do know of our services. They might be our biggest problem if they feel our miscues could expose them...

"... and the newspaper story isn't just a public perception problem. My office has already fielded calls from two other VPs in the company asking me if the article was true. Our secrets are out, both outside and inside the company now."

"We need to have a plan in place for liquidating the whole program, if that becomes our only option down the line," Jones said.

"... and exactly what would you propose we *liquidate*?" Keeps asked pointedly.

"Dave Smith to start. He's their link to Greenrock. No person, no problem. We should have a plan in place to dispatch of all the furries," Jones said.

"What about the rest of the personnel? There are a lot of people in this lab who have probably seen the article and could betray us in the future," Cooper added.

Given most of the personnel with firsthand knowledge of the furry program were mercenaries under Keeps' command, he took offense to the suggestion. "Any betrayal will not come from any of my people. I would be more worried about our non-military staff. They don't have the training and discipline my people have."

"That is understood, and nobody is proposing we eliminate your team or anyone else who works here," Cooper said while looking at Jones. "But the furries themselves are the proof that Greenrock was involved in murdering the Jackson family."

"I think we can agree, then, we must have a contingency in place to eliminate Dave and the rest of the furries. We can't eliminate the entire medical staff, but Dr. Danzel is too much of a wildcard to keep around if we make this decision," Jones said.

Cooper looked at Keeps. "We'll sort things up here on our end while you remain in Columbia with your apes for a little longer. Find something to keep them occupied. Jones, you grab Danzel and lock him up immediately. I don't want him leaving the lab until things settle down or we terminate the program."

An outsider would have left the meeting feeling that all three men were in agreement, but the opposite was actually true. Jones and Cooper were lying to each other and Keeps. Despite what was said, Keeps assumed that the other two were making plans to kill him and his mercenaries along with the furries. Jones assumed that Cooper would do all he could to blame the whole problem on him. For his part, Cooper just wanted to get out of the situation alive, he didn't care if that meant everyone else in the lab didn't.

Jones had no intention of detaining Danzel. Danzel was the heart of the lab—in many ways he was the lab. If Stirling only spared one person, it would be Danzel. He needed Danzel as an ally and knew that he could be a good ally to Danzel also. Not that Danzel cared about or paid attention to office politics, his mind was firmly planted in his work building genetic mutants.

*

Jones left the meeting feeling a sense of loss. He had dedicated the last decade of his life to HEL, first as one of CEO

Stirling's assistants and then as its director, and now that was coming to an end. Despite referring to the termination of the lab as a contingency, they all knew closing it down was inevitable now that three separate local police departments were closing in on them. With the connection between the Jackson family killings and Greenrock, and some of their other misdoings exposed by the *San Jose Dispatch* for all the public to read, their backers in Washington would all start covering their own asses and demand their own investigations into Greenrock. He imagined Cooper being hauled into a congressional hearing in the near future. The only question was when and how Greenrock would do away with them—them, but not him.

Jones's priority was to protect himself. Politicians and senior company executives loved to push the blame for their own failures down the line to the people who worked for them and did their bidding. If they tried to point the finger at him, he would point it straight back at them. If they tried to take him down, he'd expose everything, and everyone associated with the lab. Dead or alive, he'd release every document, image, and video he had amassed from the start of the furry program to the present. Jones knew Cooper would try to make him the fall guy, but he had several trump cards that would protect him. Cooper had no idea who he was really dealing with.

He also assumed Keeps was smart enough to protect himself and his team of mercenaries. He actually didn't care if Keeps ultimately took the fall for the program, but he knew if it came to that, Keeps would have to take the fall postmortem. He could implicate Jones in an effort to protect himself.

While immersed in thought, contemplating what moves he might have to make in the future, his phone buzzed: it was a text from Jurgensen. With all the morning's excitement, he had forgotten about the mission to intimidate Detective Sparks and force him to back off the case. Sparks' move to take the story to the press changed the calculus, now that the old strategy of covering up their link to the Jackson murders had failed. The new mission was to escape blame and potential death, and abducting Sparks' daughter ran counter to that.

The message was simply a link to the online *San Jose Dispatch* article. He texted back to abort the mission and leave town. Even if he had thought about it sooner, the mission was already in full swing by the time he received Cooper's call and discovered the news story. Maybe this would still work out in his favor. After Sparks' daughter was back safely in his arms, he might realize the cost of pushing further with his investigation was too much and disavow the story and claim he was seduced by a wild conspiracy theory. Maybe he could push Sparks in that direction while the scare of almost losing his daughter was still fresh in his mind.

CHAPTER 75

Cooper walked back into his office suite on the fourth floor of the division headquarters, above the underground lab. The suite consisted of four rooms. The first was a small lobby staffed only by his junior admin, whose job it was to greet guests, take calls, and do whatever his senior administrator, Sally Hastings, told her to do. Off to the side of the lobby was a private conference room where Cooper held his meetings. Beyond the lobby was a large open space that seated his staff, including Hastings and two other long-time assistants.

The newest member of his team was Kendall Cooper, his nephew. Kendall had always been something of a disappointment to the family, but in the last half a year he'd come into his own, and now he was finally showing true initiative. He was a little skeptical when Kendall had asked him the week before to increase his responsibilities at work, but he made the request to him in front of his brother. He loved his brother and knew how much giving Kendall a chance would mean to him, so he said yes. In the last week, Kendall had surprised him and was a model employee, doing what he was told and even taking some initiative and anticipating his needs on occasion.

Kendall was also the only staff member who was aware of the lab, which allowed him to help in ways none of his other subordinates could. It was actually Kendall who called him early that morning, telling him about the article. He was extremely grateful for that heads-up, since fifteen minutes later, the CEO of Greenrock, Philip Stirling, called him, and the call would have gone much worse if Stirling had been the one to wake him with the awful news that morning. He walked through the common space and gestured for Kendall to join him in his office.

Cooper sat down in his black ergonomic chair and gestured for Kendall to take a seat on his couch.

"I want to thank you for calling me this morning to let me know about the news article. That's the type of initiative I need from you."

"Thank you, Uncle Shane ... I mean, Mr. Cooper." His uncle insisted that he never refer to him as uncle at work. "I recognized Dave Smith in the article as the person I had to monitor when I worked down in the lab."

"Yes, I'm assuming you read the article?" Kendall nodded affirmatively. "Then you can imagine the pressure this puts on me and the rest of the organization. Getting through this is going to be hard and require some tough decisions."

"What type of decisions?" Kendall asked.

"That's for later. For the next couple of days while I'm in Maryland, I need you to be my eyes and ears around here. Anything that you hear relating to the situation in this office or down in the lab, I need you to report to me. Tell me everything. I'll determine whether it is important or not. Understand?"

"You can count on me, sir," Kendall confidently stated.

"Good. Your first assignment is to get a progress report from your former boss, Jones, every two hours."

Kendall looked unsure of himself. "Jones won't like that."

"I don't give a fuck. He probably won't be able to tell you much, since you don't have the clearance, but sending you down there to pester him reminds him who's boss."

"Okay," Kendall said with a slight crack in his voice.

"Don't worry. Jones's bark is worse than his bite."

Kendall wasn't sure that was true. Having spent some time around Jones, he had seen some of the things that went on down there, but his uncle was his new boss, so he would have to buck up and go harass Jones.

Cooper had a plane to catch to Dulles. He was ordered by Stirling to attend a meeting in the CEO's office in Potomac that evening. There was no reason Cooper had to update the CEO on the situation in person, other than Stirling's need to chew him out personally. This was his reward for giving Jones and Keeps so much autonomy. After they shut down the lab and dissolved the furries and Dr. Danzel—literally—he would have to figure out how to contain Keeps and Jones.

That would all have to wait until he got back from Maryland. He didn't put it past Stirling to send him back home in a box or simply make him disappear. Stirling had approved the founding of the lab and helped forge its direction into the money-making terrorist menace to society it had become. Stirling was as cold-hearted and scheming as Jones, but with a lot more power. Twenty-five years prior, it was Arthur Stirling who led the company, but he had it on good authority that Arthur's death, which led to his son Philip taking the reins of the company, was patricide.

CHAPTER 76

Jones was sitting at his desk monitoring Kendall's progress as he made his way off the elevator at level U1 and walked toward his office. Kendall's arrival was an obvious and clumsy attempt by Cooper to assert his authority over the lab, but Jones had his own plan, and it involved Kendall.

Kendall knocked on the office door, and Jones immediately waved him in.

"Look at you, my boy. In a week, you went from working the night shift to being your uncle's lapdog. What can I do for you?"

Kendall was shaking. Looking at the ground, he started mumbling out something that Jones couldn't understand.

"Speak up and look at me when you talk," Jones commanded.

Kendall snapped to. "Mr. Cooper needs an update on what you are doing about the situation," he stuttered.

Jones decided to ignore the request and ask his own questions. "What do you know about what goes on down here in the lab?"

"Not much, sir. I just watched the prisoners." That wasn't entirely true. In the last week, he had logged into his uncle's account multiple times and found files that detailed exactly what they were doing in the lab—the password was written on a sticky note in the front drawer of his uncle's desk.

Jones took a different tack. "Furries. Do they give you nightmares?"

Kendall hesitated, rocked back and forth, and looked down at the ground while answering, "I don't know what you mean, sir."

"Tell me one more lie and I'll drag your ass to their cage and feed you to them!" Jones said forcibly.

Kendall knew that wasn't an idle threat, since one of the files he read detailed the furries' response to two former members of Jones's security personnel being thrown into their cage. "No, I mean, they don't give me nightmares. The collars keep them in control."

"... and your uncle told you this?" Kendall didn't answer but kept staring at the floor. Jones was fishing for information at this point. It surprised him that Kendall had knowledge of the furry program. Did Cooper tell him, or was it common knowledge among all of his staff? It was a small lab, so what did he expect.

Jones softened his voice: "The furry program is highly confidential. Your uncle can get in a lot of trouble for divulging that information to you."

"He didn't tell me anything, I swear!" Kendall said, actually looking Jones in the eyes when he said it.

"You were poking around someplace you weren't supposed to then. Is that what you are telling me, if it wasn't your uncle's betrayal?" The kid looked down again and pursed his lips; Jones thought he had his answer. "Look, I don't really care what you've done, and your uncle and I have worked together for a long time. I don't want to see him get in trouble either. I do need to know what is happening upstairs, so I'll keep your secret if you help me, alright?"

Kendall looked back up, seemingly relieved—it was hard to tell, though, since he was such an effete kid.

"Your Uncle Cooper wants you to spy on me, so you'll report back to him what I tell you to report, and you'll keep me abreast of everything you observe upstairs. To do my job properly and save this company, I need to know what the executives, like your uncle, are doing and planning. It may seem like you are being disloyal, but trust me, you are helping him in the long run. I need to hear you agree to my offer."

"Yes, sir ... I agree."

"Good, so give me your first report."

"He asked me to come down here every couple of hours to get a progress report from you. I'm his eyes and ears while he is in Maryland at company headquarters."

That was interesting to Jones. Corporate didn't waste any time in bringing Cooper in; he wondered if he would ever see him again. If they killed Cooper, that would be a sure signal that the rest of the people in the lab's days were numbered too.

"You give me those reports on what you are hearing in his office to me too. Furthermore, if you lose contact with him and can't make your reports, I want to know that too. Your uncle is in danger, so I need your help keeping tabs on him. Now go!"

"What about your progress report?"

"Just make something up," Jones said as he waved Kendall away.

CHAPTER 77

Cooper arrived at Stirling's office on the top floor of Greenrock Solution's company headquarters in Potomac, Maryland. When he first arrived, Stirling's secretary told him that the CEO was running a little behind and would be with him shortly. After waiting for two hours in an uncomfortable chair in the lounge, he got up the nerve to walk back into Stirling's office suite and ask his secretary how much longer it would be.

When he walked in, the secretary was gone and the lights were out. He walked over to Stirling's office door and tried to turn the handle, but the door was locked. The lights then flickered on, and when he turned around, a security guard was standing at the entrance to the suite.

"This is a private space. You can't be here," the guard said.

"I have a meeting with Mr. Stirling. Where is everybody?" Cooper asked.

The guard talked into a microphone on his shoulder, asking for immediate backup. "Sir, please calmly step out of the office. I need to see some ID right now." The guard pulled out a billy club, apparently expecting Cooper to give him trouble.

"Do you know who I am?" Cooper stated presumptuously. "I'm vice president of the Special Research Division. You have no right to treat me like this."

"Sir, I will ask you only one more time to leave this office and show me your identification." The guard said it calmly, but smacked the club against his hand a couple of times to let Cooper know that he was serious.

Flummoxed, Cooper left the office and was greeted by three more club-wielding guards in the lobby. He pulled his wallet out of his pocket and then immediately dropped it on the ground; his whole body was shaking with embarrassment and anger. He finally managed to pull his company ID out of his wallet and hand it to the guard who had requested it. The guard then scanned the card with his smartphone and carefully studied the information on his screen.

"I've been directed to confiscate your company ID, credit card, phone, and keys to the company car you borrowed, and then escort you out of the building." He then held out his hand, waiting for Cooper to hand over the four items.

Cooper looked over the four guards: three were holding their clubs and one had a taser. He determined that resisting further would be hazardous to his health, since the security personnel had obviously been directed to treat him roughly if he didn't cooperate. He handed over his company credentials, phone, and keys, then let them lead him out of the building. They left him on the curb and then walked away.

Left with no keys to drive back to the airport and no phone to call for a ride, he started walking across the large parking lot fronting the building. Maybe he could find a bar and have a drink, then call for a ride to the airport from there. He had already decided that he wasn't going to stay the night. He just wanted to get home to his family and possibly warn Jones that corporate was cleaning house and his job would probably be in danger too. That could wait until tomorrow; warning Jones was way down on his to-do list, after having a few drinks, getting home to his family, and sorting out his own priorities.

He had made his way across the parking lot and was walking on the drive out of the campus when a car drove up beside him. It was an electric vehicle, so he didn't notice it coming up from behind him until it had almost passed him and came to a stop. A man opened the door, slipped out of the driver's seat, and walked a few steps toward him.

"Can I help you?" Cooper asked.

The man continued to walk right up to Cooper. Cooper took a couple of steps back and raised his hands in a defensive posture to try to push him back. The man then kicked Cooper in the knee, breaking it, causing him to fall to the ground and land on his side. He was in shock from the sharp pain in his leg and the thought that someone would attack him. Before he could react further, the assailant kneed him in the back, then pushed Cooper onto his stomach. The man then hugged his head with one arm, his face mashed into the man's inner elbow, the man's hand squeezing into the side of Cooper's head. He then felt the other hand make its way across the other side of his head, both hands, along with an arm squeezing more tightly. He briefly wondered if the attacker was going to try and suffocate him, before feeling a sharp twist to his neck and hearing an accompanying crack. Cooper then thought no more, passing out from the shock of his head being quickly turned almost one-hundred-and-eighty degrees in the wrong direction.

The assailant, a long-time member of Stirling's security detail and trusted friend, carefully lifted Cooper up off the ground, placed him in the trunk of his car, and drove off. Cooper would never be heard from or seen again, only existing in the memories of the few people who loved him.

CHAPTER 78

After leaving Jones's office, Kendall went back up to his desk and spent the rest of the afternoon poking around the lab's systems using Cooper's credentials. His uncle had left him a message to wait for his call later that evening, so being only early afternoon, he had nothing else to do for the rest of the day.

He was no longer interested in looking over lab invoices and meeting notes. He wanted to understand how the security system that monitored and governed the furries worked. After a couple of hours of digging, he found the PowerShell code that implemented the controls for the collars.

He paid particular attention to two of the cmdlets—small scripts of code that execute a task. The first was a command to turn a collar off, and the second was to unhook the collar. Removing a collar meant sending a command to turn it off, then a second to signal it to unlatch. He then found other commands that directed the collars to apply different types of stimuli to the person wearing it.

Finally, he found a command named "Kill-Subject", which called on two other cmdlets. The first was a cmdlet that initiated a shock to the subject at its top setting, and the second directed the collar to tighten itself around the subject's neck. The kill command signaled the collar to disable the furry with a powerful shock while choking it to death at the same time. The thought of Jones or his uncle killing Dave in that way infuriated him. He would never allow that to happen, now that he had access to the controls.

Kendall changed the kill code to call on two different cmdlets: the command to turn the collar off and the second to unlatch it. He then deployed the newly written "Kill-Subject" cmdlet to the collar control service and sat back in his chair, satisfied. He imagined the surprise on Jones's face when he hit the kill button on his remote and the collar unlatched and fell off Dave's neck instead; it made him giggle.

By the time he finished, it was 9:00 PM, and he was the only one still in the office. He didn't expect to have had to wait so long for the call from his uncle and started to worry. Jones specifically told him to give him a report if his uncle stopped calling in, so maybe this was a sign that he was in danger. He was tired and hungry and didn't want to face Jones again, so he sent him an email, indicating that Mr. Cooper had not called him to ask for a report, as expected. He then packed up his things and left for home.

CHAPTER 79

Stalking their human prey and hunting was fun, but it didn't fully satisfy the furries' bloodlust. Dave, acting as the furries' representative, proposed sowing a little chaos back at the jungle drug lab. The traffickers regularly sent out patrols of militia to walk the perimeter of the lab at regular intervals. Many times, these soldiers would walk within feet of the hiding furries, completely unaware of the deadly danger right under them. The soldiers were more concerned with avoiding insects and snakes than some mythical apelike creatures sent by the U.S. government to kill them. The furries wanted to start culling the narcos and blowing off a little steam in the process.

Keeps heard Dave's proposal and gave him and the furries the green light to start eliminating the traffickers, with the condition that they only eliminate no more than one patrol a day and do it quietly. He wasn't ready to start a full-scale war just yet, given that he wanted to keep his position as long as possible, and destroying the drug lab would necessitate them packing up and moving to a new location. Once the traffickers' brethren started to disappear, it would be only a matter of time before they started to aggressively search for the source of the threat. He didn't know if that would be a couple of days or a couple of weeks—though he assumed days were more likely.

He had to weigh the danger of harassing the jungle lab with the danger of living with eleven bored fiends. As an officer, he knew that one of the keys to good discipline was keeping the soldiers occupied. With the camp fully built and plentiful quantities of food already obtained, there wasn't a lot for the furries to do, other than play with the narcos. Out in the jungle, he needed his entire team kept in good spirits and working as one. He could always resort to using the collars to demand compliance from the furries, but out on mission, that wasn't the ideal way to gain their trust and loyalty—if loyalty to Keeps was something even possible. He did know that HEL was crumbling beneath him; Jones had told him that Stirling had fired Cooper and seemingly erased all records that he had ever worked for Greenrock; he also suspected that Cooper had been terminated, literally, as he was no longer able to contact him.

Like it or not, Keeps now needed the furries more than they needed him. His biggest fear at the moment wasn't what would happen to himself or Jones, but the other six members of his team still back in Johnstown. He would give Jones a few more hours to try and locate Cooper, but if it became apparent that they had eliminated Cooper and started their liquidation of HEL, he would make the call to order the six members of his team still up in Johnstown to disperse and go into hiding.

CHAPTER 80

Isla, Nu, and Hamit were the first furries out on patrol after Keeps had given them the go ahead to start eliminating the traffickers out on patrol. The three of them lay in wait near a spot where they knew a patrol would walk by that time of day. They squatted perfectly still in the thick vegetation, brimming with excitement over the possibility of killing their first victims of the trip. All eleven furries equally felt the excitement in their hive mind, so the three furries on patrol would satisfy all of their blood lusts.

Right on time, they spotted four traffickers walking in a single file through the jungle toward their position. Their rifles hung loosely from straps on their shoulders as they were busy gabbing and using their hands to swat away mosquitos. The furries suspected the patrol wouldn't even notice them if they were standing straight up and waving their arms. They had no notion of the danger they were in.

They let the traffickers continue on their way until they were adjacent to where the furries were squatting. The furries then leapt the ten feet from their cover to the unsuspecting narcos and fell upon them. Isla and Nu fell onto the first two traffickers, while Hamit, with arms spread wide, took down the last two. Isla slammed her victim face down onto the muddy trail, and immediately reached under and pulled up hard on the victim's chest while pushing on his lower back, breaking his spine. That disabled the man but did not kill him, so Isla calmly held the man's face down into the mud until he suffocated.

Nu wasn't in the mood for killing her prey so cleanly. She tore through the woman's belly with her fingers and gently pulled out the trafficker's intestines before sitting her up against a tree. Nu saw her father murdered by government troops in her home country of Miramar in a similar way back when she was a small child.

Hamit, flying through the air with his arms outstretched, grabbed the face of the man in front and the back of the head of the man behind, and bashed their heads together with all his strength. He managed to do all that before hitting the ground himself. When he and the traffickers did land on the ground, his two victims were already dead, their sculls fully bashed in.

In seconds, the attack was over, and the furries were standing tall with their chests out and their heads looking toward the sky, silently howling with joy. Back at the camp, the seven other beasts all joined in, much to the dismay of Keeps and the mercenaries, who were taken by surprise at the furries' sudden change in demeanor. Bonobo also joined in, but lifted his arms in the air and did a little jig, while yelling "That's how you do it."

"Dave, what the fuck is going on?" Keeps yelled.

"Another successful hunt, boss. Another successful hunt," Dave said with a big smile. Keeps finally got it.

Back on the trail, Isla, Nu, and Hamit loaded their prey onto their backs and ran deep into the woods away from the drug lab and their own camp to the spot by the river where Bonobo and Lud captured Jumbo. There were seven caimans, all sunning in the mud by the shore, so the three furries tossed their prey right onto the caimans' backs.

The effect was as expected, and the caimans started tearing at the bodies, ensuring that the patrol would fully disappear from the world. Unfortunately for the woman with the distended gut, she was still alive when two caimans started to play tug of war with her body. She did finally die when they managed to pull her in half, each caiman sharing in their unexpected afternoon snack.

CHAPTER 81

Rodriquez was almost through with her second week of babysitting duty. At first, she couldn't stand the thought of taking care of a kid, given that she didn't like children. It wasn't only that: stuck alone with Kate in the safe house, she was disconnected from the action. Four of her counterparts were on a mission in the jungles of Columbia, tasked with taking out a jungle drug lab, while she was stuck back home making sandwiches for a pre-teen. She was a highly trained soldier; this wasn't right!

Thankfully, after the first week, Kate settled down, resigned to her fate. She stopped sitting in the corner of her room, crying, and being in a general somber mood all the time. She still wasn't pleasant to be around, with her snotty attitude, but Rodriquez greatly preferred that to melancholy. Sometimes she even admired Kate's fighting spirit and attitude. She wasn't much different at her age.

Rodriquez was sitting at the kitchen table with Kate, eating lunch, when she heard a buzz from the device she used for private communications with Keeps, indicating a new message received. She carefully read the message and felt a moment of concern, but also gratitude; she would finally get to leave this place and go back on mission.

"Pack up your stuff in that small pack in your closet. If it doesn't fit in the pack, it stays here. We leave in five minutes."

"What are you talking about? I'm not going anywhere. Are we going to see my mom?" Kate babbled with attitude and then hopefulness.

"I don't have time to explain, but we're in danger. If you stay here, you'll die. I told you, some bad people killed your mom and brother, and now they've found us. If we don't move, they'll get you too. Go!" Rodriquez ordered.

On the third day of Kate's confinement, Rodriquez got so sick of Kate asking for her mom that she made up a story about bad people who had gone to their house and killed her mom and brother. In her story, she had gotten there just in time to save Kate, and now they were in hiding. It was actually close to the truth, if only she hadn't left out the part that it was her comrades that had killed Kate's family. Given that she was a soldier and following orders, she could envision that it was really Keeps who had killed Kate's family; she was just a soldier. In truth, she didn't know what happened to Jan and Mickey and was assuming they were dead. She hoped it would also bond Kate to her and make her more compliant; that part of the plan was still a work in progress.

Kate gathered her pack and was back in the kitchen in under two minutes. By then, Rodriquez had mostly packed up her stuff, which included two pistols and lots of ammunition, plus some food and money. They left through the backyard and into the forest adjacent to the back of the house. From there they followed a path two miles through the woods to a parking lot, where there was a car stashed for them. Keeps always made sure his people had multiple exit options if things went wrong and an escape became necessary.

Two hours later, they crossed into Pennsylvania, where they switched cars and continued on to a second safe house, known only to Keeps, in rural West Virginia. There she learned that her five other comrades who were not on mission in Columbia had all safely got out of Johnstown and away from the lab. Two of those comrades would be joining her and Kate in the West Virginia safe house. She was not privy to the location of the other three mercenaries, or if Keeps and her four counterparts in Columbia were safe—or at least safer than earlier that day.

She looked over at Kate, feeling a sudden sensation of warmth. This surprised her, but she had a desire to protect Kate, beyond what was required of her standing orders from Keeps. The message to leave Johnstown and go underground didn't specifically call for her to take Kate with her, but her last orders were to watch over and care for Kate, so she would continue with that mission until ordered by Keeps not to.

CHAPTER 82

The drug traffickers' response to losing a patrol came early the next morning, when they sent out seven soldiers, heavily armed with AK-47 rifles. Keeps sent out George, Anne, and Dell to keep tabs on the soldiers, but ordered them not to engage. The soldiers quickly followed the missing patrol's route to the point where the attack occurred the previous day. The signs of the struggle, including some blood, had not been fully absorbed back into the rainforest, so the soldiers were able to establish that the patrol was violently attacked and not simply lost in the jungle.

One of the soldiers seemed to be an expert in jungle tracking and was able to direct the rest of his squad in the direction the furries had carried their victims. Over the next couple of hours, they slowly made their way toward the caimans' abode by the river.

The soldiers' march to the river alarmed Keeps, since there they would find a well-tilled path back to his own camp. He needed more time to break camp and retreat to a new location, so he called the eight furries still at camp together to give them their new orders. When they were assembled, he looked at Lud and told him to relay to his team out in the field to take up position around one-quarter mile from the river to set up an ambush of the seven soldiers. He then further ordered Lud to send in four more furries to supplement the team already out in the field.

"Sorry, boss, but my mates didn't bring their walkie-talkies. How are they supposed to get the message?" Dave asked.

"We don't have time for games, Dave. I know you guys communicate with each other telepathically or something like that. If we don't stop that unit, they'll find the path that Jumbo forged back here and radio the discovery back to their camp. By tonight, we might have a whole platoon at our door."

Hold position a quarter mile from river and wait for back-up. Frank, Isla, Nu, Jason, go. Move to position. Kill patrol. Can't wait.

Frank, Isla, Nu, and Jason immediately left the camp and made their way to the ambush spot approximately two and a half miles away. The rough terrain would slow them down, so they didn't expect to arrive at their destination for at least fifteen minutes; just before the soldiers got there.

Keeps gave the remaining furries a nod, indicating that they were dismissed, then retreated to his shelter to keep tabs on the furries' progress via their collars. Twenty minutes after first giving the order to set up an ambush, the seven furries were in place and the soldiers were walking into the trap. The soldiers would have lost even if they were ambushed by just a single furry, but the seven furries ended the battle in seconds. It wasn't really much of a battle: the seven furries jumped out of their hiding spots and simultaneously hit each of the seven soldiers. Unusually, they did not get creative, and all ripped out the sides of each of the soldier's throats. They then carried the dead to the river and dumped them in before making their way back to camp.

*

Keeps gathered his four mercenaries and eleven furries together to give them all new orders. He had decided it was time to be straight with his team and tell them what was happening back in Johnstown and what that meant for them, hidden away in the jungle. It was obvious, to both human and furry, that Keeps was not his usual self: he seemed less focused and more pre-occupied than usual.

"Men and ladies, it is time we make our retreat. I want all of our structures disassembled and scattered before nightfall. Tomorrow, before dawn, we'll finish packing up and then hike to the hub to disassemble it. Then we'll retreat into the jungle, away from here, and determine our next move."

"Boss, why don't we just go back to plan A and take out the jungle lab? It's not like you or the lab to give up on a mission," Dave said. Gill Turner voiced his agreement with Dave, not wanting to abandon the mission. "... Oh, and I appreciate you referring to us monsters as men and ladies too. You must be in a real bind."

Keeps smiled at Dave's attempt at humor. "There is no mission any longer. Greenrock has decided to terminate HEL, including us. We are on our own, and they will be hunting for us."

"What about the rest of the team, back in Johnstown?" Wallis blurted out.

"Earlier today, I gave them the order to go underground and wait for further instructions. I'm hopeful they all made it out safely. If we are going to make it out safely, I need all of your cooperation, that includes furries."

"Well of course, boss, you still have us leashed. You want us to trust you and cooperate, maybe you should trust us and remove the collars," Dave said.

"That order can only be done from the lab. I can't remove them, but when the hub is taken offline, nobody at the lab will be able to control them—at least temporarily."

"What does that mean?" Dave asked.

"It means Greenrock and the U.S. government will be hunting for us. If they get within five-hundred miles of these collars, they'll be able to re-establish their link to them and kill you. After we disable the hub, we'll have time to try to figure out how to remove them without setting them off. I promise, that will be a priority as soon as we're away from the drug lab. You'll have to trust me on that."

We don't trust him. Kill them as soon as the hub is dissembled. Agreed.

"We'll see," Dave voiced noncommittally to both Keeps and the other furries in his mind. Bonobo didn't agree with his band. He believed Keeps was sincere; for all Keeps' faults, he wasn't shifty like Jones. But the others in the hive disagreed or didn't care if he was telling the truth.

CHAPTER 83

Jones woke up to a beeping noise in the background. Still groggy, it took him a little while to remember where he was. He reached over to turn off his alarm and then proceeded to fall on the floor. The shock knocked him back to his senses, and he remembered that he had fallen asleep on the couch of his office. The beeping was his perimeter alarm warning him that someone was making their way up to the first underground floor on the elevator.

When he got up and looked at his monitor, he realized that the intruders were actually coming up from the underground garage on U4. They had access to the garage, usually reserved for senior HEL staff and the vehicles used to transport the furries. As the intruders made their way off the elevator and toward his office, he could see that there were four armed men, plus Philip Stirling, Greenrock Solutions' CEO.

Jones hopped up and down a few times and then did a few quick stretches to knock the cobwebs out and bring himself back to full alertness. He then sat in his desk chair and waited for management to arrive. He was expecting them.

The first man to enter his office was one of Stirling's armed security guards. His door was pushed open, and one guard slid in, knees bent, eyes forward, with his gun pointing out in front of him, ready for an ambush that was destined never to materialize. Following the first guard was another guard who scanned the opposite side of the room with his gun out in front. Satisfied there were no hidden threats in the office, both pointed their guns at Jones, then called back to their compatriots that all was clear.

Stirling immediately walked into his office, cane in hand, a little hunched over, and directed the two guards to stand down and wait outside the office. Stirling was starting to get up there in age and was looking a little more gray than the last time he saw him, Jones thought. As Stirling's guards were leaving, there was some commotion outside Jones's office. Jones made a gesture to let the new interloper in; Stirling gave one of his guards a nod, indicating that it was alright, and Big Freddy stumbled into his office.

"Sir, I saw these guys coming toward your office on the security camera and thought you needed some help."

"... and what help do you think you could provide, given that they already broke into my office before you got here?" Jones asked.

Freddy didn't have an answer for that, so he just stood there looking dumb and shrugged his shoulders.

"Useless ... go back to your station," Jones ordered.

Freddy left, and Stirling closed the door after him.

"Now, if you aren't expecting any more interruptions, I think we have a lot to talk about, Bill," Stirling started.

"No, you are the only interruption I am expecting this morning. Were all the theatrics really necessary? You really think I would try to ambush you?"

"I know what you are capable of. Don't think you're safe just because you're Elanor's nephew," Stirling scolded.

"What makes me safe, Philip, is your wife's love for me and your fear of your wife," Jones joked.

"Well, you've certainly made a mess of things, haven't you, Bill?"

"I've been the one trying to clean things up. Remember, this started because Keeps failed in his mission to kill the *whole* Jackson family. A mission you personally greenlighted, I might add."

"Even as a kid, you never liked to take responsibility for anything. It was my biggest worry when I gave you this job. Well, it doesn't matter now. It's over. I ordered BlackCorp to terminate Keeps and his team, and I'm here to personally see to it that all your beasts are terminated as well. There is one problem, however. A big problem ... well, two problems, actually."

"And what are they, Philip?" Jones inquired. Every time he used Stirling's first name, Stirling winced a little. Anybody else would be immediately fired, or worse, for not referring to him as Mr. Stirling.

"Keeps' six mercenaries who were still supposed to be in the area have all disappeared, including the one in the safe house with the kid." This was all new information to Jones, but he didn't act surprised, since he wasn't. Keeps could feel that things were falling apart up here and obviously ordered his people to scatter.

"That's no surprise. Keeps was always good at reading the room. Did they take the kid?"

Stirling just nodded yes.

"What's the second problem?"

"You... in your effort to clean up the mess, you've continually made things worse. First you kill that woman in accounting, which brought more heat on us, and then you kill Sparks' daughter and her husband, which will have incalculable consequences for this company. How could you be so sloppy?"

Jones's eyes opened wide, and he briefly held his breath. His reaction was fleeting, but his apparent loss of control over his expression at the mention of the death of Sparks' daughter and son-in-law was noticed by Stirling.

"My god, Bill. The lead investigator of the Jackson murders being fired and then losing his family the same day was big news. How the fu... heck could you have missed that?

With that article that came out, the speculation that we were involved is non-stop."

Jones had a source in the Livermore police department, so knew about the deaths, but decided to play dumb to deflect his own culpability in their passings. He leaned into his clueless act.

"How did Sparks' daughter and son-in-law die?"

Stirling nodded his head in disgust but sighed and then told Jones what had happened. "Apparently, they found the daughter's car abandoned in some alley on her route to work. The husband tracked her phone to the car, and two vagrants stabbed him to death. The wife died of a fentanyl drug overdose, but Sparks insists that she didn't have a drug problem."

Jones false expression changed from worry to relief, and he even smiled a little. "So, it was just a random killing and a woman with a drug problem. Nothing that could be tied to us."

Stirling looked at Jones curiously, knowing something was up, but also knowing not to ask a question when he did not want to hear the answer.

"No, but given the newspaper article that came out the very same day, you can imagine what every conspiracy theorist is saying. Normally, I wouldn't care about that, but regular media is coming up with conspiracies of their own.

"That brings us to where we are now. I fired Cooper, which I'm sure you've already surmised. As I previously told you, I ordered BlackOps to hunt down and kill Keeps and his team. That leaves us with two things left to do—"

"Liquidate the lab and kill the furries and Keeps' team down in Columbia," Jones interjected, finishing Stirling's sentence.

"There are military jets scheduled to destroy Keeps' camp and the drug lab at exactly 0500 hours." Stirling looked at his watch. "That is five minutes from now. What I need you to do, immediately, is terminate the furries."

Jones just nodded his head. There was no use in arguing about it, since he knew this day was coming. He logged into his account on his computer and brought up the application that controlled the furries' collars, then brought up the list of all the furries and selected the checkboxes next to all of their names. Finally, he hit the button that said terminate, which brought up a dialog box with a button that said "Okay" and another one that said "Cancel." He looked over at Stirling one last time; Stirling gave him a single nod of the head, down and up; Jones then clicked on the button that said "Okay."

They both remained silent. A few minutes later, Stirling received a call; he simply said thank you into the receiver and hung up.

"It's done. The camp and drug lab have been destroyed. Surely, between the collars and the missiles launched, Keeps and his men and the furries are dead. It's over. I need you and Dr. Danzel to finish cleaning up the lab. Destroy everything. Are all lab staff in the facility, as I requested?"

"Yes ... Is the furry program over?" Jones asked.

"No, dummy! The furry program was insanely profitable and popular among the elite back in Washington. We'll set you and Danzel up in a new location down the line. Of course, you'll get some adult supervision. I can't trust you to be competent. I guess that's what happens when you hire family."

With that, Stirling turned and started to leave the office, leaving Jones slack-jawed at the parting insults. Jones was still alive, so there was that. Given the family connection and his threat to expose the lab and Danzel's work, he didn't really think Stirling would kill him, but you could never be sure.

Stirling turned back one last time. "Oh, and I assume Aliyah was not terminated when we set off their collars. I noticed I didn't see her name in the menu selection."

"She was not."

Stirling left with his entourage. Jones wasn't surprised Stirling knew that they had transformed Aliyah. He apparently didn't care, however.

Besides still being alive, he had more good news. The lab wasn't closing, only changing location. He was still employed, though he would have to report to a new Cooper, a Cooper that might be more of a micromanager if his uncle had his way—which he undoubtedly would. Finally, he still had Aliyah, Jurgensen, and Green under his entrustment. He would take Big Freddy too.

*

After packing up the few physical items they wanted to keep and loading those items into a truck in the garage, Jones and Danzel made one final stop to visit Aliyah in the furry recovery room, where she had spent the last five days recovering from her transformation. She was just starting to recover from the sickness all furries felt after the procedure, and hopefully open to reason. She was locked in the plexiglass cage as a precaution, since even though Aliyah agreed to remain loyal to Jones, and Danzel had supposedly ramped down her compulsions to kill, they couldn't be sure she would stick to her promises while in the throes of sickness.

It was time to leave, however, and Aliyah was going with them as a willing participant, so it was time to risk their lives and set her free. Jones looked over at Danzel before they entered the room and said, "Let me do the talking."

"Why's that?"

"It's just your usual spiel tends to grate people, and I'm trying to placate her."

"You can speak first," Danzel offered, not willing to fully acquiesce to Jones.

Jones figured that was the best he would get from Danzel, so they entered the room. Aliyah immediately looked up and greeted them.

"I thought we were partners, Jones, but you've locked me up in this cage and haven't visited me once. Am I just an animal, like the rest of your apes?"

"I'm sorry, Aliyah, as I told you before your procedure, the lab was in crisis, and that required my full attention. You are not an ape; your appearance has not changed. I kept my promise. You are now a super-human. I know it wasn't pleasant, but think about where you are now," Jones pleaded.

Aliyah snorted, "... not fucking pleasant! You call having needles jammed into your eyeballs, not fucking pleasant?"

Dr. Danzel decided to take over. "The pain is a vital part of the transformation. Without the pain, there is no transformation. I promised you greatness and I delivered. I know you can feel it. You really are a super-human."

Aliyah didn't believe Danzel's bullshit about pain being a vital part of the transformation, but she was happy with the changes anyway. Her new abilities would allow her to do things she had only ever dreamed of. She was a weapon, a killing machine. She also didn't want to make it easy on the two men, so she had to give them a hard time—just for fun.

"So, boys, why am I still in this cage?"

Jones nodded to Danzel, who walked over to a panel on the wall opposite her cage and pressed a button that opened the door. Immediately, Aliyah jumped out of the cage, landing within inches of Jones. She stood there staring at him, with her forehead scrunched up and mouth in a snarl. "... Boo!" she said, changing her expression to a smile. To his

333

credit, Jones did not pee his pants, but he felt his heart stop, thinking that he was experiencing his last moment of life.

The three made their way down to U4 and Jones, Aliyah, and Big Freddy boarded the truck. Danzel got into a van with his six orderlies. He trusted them and knew replacing them would be very difficult—he had already lost Powell. That meant only seven unfortunate souls were left behind to burn in HEL's fiery demise.

Earlier that day, both Danzel and Jones had called in all of their respective reports to report to the facility for an all-hands meeting. Before leaving, Jones confirmed that every staff member they were leaving behind was in the facility. After they cleared the exit to the garage, a thick metal door closed after them, sealing off that exit. Simultaneously, the elevator shaft to the division building was sealed off and the regular ventilation and HVAC system was closed off and reopened to a separate ventilation shaft located a couple miles of away in the midst of a large piece of land owned by the lab.

After the lab was sealed and the ventilation was redirected away from the shafts close to the division property, the fire suppression system started to work in reverse. While pumping oxygen into all of the lab's rooms, it also sent in gas that it lit, creating an inferno throughout the facility. Everybody and everything in the facility were instantly incinerated into ash, HEL became one big crematorium.

The group of refugees from the lab were heading into an uncertain future, but confident that they would be a critical part of whatever came next. Jones assumed that Greenrock would use its political influence and money to bully and bribe its way out of any problems the lab's actions had caused. He was eager to rebuild his fiefdom with the core of his team intact. Aliyah simply had revenge and blood on her mind. Danzel's mind was where it almost always was: in his work—

there were new mutations to test out and monsters to be made. Greenrock would learn from their mistakes and build a new and better HEL—more profitable than ever.

CHAPTER 84

Keeps, the mercenaries, and the furries were all up two hours before dawn. They finished packing up everything they planned to take, including the caiman jerky, and started their trek to the hub.

They were walking for no more than thirty seconds before the eleven furries all felt a slight ping from their collars. Next, the collar latches all released, and the collars fell to the ground. The furries were free.

The eleven furries wasted no time and formed a circle around the five humans, blood and revenge on their mind. Keeps, scared in a way he hadn't experienced since he was a child worried about the creaks coming from his closet, needed to say something to try and save himself and his men. For a moment, the fear overpowered him, and he couldn't talk, but he quickly slowed his breathing down and pulled himself back together.

"Killing us won't solve anything. We all need each other more than ever. Greenrock will be coming for all of us," Keeps stated.

"I might even agree with you, boss, but unfortunately, I've been overruled. My troop wants their blood and revenge for all you've done to them. Can you blame them?" Dave said.

Keeps couldn't and had nothing further to say. He wasn't going to beg for his life.

Just then, Est spoke up. "The village I grew up in is around four hundred miles from here. If we make it there, you'll have shelter and the protection of my people. If you let us live, we can help you."

The kid isn't wrong. We can't just live in the jungle. Well, we can, but I've had my fill of camping. We want to kill them, and me, and me ... Yes, but we also want to survive. We delay our revenge. We follow you, but disappointed. Yes, Greenrock will pay, but better chance with Keeps. Reprieve.

The invisible discussion went on for almost a minute, but in the end, Bonobo convinced Lud, who was already coming to the same decision on his own. The collective followed Lud's lead, so the mercenaries would live for now, and they would make their way to Est's village.

Dave gave Est a nod. "Alright, Est, lead the way. We'll let you live for now and won't harm the people in your village, as long as they don't try to harm us."

The relief on the faces of Keeps and his four mercenaries was obvious. Wallis fell to his knees and started vomiting from the stress of almost getting torn apart by eleven monsters. For the furries, there was some satisfaction in that.

A couple of minutes after their collars had fallen off, they heard a loud explosion coming from the direction of the hub. They were a mile away, but the shock of the explosion was still strong enough to shake the ground beneath them and knock a couple of Keeps' men to the ground. Shortly after that, they heard several large explosions from the direction of the jungle drug lab, a few miles away.

Keeps' decision to locate the hub a mile from their camp had likely saved their lives. Luck also played a role, since if the bombing had taken place fifteen minutes later, they would have arrived at the hub and been killed there.

"Our enemy really is the same now," Keeps offered. That was true, but it didn't mean that Keeps wasn't also the furries' enemy.

They needed to move out of the area fast, just in case Greenrock had sent in ground troops to finish cleaning up the area. Four of the furries dropped some of the equipment they deemed non-essential and hoisted the mercenaries onto their backs. Dave squatted down and bent over a little bit, looking over at Keeps.

"Time to hop aboard, boss." Keeps gave Dave a strange look and didn't immediately move. "We can travel three times faster if we carry you. Just until we clear the area and are out of danger. You must have played piggyback as a kid. It will be fun."

Dave then patted his ass, indicating that Keeps needed to hop on his back so they could get going. Keeps sighed and hopped on.

The new platoon, joining together human and beast, made their retreat through the jungle and on toward Est's village. There, they could regroup and strategize their next move. All sixteen were now aligned to the same goal. Find and destroy the people who were trying to kill them. Even without the collars, until their adversaries at Greenrock were destroyed, they could never truly be free.

EPILOGUE

Dave stepped out of a little shop in Barranco Minas, Columbia, holding a bag full of avocado green long-sleeved shirts, loose fitting yellowish pants, straw hats, and cheap plastic sunglasses. The ten neanderthal-like furries needed better cover than spandex shorts when they came through villages on their way to Est's hometown. He didn't bother getting them footwear, since their feet weren't that much different than the average foot of a person who lived in the jungle—maybe just a touch thicker and hairier.

To test their disguises, the furries, including Bonobo, put on their new clothes, and the squad of sixteen refugees had their first group lunch out. They picked a combo disco-bar-restaurant as the venue for the company outing. In Columbus, Ohio, the group would have attracted a lot of unwanted attention: five group members were dressed in military fatigues, all heavily armed, and the other eleven were dressed in the identical greenish, yellowish garb that Dave had purchased earlier. When they settled into their seats and removed their hats and glasses, ten members of the group looked like they were extras from a comic book movie.

In a backwoods jungle town in rural Columbia, the locals just took their strange visitors in stride. They were used to dangerous and strange people and creatures coming through their town. They were even more used to not asking questions because too many questions got people killed in those parts.

The food was amazing and a wonderful change after a couple of weeks of eating mainly caiman jerky. The family who owned the restaurant cooked them up large quantities of grilled chicken, plantains, pickled onions, and fresh tomatoes. Luckily, the restaurant had a large supply of warm cervezas, and human and beast drank heavily. Unfortunately for the furries, their enhancements made it hard for them to get drunk, but after fourteen bottles, Sigurd managed it.

Sigurd stripped down to his blue spandex shorts and started jumping around, pretending that he was a real ape. He went up to Keeps and started sniffing him and pretending to pick bugs out of his hair to eat—though he might not have been pretending. Keeps, fairly lit himself, laughed and patted Sigurd on the head like he was a pet. If the owners were shocked, they didn't show it. Keeps was overpaying handsomely for the meal with American dollars.

On the way out, Keeps gave the owner an extra monetary tip, plus a second tip, warning him to keep everything he saw that day to himself, ominously telling the owner that the hairy fiends would have their revenge if he didn't. The owner assured Keeps that he was just a simple man and had seen and heard nothing.

Back at camp, Bonobo pondered where life had led him. Four months prior, he was sitting drunk in his car, bloodied and wounded, but also optimistic about his future for the first time in a while. He hoped getting fired from his dead-end job would propel him to make something better of his life, and after many twists and turns, it had. Sometimes he missed his family and wondered if he would ever see them again, but he also relished his new family.

They were a gang of outlaws, on the run from Greenrock and the government, but free for the first time since they were forcibly pulled into HEL. HEL had genetically engineered them to do horrible things, and they had done many, but since losing their collars, they first resisted the urge to kill the mercenaries and continued to resist the urge to kill villagers they'd come across on their journey through Eastern

Columbia. He shared their mind, though, so he knew how hard it was for them to resist their urges. Violence was in their nature, and they could only suppress that nature for so long before their true selves came out again. Dave just needed to make sure that bloodlust was directed toward those who deserved it.

The group slept off their food and drink at their camp, right outside of town, then disappeared back into the jungle before dawn the next morning. Rumors of the strange outfit of soldiers and beasts spread through the jungle villages and encampments, taking on a life of its own. Were the beasts newly undiscovered creatures of the rainforest? Or possibly some new mutation of a jungle primate? So much about the jungle was unknown, and stories about mysterious creatures hiding in the canopy were as old as life in the jungle itself.

THANK YOU

Thank you for reading *Assassin Lab,* the first book in the new *Designer Mercenaries* series. The best way to support this book is to leave a review, so please go back to the book's product page at the store you purchased it at and leave a review and comment.

Visit https://sites.google.com/view/stuartdejong/home for more information.

Follow author and leave feedback at https://www.goodreads.com/stuart_dejong or on Amazon.